I0699686

DEATH'S DESPAIR

A KASSIDY SIMMONS NOVEL

DENNIS K. CROSBY

FROM THE TINY ACORN …
GROWS THE MIGHTY OAK

Death's Despair

Printed in the United States of America. For information, address
Acorn Publishing, LLC, 3943 Irvine Blvd. Ste. 218, Irvine, CA 92602

www.acornpublishingllc.com

Cover design by Damonza.com

Interior design and formatting by Debra Cranfield Kennedy

ISBN-13: 979-8-88528-050-1 (hardcover)
ISBN-13: 979-8-88528-049-5 (paperback)

For My Parents

*Thank you for your love, support,
and encouragement over the years.
Thank you for being strong, intelligent,
and giving people to look up to.
Most of all, thank you for never giving up on me
as I followed my own path through life.
My gratitude is endless! I love you!*

Also by Dennis K. Crosby

Death's Legacy

Death's Debt

CHAPTER ONE

WHEN SHE WAS HUMAN—BRUISED, BATTERED, AND HUMILIATED— praying for death, Kassidy Simmons had been told that death was like a corporation, complete with a CEO, officers, and subordinates. Those words came from Azra-El, the being that brought her into the Reaper ranks. He died poorly. Beheaded by her in a very hostile corporate takeover. In most corporations, though, the CEO wasn't on the front lines, rolling up the sleeves to get down and dirty. But this corporation was Death, with a very hands-on leader. As the Death God, Kassidy didn't just get down and dirty, she got downright bloody.

The cut across her cheek illustrated that perfectly.

As she ducked to avoid the next slash of the switchblade poorly wielded by a young wannabe gangbanger, she spun, pivoted, and followed through with an uppercut that sent the gangbanger's companion on a trip through the frigid Chicago air onto a hardened pile of snow.

"What the . . . ?"

"Not bad, eh, Switchblade?" asked Kassidy, rhetorically.

Switchblade looked perplexed. Maybe at the skill and ease with which Kassidy fought, or perhaps at the sheer power of the woman. Likely, both. Kassidy could see realization on his face. Realization that he got very lucky with that slash across her cheek. And in fact, he did. Kassidy had slipped on a snow-covered patch of ice, essentially falling into the blade rather than being cut by a person with some semblance of skill with the weapon.

He couldn't have been more than nineteen, maybe early twenties at the most. His black knit skullcap had a marijuana leaf embroidered on it. His coat was oversized. Stylish, but oversized, and no doubt restricted his ability to move. Lack of skill with a blade played a larger part. His skin was light brown with European features. Kassidy couldn't discern his nationality, but she wasn't overly concerned with that in the moment. She wasn't going to report this to the police after all. She'd come to Columbus Park for a very specific reason and these two young punks were hinderances to her primary objective.

"Look," began Kassidy, "take your boy and get the fuck outta here before you get hurt. I won't call the cops. Just leave."

"What? What did you say to me, bitch?" asked Switchblade with all the incredulity his two decades on the planet could muster.

"Oh, good god. Really? *Bitch*? That's what you're going with?" asked Kassidy, with a sigh. "You heard me. Leave. And we can forget all this happened."

In her peripheral vision, Kassidy saw Switchblade's buddy stumble off the snowbank. He moved slowly, clearly in pain, from both the impact of her punch and the landing he stuck with the grace of a diseased whale. He was about the same age as Switchblade. He wore no skullcap, which was stupid for a winter night in Chicago. His gloves were leather, and rather expensive from the look. As was his coat. It wasn't oversized, but slightly fitted. His jeans were high priced, hanging off his ass, and neatly tucked into his tan Timberlands. With fair skin and light brown hair, he screamed "rich suburbanite trying to rebel against his parents."

So cliché.

"Dude," began the Suburbanite, "let's get the fuck outta here. You know she's gonna call the cops."

Kassidy sensed a great deal of fear in him. Even without the benefit of her supernatural empathic abilities, that was clear. So, at least he was smart. Switchblade was different. There was fear there, but there was also stupidity, determination, and . . . arousal. Not so much inspired by her, but by the violence. He wanted to be a badass. He got off on it. It was likely that this entire night was more about showing off in front of the Suburbanite than asserting himself against a woman alone in the park.

It was unfortunate that they chose this night.

More unfortunate that they chose her.

"Bro, shut the fuck up and let me handle this," said Switchblade.

"You really should listen to your boyfriend," said Kassidy.

"What? He's not my boyfriend, bitch."

"Oh, I'm sorry. Right, that was insensitive. I meant to say partner. You should really listen to your partner. I'm old school. I just use girlfriend or boyfriend. I'm getting better though."

"Bitch!"

"There's that word again," said Kassidy.

Switchblade lunged at Kassidy. In the corner of her eye, she saw the Suburbanite back away. She was growing impatient and felt a sense of urgency to get her true mission accomplished. Normally, she wouldn't use her powers in front of mortals. Well, that wasn't always true. She'd certainly had some fun at the expense of others in her teens when she was just a Reaper. Back then, she didn't care if anyone said anything. She'd already been dubbed Krazy Kassie by her classmates, so in her mind, it didn't hurt to fuck with them. She had power. True power. And the power she had back then paled in comparison to the power she had now. Using it against these two idiots wouldn't bring as much joy as it had in her teens, but as was the case back then, she knew these two wouldn't be telling anyone.

And if they did, who'd believe them.

As Switchblade came at her, Kassidy shimmered out of view, reappearing behind the Suburbanite. She grabbed a handful of his hair with her left hand and grabbed at his throat with her right. When the bewildered Switchblade spun, trying to figure out what had happened, she willed her right hand to transform into an onyx sickle, the tool of a Reaper. As she touched the tip into Suburbanite's neck, she felt, more than sensed, his fear. His heartbeat was a jackhammer competing with the sound of the wind sweeping through the park.

"What the fuck are you, lady?" asked Switchblade, his eyes wide.

"I'm the one politely asking you both, one last time, to get the fuck out of here before I get really pissed," replied Kassidy.

Kassidy closed her eyes, knowing that her next bit of magic would likely close the deal. In the Reaper ranks, when a psychopomp—a being that ushered souls to the afterlife—used their power, their eyes would shine silver. Kassidy's had been silver for decades when she powered up. A couple of times in life, they'd shown black, the mark of the Wraith. Similar to Reapers, Wraiths had been created to be the secret police of Azra-El, the former Primus or Angel of Death, right hand to the original Death God, and Kassidy's father, Thanatos. After Kassidy dispatched Azra-El she became the new Death God, in the absence of her father. Now, when she powered up, her eyes shown a metallic, unearthly blue, the mark of a god.

That's what Switchblade saw when Kassidy opened her eyes.

"Run!" she screamed.

And he did.

Kassidy thought he'd make an excellent track star when his career as a gangbanger failed. The Suburbanite was still in her grip. She released him, pushing him forward a bit. When he turned to face her, Kassidy held up her scythe. For added effect she lifted her left hand, willed it to transform as well and crossed her arms with a stare that rivaled any psychopath in fiction.

"If either of you fuck around in this park again, I'll gut you both," said Kassidy. "Nod if you understand."

The Suburbanite nodded.

Then, the Suburbanite ran.

Kassidy powered down and shook her head. She couldn't believe she'd had to deal with such nonsense. After willing her sickles away, she touched a hand to the cut on her cheek. It was gone. As a Reaper, cuts, bone breaks, and other injuries healed faster than humans. As a god, depending on the severity, they healed almost as quickly as they'd occurred. At least she thought that's how it worked. There wasn't really a manual that came with being a god. At most she'd only had to deal with cuts and bruises since her ascension. Even when she fought the War God, her injuries healed rather quickly. Thankfully, her fighting skills allowed her to avoid most of his ferocity. Or he'd been holding back. That thought sent a shudder through her.

Kassidy turned to proceed through the park as she'd been doing before the Abbot and Costello of crime interrupted her. She'd been drawn to Columbus Park because of the pull of a lost soul. In the human world, the term *lost soul* meant something entirely different. For Kassidy, it was a literal lost soul. When she'd fought and dispatched Azra-El, she'd unwittingly released hundreds of souls that he'd previously absorbed in his effort to regenerate from injuries sustained in their initial battle twenty years ago. Those souls were taken before their time and had not been transitioned properly to the afterlife. The first order of business after destroying him had been dispatching all the

Wraith's he'd created. Now that that was done, her next order was helping the released souls find peace. The problem was that many of them had attached themselves to living beings. Some were strong enough to possess humans outright. Others simply hid, choosing to take over a body when a person was unconscious. She suspected she was dealing with the latter tonight.

As the Death God, Kassidy was connected to all things related to Death. From Reapers to souls, she was, for better or worse, in a symbiotic relationship with them all. She was still learning how to manage it. Throughout her childhood she had struggled to understand and manage her empathic abilities. The challenges began early, and it was hard, but eventually she found a way. Trying to manage her connections with souls was like that. Hard and frustrating times one thousand.

She followed the pull of the soul through Columbus Park, one of the many that made up the Chicago Park District. Just off Jackson Boulevard, between Austin and Central Avenue, the park took up space between the city of Chicago and the suburb of Oak Park, where Kassidy had grown up. It had little trails, a massive, centralized building for special events with a small man-made body of water behind it, and a nine-hole golf course. The soul she was tracking was on that course.

Approaching the green at the third hole, through light patches of snow, Kassidy watched as a middle-aged woman held a putter and lined up her shot. Vapor escaped the woman's mouth as she let out a breath to steady herself. She was a pleasant-looking woman. She had short dark hair, stopping just above her shoulders. She wore glasses, behind which were lovely chestnut brown eyes. The woman was wearing a short-sleeved black polo shirt, with black jeans and black golf shoes—the red glove on her left hand a beacon against her monochromatic attire. Given the attire, the lost soul was clearly in control of this body. They did not feel the effects of the elements, even when they occupied a human. A handy trick during the Chicago winter. The woman pulled back slightly then lightly tapped the bright white golf ball sending it six feet forward until it gently dropped in the hole.

"I always had a problem with my short game," said the woman.

"Seems you've worked out some of the bugs," said Kassidy.

"Yeah. Yeah, it looks that way."

For the first time, the woman looked at Kassidy, and there was clear awareness in her gaze. Kassidy sensed no malice. Nothing to indicate that the soul within the woman was going to do anything violent or unexpected.

"Are you here to take me away?" the woman asked.

"Yeah. I am. And . . ."

Kassidy didn't know how much to tell her. She wasn't even sure the soul would care. Deep inside, Kassidy wanted to let the soul know how sorry she was for all of it. For the pain of death, the confusion that came with being lost in the purgatory that was this world, and ultimately, for being the cause of it all. She wanted to say all that. She was desperate to say that to all the vagrant souls out there. But it wouldn't change anything, and in the end, it wouldn't make them feel better.

They were still dead, and it was still her fault.

"And?" asked the woman.

"And . . . to apologize for taking so long to help you."

The woman smiled. It was simple. It was pleasant. It was what Kassidy needed.

"Will it hurt?" asked the woman.

"No," said Kassidy. "Nothing will ever hurt again."

After transitioning to the Nexus, Kassidy set to work to separate the soul from the woman, careful to not disturb the living soul rightfully residing in the body. Stretching out with her power, she placed one hand on the woman's shoulder, and the other on her stomach. Concentrating, she pulled her hand away from the woman's body, and with it, came the vagrant soul. She called to one of her Reapers to escort the soul to its final destination. After transitioning back to the real world, Kassidy called for another Reaper to return the woman to her home. Once alone, Kassidy dropped to her knees at the third hole on the Columbus Park golf course and mustered a smile, trying to relish in the satisfaction of at least one job done well.

Then she felt, more than heard, a loud sonic boom, followed by a low warbling pulse. Kassidy doubled over in pain, grabbing at her stomach. Inside she felt her body being ripped apart. Her organs twisted, pulled, and contracted. The pain persisted for what seemed like hours. At times she could barely breathe.

Eventually, Kassidy Simmons, the Death God, screamed in anguish.

CHAPTER TWO

THE SENSATION HIT THE DIVA IN HER ABDOMEN THEN RADIATED OUT to her extremities. Over and over, she felt the supernatural assault on her body—an expenditure of energy that seemed to target her directly from an invisible force. It wrapped itself around her heart and squeezed. It stabbed at her. It punched her, from the inside out.

And she loved every second of it.

Loved it more, in fact, than the sex she was currently having. The man on top of her was doing nothing for her. She'd picked him up outside an Atlanta bar as it was closing. He'd said something crass. Something he thought would be funny, jovial, and flirty. It was none of those things. It was ignorant, childish, and unsolicited. But the Diva had received good news. Good news about some elements of the next phase of her plan. On a high from that excitement, she decided to entertain the uncouth tool of a man. She'd planned to entertain him, tease him, fuck him, then kill him.

She'd checked off the first two boxes of her plan. When they'd returned to her hotel, she made him shower to mask the offensive smell of alcohol and marijuana. She promised room service with good wine, some snacks to nibble on, and perhaps, if he were a good boy, she'd call a friend later. The promise of all those things made him putty in her hands. The Diva wasn't displeased with his look. If she had been, she would have likely killed him on the spot after the ridiculous comments he'd made. He was handsome, with a nice firm, fit body. It was unfortunate that his attitude was crap. Not that it would have mattered to her. Even if she liked him, she probably would have killed him later.

The Diva pushed his buttons. She teased him with her body, and emasculated him with her words, hoping that in some way, shape, or form, he'd take more control, be more aggressive. But he did none of those things. She felt nothing when he kissed her. She felt even less when he entered her, and she told him as much. The attack on his ego sparked . . . something. He moved faster. His thrusts were harder. But she still felt nothing.

Until the Pulse.

There was no sound. Only the sensation of one thousand punches to her gut. When she cried out, her companion clearly confused it with pleasure and assumed she was begging for more. She felt him move with renewed spirit and vigor, but it still meant nothing to her. The Diva closed her eyes and allowed herself to get swept up in the sensation attacking her. She moved, she moaned, she writhed . . . and then she came.

"That's right, girl," said the man.

The Diva opened her eyes and saw the bright metallic blue color reflected in his. She moved her hands up his chest, to his neck, then squeezed . . . and squeezed . . . and squeezed. He continued to move, desperate to get free, and she moved with him, his imminent death renewing excitement within her. She came again when she saw that life had escaped his eyes. The Diva tossed him onto the floor, unceremoniously. He'd brought her no pleasure. Even that last bit of frenzy was less about him and more about what she was doing, and most certainly, what the Pulse was doing to her. It was just what she needed. The perfect release.

The Diva smiled wider at the knowledge of its meaning.

"She's coming," she said.

And her laughter filled the room.

◆　　◆　　◆

"Are you all right, sir?"

"Yes. Yes, I'm fine."

And Keiron was fine, mostly. The Pulse hit him with the weight of a toppling building, which, strangely enough, had happened to him once decades ago. That time, he'd been trying to rescue people from the burning structure. This time, he'd been minding his own business carrying a box filled with six bottles of wine to add to his collection.

He'd be taking one surviving bottle home.

"Here, let me help you," said a passerby.

Keiron looked up and saw a boy, no older than fifteen. His green eyes were filled with genuine concern. Though he was no empath like Kassidy, Keiron had the experience of a couple millennia of life. It gave him a certain perspective on the human heart and soul. The boy before him was an innocent, an uncorrupted soul with the potential to be an amazing force in the world. Keiron was as certain of that as he was his own name.

But that Pulse.

He hadn't heard the boom that preceded it. No one heard it. But he felt it, as did all immortals with divine blood. Keiron was the son of Cronus, leader of the Titans, predecessors of the Twelve. He was brother to Zeus and uncle to the recently returned War God. Keiron was no god.

But he felt that Pulse.

He knew what it meant. At least, he knew what it symbolized. Someone had, or was trying, to break through from another plane of existence.

Thanatos?
Cronus?
Someone worse?

Whoever, or whatever it was, if they had the potential to break through realms, they had the potential to change the world forever. And just like that, the hope Keiron felt when he looked into the eyes of the boy assisting him, faded. The kid may never live to his potential because something bad, something evil, loomed on the horizon.

"Thank you so much for your help, young man," said Keiron.

"No problem, sir. You sure you're okay?"

Keiron nodded.

But he was not okay.

He was not remotely okay.

CENTURIES AGO

Rain fell hard as the Earth shook and mountains crumbled. Around her, trees and plants immediately perished, and death swept across the crops throughout the countryside. People fled from the shrieks and wails of the enraged goddess.

A sudden crack of thunder followed by a flash of lightning illuminated the stormy night, and as smoke dissipated, Zeus stood before the forlorn goddess. With an unexpected demonstration of tenderness, he kneeled and took her in his arms. Her sobs seemed never ending, but in the comfort of Zeus' arms, the rain eased, and the rumbles of the Earth lessened.

"I'm here, sister. How can I help?"

"She's gone!" screamed Demeter. "She's gone and I cannot find her anywhere!"

"Gone? What? Who?"

"My child," began Demeter, "my sweet, gentle child. Persephone!"

"That . . . that . . . can't be. Surely she must be near."

Demeter shook her head vigorously. She began to speak but could not find the words. Persephone was her child, her love, her light, her very life. Demeter was said to have many children, though she did not often acknowledge them in the open. Persephone was different. Of all her children, Demeter favored her. Many gods believed Demeter was so devoted to Persephone because of the girl's father. No one, except Demeter, of course, knew for certain who it was. There was speculation throughout Olympus that it was Zeus himself. To bear a child fathered by the King of the Gods was a special honor indeed. Demeter never acknowledged the rumor, which only led to its fortification in the halls of Olympus. Zeus never inquired, and that hurt Demeter most. He *was* Persephone's father, and Demeter wanted him to accept her and to celebrate her the way he did all his children. His disinterest in the truth left Demeter feeling ashamed—and angry.

"She's not here. I've looked everywhere. Searched every field, every city, every mountain, and she is nowhere. Nowhere!"

"All right, all right," said Zeus. "We will find her. She can't possibly have vanished. We—"

"I want everyone, every god, looking for her. Now!" demanded Demeter.

She pulled back as she spoke, staring into the eyes of Zeus. Few dared to challenge him. Though he was the youngest of his siblings, he was the most powerful. A shrewd and cunning warrior, Zeus was the reason his siblings were released from the hell they'd been imprisoned in by their father Cronus. If not for him, they would have all spent a lifetime in a desolate existence void of any contact, any love, any hope at all. Zeus' actions led to their liberation, and for that they respected him. His ability to gain favor, to manipulate, to inspire—it was those characteristics, along with his innate power, which led to the eventual fall of the Titans and the Olympian ascendancy to the thrones of the heavens. All of that led many to grovel at his feet. In reverence. In worship. In fear.

But not Demeter.

It was not out of refusal to recognize his power. She recognized it, she acknowledged it, and she respected it. But for her, Zeus was still her little brother. For her, blood superseded station. In this moment she made demands of her brother as his sister. But she also demanded he act—as her King.

"Of course we will help, sister. All of us. We will reach out to our priests and through the oracles. We will find her. But, in the meantime, you must stop this," said Zeus, gesturing to the fields around him and the skies above.

Demeter followed his hand and looked around. Immediately, she was horrified at what she'd done. As goddess of agriculture, nature and bountiful harvests were her charge. She took pride in helping the mortals learn and grow in their capacity to care for the fields and themselves. What had she done? In an instant she'd killed everything. Harvests that would feed mortals for months were now destroyed.

"I ... I ...," stammered Demeter.

"It's okay, sister," said Zeus. "Let's fix this, and then we'll set out to find your daughter."

As if Persephone were her problem and her problem alone. As if the gods were doing her a favor. As if *he* were doing her a favor. After all she'd done for him, suddenly, Persephone's disappearance was *her* problem. Those last two words struck Demeter like an arrow from Artemis' bow.

Your daughter.

Demeter's eyes flared a metallic blue and she rose into the air.

"I will fix nothing!" she screamed.

"Demeter, please! As your King I command—"

"You command nothing! You care more for your precious mortals than your own family? Then watch them suffer. Nothing will grow until my daughter is found!"

Demeter was unprepared for the lightning strike.

Demeter crashed to the ground, writhing, as pain rippled through her body. Electricity sizzled around her entire body like cooked meat fresh from the fire on a wooden slab. Smoke rose from her body as the rain fell over her. When the worst of the pain left her, she looked up to find Zeus standing over her.

Crackles of electricity replaced his once cool blue eyes.

"You make no demands here, sister!"

Zeus raised his hand, and a powerful white glow began to intensify. Demeter cowered from her brother, for the first time in her existence, as he prepared for another strike.

"Lord Zeus, I beg of you," said a light voice from behind.

Demeter let out a sigh of relief as she saw the Titan, Hecate, step into view. Zeus stayed his hand, heeding the request of the Titan, a woman he respected. Hecate, despite her lineage, had stood against the Titans in their war against the Olympians. In throwing her allegiance to Zeus, she sealed her fate with her Titan family. Thankfully, the Olympians won, and for her help, Zeus showed her favor.

"What are you doing here, Hecate?" asked Zeus.

"Lord Zeus, as I too am connected to this Earth and the skies above, I felt the anguish of your sister. I understand what she's going through and humbly beg you forgive her considering the circumstances. She's lost her daughter. She hurts because of that. Please, I implore you, show mercy and consider that before you cast judgement."

Hecate's eyes brightened. Moments later, the rain ceased. Hecate was the goddess of witchcraft, magic, and sorcery, but held some dominion over the sky and earth, too. As the rain stopped and the clouds slowly parted, Hecate walked toward Demeter and extended a hand. Out of fear, or confusion, Demeter glanced at Zeus who gave a light nod. Demeter took the hand given to her and rose to her feet. Soaked to the core from the rain and still reeling from the assault of lightning, Demeter winced, but leaned on Hecate for support.

"Lord Zeus, allow me to accompany Demeter on her search. With our shared love of the earth and my magic, I'm sure together we can find Persephone."

"Would this . . . please you?" asked Zeus through gritted teeth.

Demeter nodded.

"Very well," said Zeus. "I will alert the other gods as I said I would. I'm sure we will find your daughter soon."

Those words.

Again.

Demeter held her tongue and acknowledged her brother. It pained her to do so. Not physically, but spiritually, for so many reasons.

"Zeus . . . brother," began Demeter, "I . . . apologize."

Zeus again responded with a slow nod and vanished in a flash of lightning.

Demeter slumped into Hecate's arms. She'd never been struck by Zeus' thunderbolt before. She'd seen it and witnessed the devastation it could cause. Had she not been a god, her life would have ended immediately. But she was a god, and she was his sister. Perhaps, because of that, he'd held back a portion of his power. She'd likely never know.

"Thank you, Hecate. I am in your debt for coming to my aid."

"Of course. I could not allow that to go on."

Hecate helped Demeter to a large rock, where they both rested. Demeter held Hecate's hand in friendship, in solidarity, and in gratitude. She could tell in a gentle squeeze that the feelings were reciprocated.

"Do you think we'll find her? Do you think we'll find my Persephone?"

"We will find her," began Hecate, "and we will punish whoever is responsible for this. You have my word."

CHAPTER THREE

TRACI OPENED THE BAG OF SUPPLIES SHE'D PURCHASED FROM A LOCAL occult shop. If there was one thing she enjoyed about living in the Chicagoland area, it was the plethora of occult shops in the city, and surprisingly, in some of the local suburbs as well. Despite the limited time she had remaining on Earth, she found some comfort in the knowledge that *some* of the sisterhood thrived and ran legitimate shops. There were, of course, *others* who were trying to make a living selling little trinkets they'd found on eBay or procured through some makeshift black market during their international travels. They were non magic wielders on the hunt for knowledge on the craft, and all things supernatural. Traci didn't necessarily begrudge them. At the very least, they kept the lore alive. In the end the legitimate practitioners would set the record straight. And they'd do so happily for those that sought true knowledge and understanding of their practices.

They should all be made to suffer.

Traci dropped a jar of lavender on the kitchen table at the words, turned, and saw nothing. It had sounded like it was in her head, but she scoffed at that notion. She ran to the back door, peered outside, and saw no one, nor any sign that someone had been there. The vapor forming in front of her eyes alerted her to the fact that she was breathing heavily. The hard thumping in her chest was almost painful. Traci closed her eyes, took a deep breath, and held it for a beat before releasing it.

"Calm," she whispered to herself repeatedly.

Her breathing slowed, her heartbeat returned to normal, and her mind cleared. She took one more cleansing breath, then slowly opened her eyes. Looking around once again, she saw nothing, no one. There was a chill in the late-night winter air, but the skies were clear. The moon shone bright. Not quite full, but still beautiful, and enough to illuminate some areas of the yard. As with many things in nature, Traci felt a closeness to the sky, especially at night. There was a connection that she did not feel in the daylight hours. As a witch, it seemed terribly cliché. Nevertheless, she relished the moments she could enjoy a clear moonlit evening.

"That's weird," she said to herself, looking at the near-full orb against the black sheet of pin-pricked sky. She'd noticed a slight tint to the moon. It was light pink. Very light. A hue one might see when the moon shared the sky with the sun moments before the fiery ball of gas set in the western horizon. Sunset had been hours ago, yet the moon had that tint. There was no blood moon due. In fact, the next was not due for another decade.

And this was not how it would occur.

My power grows.

Traci jumped once more, this time, stumbling back against the old metal storm door. As she tried to balance herself, she reached out and caught her hand on a jagged piece of aluminum from the door's dilapidated frame.

"Ow! Fuck!" she exclaimed.

In the back of her mind, she heard low laughter. It was not a television or radio. It was as though someone were near, very near, and trying to keep their presence quiet.

"Who's there?" she said, holding her injured hand.

Almost immediately the laughter stopped, though there was an echo, lessening with intensity after several moments until silence finally prevailed. Whatever was happening, she didn't like it.

Traci wasn't a control freak. As a witch, and one with some considerable power and skill, she knew that there were energies in this world she could not control. Wisdom was found in not attempting to control them, but instead, in understanding them and finding a way to harmonize with them. Whatever this was that she was experiencing offered no hand of friendship or kinship. It offered no fellowship or sisterhood. Something was happening that went well beyond the understanding of her practice.

"Ow!" she exclaimed at the sensation assaulting her abdomen. She felt as if something had cut her open and was slowly pulling at her insides. The feeling was brief, but the intensity was enough to cause her to double over. Between the cut on her hand, the pain in her stomach, and the voice, Traci was altogether coming unhinged.

"Dammit!" she exclaimed, slamming her hand against the side of the Simmons family home out of frustration.

Fortunately for her, this section of the house had vinyl siding. Otherwise, she'd be in an all new world of hurt.

"Fuck this," said Traci.

She walked back into the house, closed the door, and immediately moved to the sink to run her injured hand under cold water. She whispered a witch's prayer for speedy healing, taught to her by Myra Hutchens, the healer of her coven. While it did not automatically repair wounds of the flesh, it did offer respite from the pain, both frequent and occasional. She closed her eyes as she spoke the words.

"Goddess, hear my prayer, and deliver my body from this pain of flesh. In this hour I ask your favor, as sister, as daughter, as child of light. Heal me through the power of night."

After several minutes of the repeated prayer, Traci opened her eyes and removed her hand from the running water. She grabbed paper towels to dab it dry. Once done, she took notice and gasped.

The wound was healed.

"What the . . ."

My power grows.

Traci shuddered.

As the words and laughter once again echoed in her mind, she stared at her reflection in the kitchen window and saw an image that was not her. In place of her chestnut brown hair were brown curly tresses highlighted with gold. Her eyes glowed blue. Her lips were fuller, and her skin held a bronze tint. The woman in the reflection was not her. She was beautiful, she was powerful, but she was sinister and full of malintent.

And Traci knew her.

Goosebumps rose on her arms and the hair stood up. She felt a rush of cold air against her back and felt her own long tresses move in the breeze. Traci watched the image in the window continue to laugh. Frozen, captivated, and terrified, several beats passed before she regained some control and closed her eyes.

"Calm," she said.

She repeated the word again.

And again.

And again.

The laughter finally passed. Traci opened her eyes and breathed a sigh of relief at the sight of her own face staring back at her. She rested her hands on the edge of the sink, and the sensation of her previously injured hand against the cold metal of the sink's edge triggered her to examine it once again. She saw no sign of injury. Not so much as a scar.

Traci finished removing the items from her bag and made her way upstairs to the room she shared with Kassidy. She needed a shower. Traci stripped off her clothes and walked to the bathroom. She turned on the shower to let the water warm up and stared at herself in the mirror. In part, she wanted to ensure her reflection was her own. But she was also asking herself several questions. Was this how the end was going to come? A string of auditory and visual hallucinations? Would she spend her remaining days on this earth going mad? She couldn't fathom anything more torturous.

"God. I'm so sorry, Kass."

Amid thinking about the end, her thoughts had drifted to Kassidy, a woman she'd loved long before she truly knew her. What would this do to her? What would the truth do to her? Traci felt her eyes well with water.

Traci stepped in the shower and let the tears blend with the warm stream. She didn't cry out, just let the emotions manifest. She embraced them, each and every one. She respected each of them. She loved each of them, recognizing that they were all a part of her.

Poor, sad, helpless little witch.

Traci froze. She looked around and saw the steam from the shower's heat. On the other side of the shower glass, she saw a shadow.

"Kass . . . ?"

The shadow moved closer.

"Kass, is that you?"

As Traci reached for the bar to slide the shower glass back, hands phased through and grabbed her arms. Traci twisted and turned, trying desperately to free herself. In her mind she heard that sinister laughter, over and over. She pushed and pulled but the hands held on like a vice. Traci made one final pull backward before she was pulled through the glass completely. The cracking and breaking were the only things louder than the laughter in her mind. As she crashed to the cold tiled floor, she heard her name shouted.

"Kass . . ." she whispered.

As darkness took her, the image of the woman she saw in her reflection returned to her mind. She'd stopped laughing and spoke.

This is the end, little witch.

CHAPTER FOUR

KASSIDY SHIMMERED INSIDE HER HOME AND IMMEDIATELY COLLAPSED to the floor. The pain she'd experienced at the golf course was so intense that, even as it subsided, the remaining aches left her feeling as if she'd been hit by a car.

"What the fuck," she whispered, gasping, searching for air. "This Death God shit fucking sucks, man."

She'd only been a god for about two months.

The downside to everything she'd been experiencing was not knowing fully how to use her abilities. She wasn't certain what she was truly capable of. Most things came to her instinctively. Other things through trial and error. Now was one of those times she wished instinct would kick in.

Kassidy crawled to the couch and pulled herself up, each movement more painful than the last. When she was a child, she'd bargain through prayer for pain to go away. She'd promise to never do something again if God would just make it vanish. She'd done the same with more than one hangover, too. After she'd become a Reaper, she often retreated to the Nexus whenever pain hit. It was usually emotional pain she'd be battling, but it helped, nonetheless. It had, in fact, helped her heal faster from a few physical wounds, too.

The Nexus!

A wave of pain hit from the sudden movement of her head as some clarity manifested. Closing her eyes, she willed herself to enter the Nexus. It took a little longer than normal, as she maneuvered through the discomfort, but she soon found herself in the greenish-gray weigh station for souls. It was on this plane, a supernatural mirror of the real world, where Reapers met souls and escorted them to the Beyond, or the Void.

It was also in this place that Kassidy was born.

She'd only recently been made aware of that fact, and the knowledge led to some realizations about the nature of her abilities, particularly her empathic power. A psychopomp was inherently connected to all souls. That connection was exponentially stronger, though, in the Nexus. As a being born in the Nexus, Kassidy's connection to souls was immediate, and it was strengthened because of her heritage. As the daughter of Thanatos, the Death God, she was destined to be connected to death in some way. Destiny can also be cruel sometimes, and Kassidy often felt as if she'd been dealt a raw deal. In this moment, she was happy to have the connection to the Nexus, because she felt the pain subsiding. Her breathing steadied. The trembling stopped. Her strength returned.

"Whaddaya know about that?" she whispered.

Kassidy stood at full height and let her power fully return. Out of the corner of her eye, she saw her girlfriend, Traci, walking from the kitchen and heading up the stairs. She was mumbling something. Kassidy couldn't make it out, but to say she was curious would be an understatement. Ever since Kassidy had dispatched Solomon Steele, a rogue wraith who'd been siphoning god power from an amnesiac War God, Traci had been different. Kassidy wondered if it was because of what she'd eventually done for Ares. To pay a debt for the harm her father had caused the War God, Kassidy used the Scythe of Cronus to resurrect the woman he loved. The universe has rules. Kassidy broke one. The universe craves balance. Kassidy tilted the axis. That act, even though it was small, was bound to have a ripple effect.

Kassidy feared that ripple would pass over to Traci.

It was probably a silly thought. But given the way her world of Reapers, Wraiths, and death took her adoptive father, her ex-girlfriend, Lynn, and most recently, Octavia, Kassidy couldn't help but consider the possibility of spill over.

Feeling her strength fully return and the pain completely gone, Kassidy, hesitantly, transitioned back to the real world. She braced herself for the return of the sensation, but there was none.

"Thank you, Nexus," she said, drawing out the word "you" and clicking her tongue.

Kassidy removed her coat and tossed it over the back of the recliner. She walked to the mini bar and poured herself a very healthy dose of Elijah Craig bourbon. When Kassidy drank recreationally, whatever form that took for her, she'd drink her bourbon on the rocks. She preferred the taste and the lesser burn down her throat as the ice melted. Nights like tonight, though, called for bourbon unmolested. She wanted the taste, the smoke, and the burn.

Holding the rocks glass, Kassidy held it to her nose and inhaled. Her mouth watered. She took a small sip at first, let it settle on her tongue, and let the aroma fill her from the inside before swallowing. Satisfied, she took a second, larger sip, and swallowed immediately, relishing the feeling of the liquid heat sliding down her throat.

"Fuck that's good," she whispered.

The glass wasn't cold, but she nevertheless held it against her cheek. Her ear tingled as she heard the shower switch on upstairs. A part of her was tempted to go up and join Traci. But something inside held her back. The soothing water would help. Other things in the shower might help, too. But Kassidy was still shaken from the events of the night. The memory of pain and helplessness did not dissipate in the Nexus as the physical pain did. To say she was shaken was an understatement. Deep down, she was scared. Not just of the feeling, but of what it might all mean.

As the thoughts filled her mind, she looked at her glass and emptied it in two very healthy swallows. She needed more. So, she poured more. She took a sip. Then another. And still another, before walking to the recliner and placing the glass on the coffee table as she sat down. After a beat, she sat back, melted into the chair, and let out a long sigh.

CRASH!

"Shit," she said, startled by the sudden noise. "Traci!"

Kassidy shot out of her chair and ran up the stairs in a blur. Bursting into the master bedroom she heard the shower still going. Moving quickly, she pushed the door open and found the glass shower door shattered, and Traci laying on the floor.

"Traci! Oh my god!" screamed Kassidy, rushing to her girlfriend.

Kassidy gently brushed the hair away from Traci's face and called her name.

"Traci! Trace! C'mon babe, say something! Traci!"

For what seemed like an eternity, there was no response. Finally, Traci let out a low groan. Kassidy called her name again, and the groans were louder, with slight movement in the fingers.

"Oh god. Ok. Ok," said Kassidy. "Don't move, babe. I'm gonna get you over to the bed. Don't move. There's too much glass."

Kassidy placed Traci's hand in hers and shimmered, taking

them both from the bathroom floor to the bed. Traci began to move almost immediately, and Kassidy tried to soothe her, helping her to roll over onto her back.

"Okay, don't move, just stay put," said Kassidy.

Returning to the bathroom, Kassidy turned off the shower, then grabbed Traci's robe from the back of the door. When she got back to the bed, she found Traci sitting on the edge of the bed, staring straight forward.

"Trace?"

There was no response. There seemed to be no awareness either. Traci seemed to be in a trance of sorts. Kassidy wasn't sure, but guilt flooded her mind followed by her body. Her stomach tightened in response to what was happening, and not happening. The bedroom door suddenly slammed shut. Seconds later the bathroom door followed suit.

"What the . . ."

Kassidy's words trailed off as a cold wind flew through the bedroom. Kassidy's gaze immediately moved to the window. It was closed. Loud knocking started on the walls, an off-rhythm symphony of chaos. The doors opened and closed on their own. Confused, Kassidy just stood, listening to the supernatural disruptions. She felt some connection to it. This was god power, at least some of it. But there was something different about it. This was not anything she was familiar with or accustomed to. Her eyes settled back onto Traci, who was unflinching through the madness.

And then, all at once, it ceased, and Traci fell back on the bed.

Kassidy rushed over to her, calling her name. She got no response. Kassidy then lifted her to put her fully on the bed and covered Traci with a robe. Once again, she brushed hair from her face and for several moments just stared.

"I'm so sorry, babe. God. I'm so, so sorry," said Kassidy, convinced her actions were responsible for the madness.

Kassidy, propped on an elbow, leaned forward and kissed Traci on the forehead, then the cheek. She felt as if she were on the verge of tears. The sensation in her stomach was followed by a lump forming in her throat. Yet nothing came.

"Mm."

Kassidy perked up as Traci began to stir.

"Trace? Hey, babe."

"Hey," said Traci, letting the word drag out. "What are you doing?"

Traci's speech came out lazy, drowsy, as if climbing out of a deep dream, but Kassidy was happy to have anything at all.

"Are you okay, sweetheart?" asked Kassidy.

"Yeah. Yeah, I'm good. Just sleepy as hell. I took a shower, I think," said Traci, lifting her head long enough to see that she had a robe covering her. "Man, I must have been exhausted. I don't even remember getting out and coming to lay down."

Shock ran through Kassidy. Traci didn't remember it. Any of it. *What the hell is going on?*

"It's okay, babe. Let me get your nightshirt, and you can put that on and fall back to sleep," said Kassidy.

"Mm-mm," began Traci, "it's hot. I'll just sleep naked. I know you don't mind."

A soft giggle escaped from Traci as she moved the robe away and slowly wiggled up the length of the bed to make her way under the covers. As she did, Kassidy noticed that Traci did not have a mark on her. Through the shock of finding her on the floor and the subsequent chaos in the bedroom, the lack of cuts on Traci's skin was the furthest thing from her mind. She'd been careful when moving Traci for fear of fractures or possibly exacerbating some unseen trauma. Now Kassidy's thoughts drifted to missing cuts and absolutely no blood. "No babe. I don't mind at all," said Kassidy, pulling the covers up farther, then leaning to kiss Traci on the forehead again.

As Kassidy propped herself up on a pillow and began stroking Traci's hair, the bedroom and bathroom doors opened.

What. The. Fuck.

CHAPTER FIVE

THE DIVA MATERIALIZED ON THE ROOFTOP OF THE CENTERS FOR Disease Control and Prevention in Atlanta. The daylight hours offered no protection from possible onlookers, but she cared little of what others saw, or thought they saw. Soon, it wouldn't matter. Soon, her plan would take shape and the humans of the world would see exactly what she wanted them to see—a world made in her image. A world without gods, goddesses, and would-be heroes seeking to save everyone. The humans would see the world for what it was—a ball of gas infested with beings who cared only for themselves and their own self interests. It was one of the primary commonalities between gods and men, and while she was exhausted from it, she would use it, because she knew that even those invested in themselves needed a leader or a deity to follow.

She watched from her perch as people walked, talked, and laughed, and she wondered what they would do if they knew the end was near. The War God was alive and well. And after the Pulse the previous night, the prophecy of The Four was even closer to fruition. The prospect excited her. The thought of that power coming together, under her command, to bring about the end so that she could rebuild the world as it should have been. As it was meant to be.

With a single god on a throne.

She looked beyond the building she was atop and watched

people go about their day at Emory University, just opposite her. The Diva was fixated on a family walking the grounds. A young man, perhaps nineteen or twenty, walked and talked with excitement as he pointed out different areas of the campus to an older couple, presumably his parents. Next to them were a younger boy and girl, grade school age at best.

"Must be family day," said the Diva with great disdain.

She didn't hate families per se. But the concept was so foreign to her that she found it laughable. Among the gods, there was no such thing as a nuclear family. They were beings of great power, and even greater ego and vanity. Jealousy, lust, anger, loathing, these emotions seemed to be the driving force for deities. These emotions fueled their decisions. They were what started wars.

They were what got her banished.

The Diva thought back to her own family. All gods were related in some way, but some closer than others. She was among the early gods of creation, a child of primordial deities, the very beings that had shaped the earth and the heavens above. That in and of itself should have afforded her some respect. Instead, she had been forgotten. She was ignored. And those moments when her presence was acknowledged, she was ridiculed. Her parents, her siblings, gods that came after her, that should have revered her, relegated her to the role of black sheep. They thought of her as nothing more than a petulant child seeking attention. Sure, when they needed her, they called. Hera certainly had no problem seeking her counsel and her help in dealing with her own hedonistic husband. Once that help was offered, the Diva was forgotten. In retaliation, she used the prize of the gods, the mortals, as her playthings.

Until the moment the gods felt she'd gone too far.

A part of her respected them for their approach. Well, she

respected one. But the others, especially the male gods, cowered behind rank and power and issued verdicts of guilt without so much as a trial.

"They should have killed me," she whispered to herself as her thoughts took her back.

"Um . . . Mistress," said a voice from behind.

The Diva turned quickly, extended an arm, and used her power to grip an unsuspecting man by the throat with an invisible hand. She gritted her teeth as he clutched at the force around his neck. He rose into the air as she lifted her arm. Stepping down from the ledge of the rooftop, the Diva walked toward him, awareness of his identity setting in. She lowered him to the gravel, released her psychokinetic grip, and smiled.

"So sorry," she began, "you caught me off guard. A girl has to protect herself in this day and age, you know."

"Yes . . . of . . . of course," said the man, coughing, trying to recover from his fright.

"Do you have what I need?"

"Y-y-yes, Mistress. Here you are," said the man, extending a vial of colorless liquid to the Diva.

The Diva held the vial in her hand, examined it, and grinned.

"And you're sure this will do what I need it to?"

"Mistress, I . . . I . . ."

The Diva turned her gaze to the man standing before her. Doctor Robert James was a Nobel Prize-winning scientist who specialized in the field of cell regeneration. He sought the secrets of science that would allow amputees to regrow limbs. He explored the science that would slow the growth of cancer cells to give other forms of treatment time to act and heal the body. His most recent research had successfully reanimated cells in the bodies of dead animals. It was this that had caught the Diva's attention.

"Please don't tell me you're going to give me excuses," said the Diva, her eyes turning bright blue.

"No, Mistress. It's just that—"

"What?!"

"It's just that this has only been tested on animals, Mistress. I have no idea what impact it will have on a human. Especially . . . especially one that's been expired for so long," said the doctor, shakily.

The Diva laughed.

"Rest assured, Dr. James, I am under no illusions that you've tapped into the power of a god to reanimate a corpse. In fact, there are only a few gods capable of such a feat, so please, calm your delusions of grandeur. You're onto something, I'll give you that. But your simple science is centuries away from true power."

"Yes, Mistress," said Robert.

The Diva again stared at the vial. It wouldn't re-animate the way she needed, but it would serve her purposes. Despite her power, despite being the child of the primordial gods, the Diva did not possess the power to bring back the dead. Only one in her line did, and he was indisposed. The science, combined with the power manifesting following the Pulse, would bring back a *corpse*. A very particular corpse.

A member of the Four.

The thought of it excited her. It had her happy, hopeful, and feeling more devious than ever. She was distracted by the realization that the doctor was still present.

"You may go now," she said to him.

"Oh, um . . . yes, Mistress."

The doctor turned and started toward the door. Strangely, he stopped and returned, his head down in reverence . . . and fear.

"M-m-mistress? Um, will I see you again?"

The Diva smirked, then let out a giggle.

"Oh, my dear Dr. James, we um . . . we don't do that anymore. I'm done with you. Until I'm not."

The doctor nodded, clearly saddened, most assuredly emasculated. After he walked away, the Diva returned to the ledge and looked again at the people walking the campus across the way, then at the scientists in the lot below. She saw the family again walking about. One of the grade school children, the boy, jumped on the back of the tour guide, the big brother. The Diva felt a pang of emotion. A coil in her stomach of longing. She longed for a feeling she'd never experienced. The feeling that young boy was likely feeling.

Pride.

Adoration.

Love.

She'd never felt those things from others. The pride she experienced was her own. Rooted in perseverance and dedication to her plan. She was a survivor, despite those who wished otherwise. There had never been adoration from anyone. There was support—reluctant support, from those who saw, just as she did, that the patriarchal rule of the Twelve needed to end.

Love was another story.

The Diva had never truly felt it. She understood the concept. She'd witnessed what she assumed to be love. But in the end, no one loved her, and she loved no one. There was a time, though, when that could have been different. A time when she had been not unlike the grade school boy jumping on the back of his older brother. She too had a brother. She had many siblings, but one, only one showed her compassion and took an interest in her life. Only one dared show an emotion toward her other than disdain. There were times when he was disappointed, sure. But he always returned to show her some semblance of support.

Until the end.

Until he imprisoned her.

That betrayal was the final insult. When that happened, she understood that she could trust no man, whether he be god or mortal. Bonds of family meant nothing. Nothing mattered but power and the ability to wield it and bend others to your will. She wondered if the boy below would one day learn that lesson, as she did. Unlike him, she was born to chaos. She was born to darkness. She was destined to be a shadow across creation. Early on, she had tried to fight her nature. She tried desperately to be something other than what she was born to be. But they would not let her. The Diva was always reminded just who she was. Eventually she tired of it. Eventually she decided that if that was how the world saw her, then that's what she would be. She would no longer regret it or feel embarrassment. She would embrace her role.

And for that, she had been imprisoned.

"Thank you again, brother," she said to herself. "You opened my eyes to truth, and each day that's passed I am grateful. In the new world, in my world, those lessons will lay the foundation for *my* rule."

The Diva turned her attention from the family walking Emory University to the vial of liquid in her hand.

"The ignorance of man and his hubris has brought me a powerful tool that will only aid in their subjugation."

The Diva smiled.

Her eyes shone bright blue.

"Oh well, off to Ki'lal."

And with a brief but terrifying laugh, she shimmered away.

CENTURIES AGO

"I feel . . . so . . . foolish," said Persephone.

"Oh, my dear, it is not your fault," said Hecate.

The two goddesses stood across from one another in Persephone's sitting room. The room was dark, as one might expect in the Underworld. There was a fireplace that roared, sending light to the blackened walls which were adorned with the heads of various creatures killed by Hades and his minions. As consolation for her abduction and subsequent imprisonment, Hades acquiesced to two requests from his new bride. She asked for a sitting room, and a companion, a friend to serve as confidant and support in the dark desolate existence that was the Underworld. And so, he gave her a room and allowed Hecate to remain as guest and resident for as long as she chose.

"Isn't it? I mean—"

"No!" demanded Hecate.

Persephone reacted to the sharpness of the tone. Hecate softened her edge appropriately. The girl was a victim after all. She was not to blame. There was no sense in exacerbating her fears. Her abduction, a selfish act that now resulted in her holding the undesired mantle of Queen of the Underworld, had been orchestrated by men. Men who acted with only the thought of power and sex as commerce. No, this was not Persephone's fault, and Hecate was determined to help her see that.

"I'm . . . sorry," began Hecate, "but for as long as I can remember, we've always been at the mercy of the male gods among us, and their ferocious, primal natures. They would have us believe that they have the best interest of gods and men in mind with every decision they make. But it's always about them. Them and their . . . needs. Needs that change as quickly as the winds change direction."

"You've dealt with this for some time," said Persephone.

"Longer than I care to think about," said Hecate.

Hecate had met Persephone when she was a young girl. The young girl's spirit was remarkable, and it was that memory that spurred Hecate to help locate her. She and Demeter not only found the poor girl, but learned that Hades, God of the Underworld, was responsible. While the betrayal had not surprised many gods, it had surprised Demeter. She'd always supported her brother. Through war, through argument, through every discord, she'd supported him, and in the end, she'd learned that she was just as much a pawn as the humans.

"Perhaps it's time for women to rule," said Persephone. "Perhaps it's time for us to be the mothers of the world. The mothers worshipped by man and god alike."

"Perhaps," said Hecate. "You are ambitious. But you are not wrong."

Hecate had long thought the same. The universe, the world, was the creation of Chaos, and from that Gaia was born. She was ultimately responsible for the birth of all gods. So how was she not more revered? How were all goddesses not more revered? It had long bothered Hecate. It had long bothered many goddesses. For now, there was little to be done. For now, they would simply bide their time.

For now.

"Enough of this," began Hecate, "we should try our best to focus on the pleasant."

"What pleasantness is there in the Underworld?"

"Well, there's you, my dear."

Both women chuckled. It was a light chuckle that grew into laughter. Hecate walked over to a table in the middle of the sitting room and poured wine from the pitcher into two goblets.

"Thank you," said Persephone, accepting the goblet of wine.

Hecate nodded, then looked around. The situation they were in was not ideal to be sure. Unlike Persephone, she could come and go as she pleased. Her power permitted it even before she was allowed to remain as Persephone's companion. Much like Hermes or Thanatos, the Death God, Hecate was a psychopomp, a being that could travel between the real world and spirit world. She didn't do it often, but she didn't want Persephone to feel abandoned and left to a lonely and dark existence.

"We need some color in this room," said Hecate.

"Sure. Let's kill some artists. Some to paint, and others to create some beautiful sculptures down here," said Persephone, sarcastically.

Hecate gave a look, then a chuckle and smile.

"We can do better," she said. "While the mortals may be able to turn nothing into art like it's magic, we . . . have actual magic."

Hecate eyes turned bright blue, and with outstretched hands she allowed energy to flow through her. She mouthed words in an ancient tongue to augment her spell. As goddess of witchcraft and magic, she needed no totem, no conduit to direct her magic, and no words to create a spell. But she could use any, or all of those things, to strengthen her power and change the very fabric of reality.

As she was doing now.

Instead of blackened walls with heads of hideous creatures, there was bright sky, blue, with pillowy clouds. In the distance there were rolling hills and beyond them, snowcapped mountains that reached the heavens. Off to one side, there was a small lake, surrounded by beautiful trees and bushes. The once dark and dank sitting room had transformed into a beautiful countryside.

"How is this possible?" asked Persephone.

"My dear, anything is possible," began Hecate, "if you want it bad enough."

Hecate watched as Persephone reached down to touch the grass. The light in Persephone's eyes as she looked up at the sunny sky and smiled filled Hecate's heart. And when the girl closed her eyes and danced in the field, Hecate's heart melted. They'd spent much time together in the months since she'd been found. Most of that time had been spent in sadness and despair. But finally, Hecate saw a glint of light and hope that had not existed before. Instead of a sad goddess filled with dread as the result of selfishness and betrayal, she saw a beautiful woman dancing on the winds. In her, Hecate saw a daughter. She wondered what it would be like to raise her own, to spend time with her own, to openly love her own.

"Where are we?" asked Persephone.

"Still in your sitting room," replied Hecate. "Only now, when you go through the doors, you come to light and life instead of dread."

"This is so wonderful. Can you teach me this power?"

"I can teach you a great many things," said Hecate. "For now, we sit, we enjoy our wine, and we talk of pleasant things."

Persephone inclined her head and raised her goblet in agreement. She drank, she smiled, she laughed. Neither of the goddesses felt the weight of their station. Neither of them felt the obligation that came with their abilities. Neither of them felt the pull of family and responsibility.

Neither of them saw Hades as he hid in a darkened corner.

CHAPTER SIX

KASSIDY WAS EXHAUSTED. NOT OF THE BODY. NOW, AS A GOD, SHE didn't feel physical fatigue the way she once did. Not only was her strength augmented, so too were her reflexes and stamina. If there were perks to her current station, those were surely among them.

The fatigue she felt was of the spirit. It was ever present. And like many things in her life, she largely ignored it. Or at least, she tried to. It lingered about—a sly specter ready to grow and become an even greater nuisance. It was much like her relationship with alcohol and Vicodin. And her relationship with herself.

She pushed those thoughts away and focused on the task at hand. She'd managed to sleep for about an hour after finally settling down from the incident with Traci before being awakened by the particularly strong pull of a soul. This soul was old. Not powerful, but strong, and wily. It was a trickster, and this was clearly not the first time it had escaped and inhabited a human body. There was a playfulness to it, but with that playfulness, just under the surface, a malevolence. She'd followed the pull and found the body it inhabited.

"If you just let me be, I promise not to cause any trouble or harm. I'm just trying to live," said the man standing before her.

Kassidy had no idea who he was, the man. She only knew that the voice and the behavior were not his. She also knew that she needed to cleanse him of this vagrant soul soon before it became near impossible to do so safely. If it came down to it, she would let the body die to evacuate the soul and escort it to its final destination. But she wanted to avoid that.

"I've heard that shit from others before," said Kassidy.

Without saying another word, Kassidy threw her fist forward and allowed it to phase through the chest of the man. Once inside, she opened her fist, letting her power build. She sought the essence of the vagrant soul and once she found it, she concentrated, and called it to her.

"Gah!!"

The voice was still that of the vagrant soul, likely feeling the pain of being torn from its host. The soul was in so much agony that she felt the pain, too. A part of her, a small part of her, considered stopping. Ripping a soul the way she was doing was an act of violence. She'd never had to do it as a Reaper. She'd heard of Azra-El doing it in the past, but she, and a few other Reapers, dismissed that as bravado. They thought it was a story to scare and impress young Reapers and show just how powerful the Primus was.

It worked.

Each time she dared challenge him, those stories lingered in the back of her mind. He was so powerful that he did not have to wait for a human to die before taking their soul? It made her wonder just what else he was capable of. It made everyone wonder. To that end, the stories fulfilled their purpose. In her role now as Death God, Kassidy wondered if he had indeed been powerful enough to rip a soul from a human, because she was having a difficult time with it. But she quickly dismissed the thought. Whether he was or was not was irrelevant. He was gone. That was then. This was now. And in the now, there was no question that Kassidy's power, and her word, were final.

She continued to pull the soul until she felt its essence in her grasp, and she squeezed. Then she pulled. Feeling some resistance at first, she doubled her efforts. This was her first attempt at this. She wondered what trauma might imprint on the host's soul. She wondered, but she pressed on. This soul needed to be extricated. Gathering more power, she channeled energy into her free hand, pressed it against the torso of the host body and released it. The host was propelled backward, and all that remained before her was the vagrant soul.

Kassidy immediately transitioned them to the Nexus.

"Well," she began, "that wasn't so bad, now was it."

"How did you do that?"

"With style. With flair. And with no remorse," said Kassidy.

She still felt some fear emanating from the soul. Perhaps that level of power was unexpected. The soul was old, but in its time had likely only encountered Reapers, and they were certainly not powerful enough to rip a soul from a body.

"You've been around a long time," said Kassidy. "You've caused a lot of problems in the world, too. I think it's time that comes to an end."

Once again, fear wafted from the soul. Perhaps it felt stronger in the Nexus because of her station and her connection to the place. Whatever the case, she needed to end this, and she needed to get back to Traci.

Kassidy stretched out her hand, closed her eyes, and tapped into the power within the Nexus to get the vagrant soul to its next plain of existence. In this act, the Nexus would decide where the soul would go. Those that led a good life went to the Beyond. Others, the ones who'd lived particularly wicked lives went to the Void. She felt pretty certain she knew where this soul would end up.

"No. Please, no," pleaded the disembodied entity.

"Your time is up," said Kassidy.

In the distance, a swirl of light manifested. It was dark, and even in the Nexus, a place with no atmosphere, no weather, it felt cold. Kassidy felt its pull, and she released the soul. She watched as the Void pulled in its next member. The image brought back the recent memory of her own time there. She wasn't sure how or why she had appeared there. She'd not led the best life, but certainly not one worthy of the Void. Perhaps all those things she'd done at the behest of Azra-El had added up over time. If not for her heritage, if not for her father, she'd still be trapped there. A shudder ran through her. Even now she wasn't all that certain how she'd escaped. Given her recent actions, she wondered if she'd be able to escape again.

You're the Death God now, girl. Stop it. Neither the Beyond nor the Void can hold you.

As the soul finally went fully through, the portal closed. The swirling light dissipated. And Kassidy, once more, felt the weight of the real world take hold. She had to return to Traci and find out what was happening to her. She desperately wanted to end Traci's torment and make things right with the universe.

She could do these things.

She could do anything.

She was the Death God, and her power was absolute.

CHAPTER SEVEN

"Hello, I'm Marilyn Simms. Aggressions persist in Ki'lal following the assassinations of Ambassador Hassan Davis and General Kareem Nasir. Neither the Shihadi nor the Jen'ai, show interest in a cease fire. And now there are reports of biological weapons being used to poison food supplies on *both* sides. Once again, we welcome General Marcus Kelly, former Chairman of the Joint Chiefs of Staff, to weigh in on this frightening situation. General, welcome."

"Good to see you again, Marilyn."

"General, let's jump right into things. During one of the last times we spoke about the issues unfolding in Ki'lal, you indicated that it would be foolish to imply that the assassinations of General Nasir and Ambassador Davis were orchestrated by US intelligence. In fact, I believe the word you used was 'hogwash.'"

"Yes, that's right, Marilyn. It would be absolutely foolish to think that our government would be responsible for something like that. The repercussions of America's involvement would be too great."

"Yet there are growing reports that show that the assassinations were ordered by none other than Charles Cartwright, one of the richest and most influential men in the country."

"Rich, influential, and very dead."

"Yes, but presumably by the assassin he hired to carry out the murders, Jaxon Burke."

"Well, see now Marilyn, that's just the thing. Cartwright's

involvement, Burke's involvement, it all stinks of cover up and scapegoating. Look, further investigations into this Burke character indicate that he's been a gun for hire for almost two decades, a private contractor beholden to nothing and no one, save the almighty dollar. To think that he cared enough to cause an international incident is preposterous."

"And Cartwright? I know he's been a close friend and ally to both you and the military in the past. Is it impossible to believe that he may have orchestrated all of this for financial gain?"

"Cartwright was a friend, and a patriot. His death, no, his murder, is a great loss to this nation. I cannot fathom a reality in which *he* is responsible for any of this. The bottom line is, like many things across the planet, what's happening in Ki'lal is a matter of land, resources, and religion, nothing more."

"Who do you think, then, is responsible for the unrest in the region?"

"I don't even want to speculate, Marilyn. But I'll tell you this, seeing France, England, and Russia, gear up to take sides is not good."

"And why is that?"

"Well, it drags more of the world into a situation that we don't need to be involved in and it causes people to take sides. The Russians are supporting the Jen'ai, France and England are supporting the Shahidi. There's already tension between the western nations and Russia. Russia is picking up allies here and there to support their middle east movement. All of this is a precursor to worldwide aggressions."

"Are you suggesting now that we're on a path toward a third world war?"

"Marilynn, I'm suggesting that if something isn't done now, we'll all be in a world of hurt, from which we may never recover."

"One last thing, General. We're getting reports now of poisoned food supplies. Now, if it were one side or the other, it might be easier to place blame, but this is an issue that will affect both the Shahidi and the Jen'ai, and there's speculation that a third party is responsible. Do you think it's possible that an unknown force is orchestrating this unrest?"

"See, now you're trying to drag my good friend into this again. Let me say again, neither Charles Cartwright, nor his family or company, is responsible for any of this."

"Well, I didn't name him directly, General. But I think it's telling that you did. I wonder if you're hearing the same rumors."

"Rumors are just that, rumors. No matter who's spreading them, they're almost always unfounded in situations like these."

"So, it's your assertion that there is no third party orchestrating these events, and there's no third party deliberately poisoning the food supply? A phenomenon that's spreading throughout the middle east, by the way, and even affecting areas of India and Southeast Asia."

"I'm a soldier, Marilyn. I believe in what I can see. Right now, I see countries colluding to potentially mount massive campaigns against one another that will have global repercussions for years to come. If something isn't done soon to quell the hostilities, we're in trouble."

"That region is on the brink of war, and with famine and drought looming, disease can't be far behind."

"The only part of the quartet left is death, Marilyn. Saying the apocalypse is on the horizon is a bit dramatic. And yet . . . it's unfolding before our very eyes."

"What can we do, General?"

"Pray, Marilyn. Pray."

CHAPTER EIGHT

KASSIDY MADE A POINT OF NEVER WATCHING THE NEWS. WHEN SHE did, it was sports and weather, and only because those two things were typically matters of fact. The sportscasters would report the scores, tell you who got hurt, and the meteorologists would give you an idea of what to wear each day. There was little to no opinion. There was no speculation—well, except during playoffs and drafts. Otherwise, there were only facts.

Now, though, she watched the news intently.

Ever since that damned prophecy about the Four returning, she watched the news to keep an eye on what was going on in the world. And this woman, this Marilyn Simms, literally called out the Four by name. War, Famine, Disease, and Death. Two of them were already here. Were the others as well? Was there some entity out there, a personification of famine, poisoning food supplies?

"Where the fuck are you, Burke?" she whispered to herself.

When she last left Jaxon Burke, the name assumed by Ares, the War God, following several hundred years of amnesia, he said he was going to the site of the unrest to try and quell tensions. He was, traditionally, prone to succumb to an unparalleled bloodlust, though. He said he'd found ways to manage it. But with war escalating around him, could he truly resist those primal urges again—the urges that led to him being a deadly warrior and one of the most hated gods among the Twelve?

As if the prospect of the apocalypse wasn't enough, Kassidy had to deal with whatever was happening to Traci. Something sinister was afoot, she was sure of it, but between the Four and vagrant souls possessing innocents, Traci's witchy issues were just . . . inconvenient.

"I'm the worst," she said to herself, thinking about how selfish she was being. Kassidy very much wanted all the nonsense to go away, especially given that she may very well have been the cause of said nonsense. Despite recently coming to terms with her station and her duties, deep down, it was still too much. She didn't want to be a Death God, but who else could be? She didn't want her girlfriend to be going through hell, but there it was. A large part of her wanted to escape, if only for a little while. Her typical coping mechanisms were bourbon and sex. Both had gotten her in trouble a time or two, and Kassidy was determined to manage her stressors. Typically, when she craved alcohol, she'd clench her fists absently, or rapidly tap—either her foot on the ground, or her hand against her thigh. So far, none of that was happening, which was a *very* good thing. There was no telling what an out-of-control Death God could do to the world. Especially in its current state.

"Babe, have you seen my blue Nikes?" shouted Traci from upstairs.

"Yeah, they're down here by the recliner," said Kassidy after briefly scanning the area. Traci had a habit of kicking off her shoes anywhere. It was a bit of a pet peeve for Kassidy, but considering the amount of disrepair in the house, shoes being deposited virtually anywhere was a minor nuisance at best.

For now, at least.

Kassidy heard Traci bound down the stairs and caught a glimpse of her as she walked by toward the recliner. Out of nowhere she was hit with a sensation of lust that she'd not felt in ages. And it was solely her emotion.

"Whoa!" exclaimed Kassidy as the sight of Traci in black leggings and the gray V-neck T-shirt, took her to an entirely different state of excitement.

"What?"

"Where are you going dressed like that?" Kassidy asked.

"Like what?" Traci asked.

"Like . . . that. All . . . yummy," said Kassidy.

"Girl, stop," said Traci, giggling. "You've seen me in leggings before."

"Yeah, but something is . . . different today."

Kassidy got off the couch and stalked toward Traci, their eyes locked. She felt something instinctual, almost primal, surging within. Normally, when she felt this way, it was the result of her empathic powers channeling competing arousals in an enclosed space. Bars and nightclubs often assaulted her senses, and her libido. But this was no bar. This was damn sure not a nightclub. This was her living room, and she was inexplicably lost in desire.

"What are you—"

Kassidy cut off Traci's question with a kiss. A deep, sensual, probing kiss that seemed unyielding. She cradled Traci's face at first, then allowed her hands to slip down to her waist, where she pulled her closer. The vibration of Traci's moan against her mouth sent tingles through Kassidy's body and she pulled her even closer. She moved her hands up and down Traci's back before settling them on her ass, where she squeezed, causing yet another moan. Her urges intensified and she knew Traci's desire had joined hers and it sent her over the edge.

Kassidy pulled Traci back to the couch without losing contact with her lips. At the edge of the cushion, Kassidy worked her thumbs into Traci's leggings and began to slide them down. For the first time, in what seemed like years since their kiss began, Kassidy pulled back, but her eyes were still locked on Traci's. Kassidy lowered herself, continuing to pull the leggings down. Traci helped by stepping out of them. Kassidy broke eye contact, allowing her eyes to drop down to the light, wispy, hair between Traci's thighs. She lightly pushed Traci back onto the couch. Her gaze returned to Traci's eyes, and she lifted a leg and put it over her shoulder. Kassidy kissed Traci's inner thigh, nibbled lightly, then ran her tongue along the length until she reached her middle. Kassidy looked up at Traci as she lowered her head and claimed her. The heat, scent, and sweetness on her tongue enveloped Kassidy. In a blanket of warmth, comfort, love, and lust, she devoured Traci, allowing shared moans to serve as their afternoon soundtrack.

◆　◆　◆

Traci was stretched out on the couch, her head against a pillow, her forearm draped over her forehead, as she worked to catch her breath. Opposite her, Kassidy was leaning into the couch, her head resting against the soft cushions, staring at Traci as she teasingly licked her fingers, before offering the Cheshire Cat like grin. Traci giggled shyly then sent her lover a kiss through the air.

"So, you like those leggings?" Traci asked.

Both women laughed.

"I like them better balled up on the floor," said Kassidy, gesturing to the mass of fabric on the rug. "But, yeah, they uh . . . did something for me."

"I may have to write a letter to the manufacturer. Maybe I'll become a spokeswoman and start raking in dough from my many, many commercials."

"That's not a bad idea," said Kassidy. "Happy to act it out in a pitch meeting."

"Ha! Freak!" said Traci.

"Only for you."

Traci blew another kiss.

"I'm going to grab something to drink," said Kassidy. "You want anything?"

"Just a bottle of water. That would be great, babe."

Traci stretched her hand out as Kassidy arose and walked past her toward the kitchen. When she felt Kassidy's hand in hers, she pulled it in, kissed it, and held it against her cheek for a beat, before letting it go. Traci laid there, naked, exposed, and feeling more comfortable than she'd ever felt in her life. A life that had been challenging, scary. No. Terrifying.

A life that now belongs to me!

Traci bolted straight up at the sound of the voice in her head.

"Who's there?" she asked absently.

"What babe?" asked Kassidy from the kitchen.

"Um, nothing, Kass. Just talking to myself."

Oh no. You were talking to me. Tell her . . . you're talking to me.

Traci began to shiver. Suddenly a sense of cold dread washed over her. She pulled her knees up, close to her chest and wrapped her arms around them. That voice. Could it be?

Oh, yes. It's me. My time is coming. Soon, it'll be me your little girlfriend is tasting on her lips.

"No," began Traci, "Not yet. It's too soon. I have—"

You have no more time! Only what I give you.

Traci shuddered at those words. She was supposed to have more time. It wasn't supposed to happen this soon. It wasn't supposed to feel like . . . this.

Too late for regrets. Too late for tears. You made your bargain and I'm coming to collect what's mine, little witch.

Tears welled in the corner of her eyes. She shuddered again as if a frigid wind had run over her body. Outside, she heard a clap of thunder and once clear skies suddenly turned cloudy. Rain fell almost immediately followed by the violent pelting of hailstone.

"Holy shit," said Kassidy, walking back into the living room. "Where the hell did this storm come from?"

Traci said nothing. She knew where it was from. She knew what it signified. She knew she was running out of time. Tears began to stream down her face as the rain intensified. A loud crack of thunder caused her to grab her stomach in pain and she cried out.

"Traci!"

Another crack of thunder and she threw her head back in agony.

"Oh my god! Babe!" screamed Kassidy as she dropped the drinks from her hand and ran toward Traci.

Traci began to tremble and shake, throwing her head back and forth, screaming in agony with each crack of thunder. Over and over throngs of pain and electricity ran through her. Any awareness of Kassidy's presence had long since gone. Coupled with the loudest crack of thunder, Traci shrieked.

And then there was silence.

Outside, the skies cleared, and the sun returned to prominence. Inside, you could hear a pin drop. Traci sat on the couch, upright, staring at nothing.

"Traci?!"

At the sound of her name, Traci turned her head to Kassidy and smiled.

"Hey baby! Did you get my water? You made me work up a hell of a thirst. Damn. I gotta wear those leggings more often."

TWENTY YEARS AGO

Traci sat on the floor in her basement, cross-legged, enthralled, and read the words again and again. She wasn't sure what to make of them. On the surface, it seemed plain and simple. But as she began to understand more about witchcraft, her lineage, and her power, or at least, her potential for power, she knew that nothing in the books was ever plain and simple. She was diving into a magic that was forbidden by her coven, thus defying the head of their order—her mother. But it didn't matter to her. From her point of view, this was her only choice. She wanted to impress her mother. Traci's lack of magical prowess left her feeling shame, and she was certain her mother, as coven leader, felt it, too. Her lack of power was a source of tension between them. This was the way to finally make her mother proud. But she was also desperate to find the one who'd saved her and her cousin Carmen, along with half a dozen other young witches. The girl who'd saved them from whatever that man truly was.

The girl with the black eyes.

The moment replayed in her mind as it often did. While the girls stood together, holding hands to try and spark some sort of collective magic to escape, they were shocked when another girl appeared. She wasn't that much older than any of them. The dark-haired girl also seemed shocked to see them all, and at the same time, seemed determined to help them. Their freedom would have come sooner had he not returned.

When Traci and Carmen had first met him, he seemed harmless. He was just a guy who seemed to be having a perfectly peaceful time reading a novel in the park. They'd seen him there many times before, reading, with a notebook and coffee at his side. He was nice to kids as they played. He tilted his head and smiled in acknowledgment to people saying hello to him. So, when some punks from the neighborhood started to bother him and tease him, Traci and her cousin came to his aid without hesitation.

They didn't fight the three boys. They didn't use magic against them. Their powers were still very latent. Carmen had little control and could not summon them at will. Traci had not yet been able to tap into her powers at all. It caused great anguish in the family. She was sixteen. Her powers should have manifested years ago. Carmen and Traci were among a number of young witches who would come into their abilities later in adolescence. Even without their powers, Traci and Carmen were strong. They fought. Not a lot, but well enough to be a thorn in someone's side. Their shared ability to fight gave them the confidence to stand up to any bully. And so, they did. They stood up to three high school boys who'd felt the need to pick on a nice, innocent, middle-aged man, who wanted nothing more than to enjoy his coffee and read.

If they'd known then how wrong they were, they likely would have left the man alone.

Later in the week, they'd encountered him again. They sat with him, talked with him, and shared their love of books and pop culture. Of course, when the subject of books on magic and witches came up, their eyes widened. When he'd offered to show them his collection at his home, Traci was only slightly hesitant. She didn't believe he would do anything sinister, and she felt herself capable of fighting back against him if he did.

She was wrong on both counts.

Shortly after arriving at his home, she found herself awakening next to Carmen in a cage with other young girls. It wasn't long before they learned they were all witches with latent abilities. And it wasn't long after that realization that they learned their captor had a few surprises of his own. Namely, the fact that he was not human.

His eyes turned coal black, and he shrieked at them all as they made noise to arouse neighbors and passersby. This form, this . . . whatever he'd become was ghastly. They didn't know the extent of his abilities, but they knew they did not possess the power to stop him. Each day they prayed to Hecate for someone to come and liberate them. Each day they prayed for someone that possessed the power to fight him, to destroy him, and to free them.

And then she came.

She fought him, with some difficulty at first. At one point, the young girl seemed shocked at what she saw. Shocked at his power. She clearly hadn't been expecting it. Yet she found some way to best him. When she'd first arrived, she had wild silver eyes and fought like a seasoned warrior. At least, to Traci's limited understanding and standards. When that girl's eyes turned black though, something else was unleashed. Now, it was their captor who was shocked. The young girl ended the battle quickly after that, and then, without warning, turned into smoke and vanished.

Before she'd disappeared, Traci saw a look in the girl's eyes that was one of horror, anger, disgust, and confusion. She appeared to be as lost in her power as Traci and Carmen were in the search for theirs. Hours later, help arrived. Police broke in and freed the girls. Parents were contacted, statements were given, and the nightmare was over. Only, it wasn't so much a nightmare for Traci as it was an awakening. In the instant she'd lain eyes on the young girl who'd saved her, she felt something. A connection. A kinship. Admiration. Attraction.

She desperately wanted to know that girl. She was determined to find her by any means, and she knew her best chance was through magic. The girl, while likely not a witch, possessed some kind of magic. There had to be a spell to find her.

Traci threw herself into the study of magic. She attempted to cast spell after spell for months, to no avail. Her power just wasn't there. She tracked her lineage and studied every witch that had come before her. Traci studied more texts—each book older than the one before it, until she found *the* book. The book no one her age was allowed to see. There were rumors about it. It was said that it was the grimoire of Hecate herself. Made from her. Written by her. Blessed by her. There were stories about its power and the things it could unleash on the world, but most of the young witches chalked it up to simple tales you tell children to teach them the importance of using their powers wisely.

But she'd found it.

Hidden in plain sight among her mother's treasures. Jewelry, chalices, charts, scrolls, all things entrusted to the coven leader. The grimoire was there. Traci found it, read it, and once she realized what it was, she absorbed every word of it. But these words stuck out like beacons and left her uneasy.

She who reads these words must only do so in times of dire need for the magic in these pages releases the power of the mother into her.

Despite the warning, a warning she had not fully understood, she pressed forward with her self-study. She practiced ceaselessly, desperate to find the spark that would ignite her abilities. That spark came on Halloween night just before her eighteenth birthday, and it came with force and authority. To the shock of her mother and others in the coven, she was able to handle every bit of it. All of her study had prepared her—mind, body, soul—

for that moment. She felt her mother's pride, and the pride of her sisters in the coven. More than that, she felt she was one step closer to finding her savior.

It was strange. As Traci read the grimoire over and over, she understood it more and more, and for some reason, she worried less and less. When her mother found her, in the basement of their home, practicing the forbidden magic, Traci was not prepared for the anger unleashed upon her. After a time, her mother found her center and, realizing how advanced her daughter was, decided to explain instead of yell.

"Your abilities are growing fast. It stands to reason that your curiosity would, too," said her mother. "I'm sorry for coming down so hard, but there is power in this book that, if unleashed, could have deadly repercussions."

"How so?" asked Traci.

"While we pray to and honor the goddess, Hecate, we are careful not to unleash her power."

"But why? She could use her power to make the world better," said Traci.

"It's not that simple," began her mother, "because in order for her to come back, she would have to live in the body of someone, likely the person who released her by reading the words in this book."

"So, if I read them, I'd die? She'd take over my body?"

"It's possible."

"But no one knows for sure?"

"No, no one knows for sure," said her mother. "But if there's the slightest chance that it's true, we cannot risk using this book. Unleashing that kind of magic could trigger a change in the natural order. The balance between life and death could be destabilized."

Traci's mother was not sure of the exact repercussions, but

she knew they would be many, and they would likely affect more than just her daughter. Traci had listened, and she'd promised her mother she would not practice that magic.

But it was for her.

The dark-haired girl with the silver eyes.

So Traci continued to read.

CHAPTER NINE

KEIRON KNELT AT OCTAVIA'S GRAVE, ONE HAND PLACED ON THE headstone. He'd seen death over and over in the centuries he'd been alive. None affected him as much as this one. She'd been his oldest friend. They could have been more. It would have been easy, almost too easy. Perhaps that had been part of the problem.

"I feel . . . empty. It's strange. Death isn't new to me, as well you know. But this? This is just . . ."

Keiron let his words drift off on the wind as he spoke to Octavia. From what he knew of death, the afterlife, he was certain she could not hear him. She had been killed by the Scythe of Cronus, the only weapon that could kill a god. Octavia was no god, but she was immortal. No one knew exactly where immortals went after death by that blade. So, maybe she could hear him. Regardless, he spoke to her. Deep down he knew it was more for him than her.

"I think Kassidy is still feeling guilty," said Keiron. "On the surface, she knows it was an accident, so it's not that. It's that she brought back Anna DeBartolo and left you. She broke the rules for Jaxon and not you, her family. She's anticipating repercussions from her actions. This is . . . unprecedented. At least as far as we know. But she'll suffer those repercussions over a stranger, instead of someone she's related to. I think that's what is hitting her the hardest."

Keiron lowered his hand and touched the ground. He closed

his eyes and hoped to feel something. He'd seen Kassidy do it before. As a Reaper, she said she was able to recall images or emotions of the people associated with the spot she touched. He didn't know how it worked. Honestly, she didn't either. Keiron didn't know what to expect from what he was doing. He was simply hoping for something. Anything. Any connection to his best friend. All he heard was noise from the traffic on the streets. The cemetery was located at the intersection of Roosevelt and LaGrange in Westchester, Illinois. It was a busy, chaotic thoroughfare.

"I am . . . sorry. For your loss," said a voice from behind.

It took a lot to catch Keiron off guard. He was a skilled warrior. He'd trained scores of warriors in his time. Getting the better of him, sneaking up on him, was unheard of. This was now the second time Jacen Lucas had done it. Despite his surprise, Keiron didn't move.

"You sound like a man unaccustomed to death," said Keiron.

"Less . . . unaccustomed, and more uncomfortable. I think, in hindsight, it was the x-factor in my decision to become an Advocate," said Jacen.

"Discomfort with death?"

"Fear. Fear of death," said Jacen.

"But not Death Gods?"

"They're no different than other gods."

"Accept they have the ability to kill other gods and immortals," said Keiron.

"Most," replied Jacen.

Keiron hid his shock. He still wasn't sure what to make of Lucas. He'd never heard of the Advocates. He didn't know what they were or how they came to be. They had power and, based on things he'd heard from Kassidy, that power seemed unlimited.

"What are you doing here?" asked Keiron as he stood and turned to face Jacen.

"Did you feel it? The other night. Did you feel the Pulse?"

Keiron nodded.

"Do you know what it means?" asked Jacen.

Keiron nodded again.

"You have to prepare her," said Jacen.

"Kassidy?" asked Keiron.

"Yes."

"She's not ready. She's still reeling from the events with the Wraith and Jaxon. She's still trying to process the prophecy of the Four," said Keiron.

"The Pulse may, in fact, be related to prophecy."

"But of course, you can't say more," said Keiron.

"I'm already telling you more than I should."

"You're telling me nothing."

"Listen, I am more involved in this than any Advocate should be. I've broken oaths because I believe helping Kassidy is the right thing to do. That alone could have serious consequences for me, but I'm willing to accept this to stop—"

The words hung there. Had the Advocate slipped? Had he said more than he should have? Keiron wasn't sure, but his words certainly alluded to knowledge that something big was coming.

Or someone.

"Stop what?" asked Keiron.

"Stop . . . what's coming," said Jacen.

"The Four? Or something more? Something worse?"

Keiron felt his anger rise. He wanted to beat the truth out Jacen Lucas. But he didn't know if he could. His logical mind reminded him that he had no idea about the extent of this man's power. So, he stood there, allowing his anger to boil just below the surface.

"Damn you!" exclaimed Keiron.

"I'm sorry, my friend," said Jacen.

"Friend? Friend? You dare call me friend? You don't know me. You come here, offer nothing, are nowhere to be seen during battles, and you dare call me friend?"

A beat passed with nothing.

"Can you at least answer some yes or no questions?" asked Keiron.

"I can try," said Jacen.

"Does the Pulse have anything to do with what Kassidy did for Anna DeBartolo?" asked Keiron.

"Not entirely."

Keiron sighed.

"Is it related to the coming of the Four?" asked Keiron.

"Yes."

"Was the Pulse, in fact, a broken seal?"

"Yes."

"Can Kassidy stop it?"

Keiron was answered with silence. It seemed a simple enough question. Especially for someone who seemed to know a great deal more than he would admit. Yet, the Advocate stood, motionless, silent, simply staring at Keiron. Seemingly speaking a non-verbal language for which Keiron had no translation.

Finally, he broke his silence.

"I believe she can. But if she doesn't believe it herself, if she simply gives up, we're all lost."

"Why would she give up?" asked Keiron.

"She's about to be tested . . . again," said Jacen.

"Everything about the last few months has been a test. Hell, her whole damned life has been a test, Advocate."

"True. But what's coming could break her," said Jacen.

"And how do I help her?" asked Keiron.

"Just as you always have. Be there. Support her. Fight with her. Remind her who she is."

"More riddles," said Keiron as he threw his arms up in frustration and spun around. He closed his eyes, just as he'd taught warriors he'd trained over the centuries. He took deep breaths, just as he'd taught warriors over the centuries. And like those warriors over the centuries, all he thought about was how best to strike his opponent rather than finding a peaceful solution. He didn't strike, of course. For all the reasons that had come to mind earlier, he stayed his hand. Instead, he thought to pose another question and turned to ask.

"I don't suppose—"

Keiron stopped mid-sentence. Jacen was gone. Again. With him went a little hope. Replaced by him was a little fear. Keiron didn't like either feeling. He was not accustomed to them. He was even more certain that Kassidy would hate those feelings, too.

CHAPTER TEN

TRACI SAT AT THE KITCHEN TABLE, STARING INTO HER TEA AS SHE absently stirred.

And stirred.

And stirred.

After what had just occurred in the living room, she needed something soothing. She'd lost time, and once again Kassidy was present for it. It was probably a good thing she was there. Who knows what would have happened otherwise.

Her thoughts were many. Her thoughts were unfocused. Her thoughts . . . were not her own.

While Kassidy was upstairs, Traci tried to sort through the images in her head. She felt a constant battle for control. Something inside her wanted out. Not just out, though. Something inside wanted to take over. It wanted to own. It wanted to dominate. Traci knew exactly what it was, or rather, who it was. She had not expected this. She didn't know what to expect, but it certainly wasn't chaos or living her last days under a cloud of fear. Traci recognized just how much she underestimated the power she'd unleashed.

You don't have much time.

"Shut up. Just . . ."

You brought this upon yourself, young witch.

"It's not supposed to be like this," said Traci.

And what exactly did you think it would be like?

"My . . . my . . . life . . . was just supposed to . . . end," said Traci.

Oh, my dear sister, it will end. It will end and mine will begin . . . anew. You should feel honored.

"Honored?"

Yes, honored. You're about to be the vessel for my return. You will be the gateway to the return to dominance for witches all over the world.

"No. No, no, no, no. Not like this. This isn't supposed to happen like this. Please, I beg you, stop this. Just take my life and be at peace."

Be at peace? There was a time when that's all I wanted. I fought hard for it. But I was lied to. Betrayed. Banished. Killed. There will be no peace, until I have justice.

Traci's hand shook. She could feel the power within trying to take control of her body again. Today, she would be overtaken by the most powerful witch to ever exist. The mother to all witches. A being once revered, worshipped, loved, and honored for her strength and courage. The narrative that she died protecting others was legendary. Every witch heard the story, and every witch praised the goddess because of it. Now, though, she knew the truth. Their connection was two-way. Traci gained memories, thoughts, and feelings that were not hers, and when the elder witch took over, the being that was Traci Leeds shrank in the background, fading away like centuries old ink on a page.

"She'll stop you, you know?"

The child of Thanatos?

"Yes," said Traci.

Oh, how I hope she will try.

Traci could hear the sinister laughter in the back of her mind as darkness slowly began to overtake her. Shadow creeped around the fringe of her vision, closing like the aperture of a camera. The remaining point of light, her only way back to the real world, got a little smaller. She held hope though. As long as some light remained, there was always a way back. Traci continued to fight hard for control, but it was too much. The hand stirring the tea was no longer hers. Her heartbeat and breathing were echoes—sounds now coming from another. An invisible door closed, and she slipped away.

The being now inhabiting Traci's body looked down at the tea and stopped stirring. She removed the spoon, waved her hand over the teacup, and willed it to change into a glass of wine.

"Sleep now, little witch. I've got work to do," she said as she raised the glass to her lips and drank.

"Babe?" said a voice from the other room.

A smile spread across Traci's face.

"Here we go," she said to herself.

CENTURIES AGO

Hecate materialized outside the halls of Olympus. The home of the gods was beautiful, but not extravagant as mortals believed. The walkways weren't lined with gold. While the columns were marble, there was nothing unearthly or magical about their construction. As humans did, the gods used limestone, marble, wood, iron, and other ordinary materials to construct their homes and meeting spaces. They used the same fabrics, albeit finer fabrics, that humans used to make clothing and draperies. The main garden of Olympus held a pond of water in the center. It was filled with life, and often some gods would use it to swim or relax. Around the pond was a beautiful and well-manicured garden, complete with a lawn, hedges, fresh flowers, and benches for sitting. A walkway surrounded this central garden, and it led to the main hall where official meetings and important gatherings took place. Today would be such a gathering as the gods convened for the trial of Hades.

Persephone's abduction was the result of a male god exerting his will and desire. The males seemed to live in the belief that everything belonged to them. The skies, the seas, the earth, and everything that dwelled within those domains. That belief of dominance extended to humans, as well—particularly to the women. The number of demi-gods frolicking below on Earth was comical in Hecate's eyes. She too was guilty, and she recognized that. She had several children herself fathered by men, and she'd had several romances with women as well. But this had been the way of things for as long as she could remember. Because gods acted on their impulses whenever they chose, she was not shocked when she discovered Persephone had been taken by one. Surprised to learn it was Hades, for sure. But not shocked.

As she strolled down the walkway toward the large hall, she took a brief respite on a stone bench overlooking a beautiful garden in the courtyard of the home of the Twelve. A part of her wanted to live on Olympus. And she could have. Given the aid she'd offered the Twelve during their battle with their forebearers, the Titans, she'd been offered a place among them by Zeus himself. The King of the Gods offered more than that, as he often did, and Hecate succumbed to his charms a time or two. Perhaps more. But in the end, she had no interest in being yet another of his conquests. Had she stayed on the Mount, she'd be at his beck and call. She supported him and she supported the Twelve when they fought the Titans because she believed he'd truly offer change in the misogynistic traditions of the gods.

In the end, he was the worst of them.

Hecate remained an ally, but deep down, she wanted change, and she would not rest until something shifted. She didn't quite know what that meant, what it would entail, but it would come, and somehow, she knew she'd be integral to it.

As she sat, staring into the beautiful garden, she heard whispers approaching. It sounded like Zeus. Hecate shimmered away behind a bush and, calling on her abilities, made herself invisible. Through the bushes she watched Zeus and his brother, Hades, walk together as they prepared for the trial.

"Brother, I did not wish to be made lord of the underworld, but I accepted it, out of respect for you, and the aid you provided in freeing us from Cronus, and the leadership you displayed in the battle against the Titans. To hold me liable for taking a bride—"

"You did not just take a bride, Hades, you took a goddess, the daughter of Demeter."

"With your blessing!"

"Keep your voice down," Zeus whispered.

Hecate's eyes widened in shock. She had never suspected Zeus played a part in the abduction of Persephone. Overhead, the skies rumbled, a sign that Zeus was displeased. His power was infinite. So much so that the heavens spoke for him. He did not need to raise his voice to express his anger or displeasure. If he did, there was literal hell to pay. Hecate had seen it. So, she was not surprised when Hades backed down.

"Apologies, brother. I'm just so . . . confused. You said she could be mine. You said you would support me, and yet I'm to stand trial? Among gods who are lesser?"

"You are a member of the Twelve," said Zeus.

"A senior member," insisted Hades. "I am the eldest of the sons of Cronus. The *first* imprisoned, the *last* released, and yet I stand in *your* shadow, banished to an underworld I wanted no part of. And you would put me on trial in front of those who came *after* me? They should bow *down* to me!"

This time, the ground shook, a sign of Hades' anger. But it was overshadowed by the rumble in the skies. Hecate wasn't sure how much more insubordination Zeus would tolerate. She was curious to find out, though.

"If you wish to strike me down, then do so, brother. You need not try to intimidate me with your power," said Hades, looking up into the heavens.

"You are powerful indeed, Hades," began Zeus, as the clouds above cleared, "and you have been loyal—as brother, as soldier, and as sovereign of your domain. It is that very reason that I agreed to allow you to take a bride in Persephone. And it is for that very reason that you will not be found guilty of any wrongdoing."

Once again, Hecate's eyes widened. She felt her own anger mount. She wanted to lash out and scream, but she stayed her hand and continued to listen.

"Brother?"

"As you know, being a ruler, a sovereign, means that you will have to do things that you do not wish in order to keep the peace. This trial was called by Demeter. Celestials are divided over your actions, and if I did not grant this trial, we'd be at war . . . again. And I cannot have that. This," said Zeus, gesturing with his hands, "is all to keep the peace. It is a formality to appease. But trust me, son of Cronus, lord of the underworld . . . brother . . . you will not be found guilty of wrongdoing. And you will return to your domain with your bride."

Hecate watched the sons of Cronus shake hands. Inside, she was seething. She wanted to unleash her fury. As a Titan herself, she had struggled with turning against her kind, but in the end believed it was for the greater good. Now, she questioned everything she believed, everything she knew. Now, she hated herself for being complicit in the narrative of the Twelve.

"There's another matter to discuss, brother," said Hades.

"Hecate?" asked Zeus.

Hades nodded.

"Let's speak about her later, Lord Hades. We need to move to the main hall," said Zeus as he gestured for them to walk.

As the two gods walked away, Hecate backed up and moved in the opposite direction. At a safe distance she materialized again. It took everything inside to hold her rage at bay. She wanted to scream, to shout, to destroy . . . something. Instead, she held it in, closed her eyes, and said the word.

"Calm," she whispered.

Why are they talking about me?

What they did to that poor girl. To their own sister. And they have the nerve to speak of me behind my back?

"Calm," she whispered aloud again.

And again.

Power flowed through her, and she felt peace fill her. She steadied her breathing. Her heart slowed. And she opened her eyes.

"Feeling better?" asked the goddess standing before her.

Hecate was taken aback. The woman before her was no friend, but she was no enemy either. A primordial goddess, largely absent, lost among the names of so many that had come before. Without her though, without her siblings, without her parents, Hecate and the others would not exist. They'd only met a few times before, and she was the last being Hecate expected to see on Olympus. The Lost One. The Trickster.

"I know. It's shocking, right?" asked the goddess.

"What . . . are you doing here?" asked Hecate.

"I heard there was an event for the ages taking place today. I thought I'd check it out."

"An event?" asked Hecate, rhetorically. "It's a farce. A sham. A slap in the face to women, celestial *and* mortal."

"Hmm, sounds like you've got some strong feelings on the matter."

"That, dear goddess, is an understatement."

Hecate went on to tell the ancient deity what she'd overheard from the sons of Cronus. She surprised herself by remaining calm through the retelling. At least on the outside. Inside, her blood boiled.

"That is . . . interesting."

"Interesting?" asked Hecate.

"Well, certainly devious. I dare say, that's worse than anything I've ever done."

Hecate inclined her head.

"Okay, so, maybe not," agreed the Lost One. "Still, this is a betrayal of epic proportion. I admire you for remaining calm."

"I don't want to, believe me," said Hecate.

"Perhaps you won't need to."

"Meaning?"

"Meaning... we should not allow our estrangement to continue. Let's walk, and talk, as we head to the event of the century."

Hecate was hesitant. Gods and men were wary of this primordial goddess. But Hecate was angry, and in anger, anyone was prone to make decisions that seemed good in the moment.

It was the nature of gods and men.

CHAPTER ELEVEN

"WHAT DO YOU MEAN YOU COULDN'T SENSE ME?" ASKED TRACI.

"I mean, I couldn't sense you. Like anything. Nothing."

"What, like I was dead?"

"No. That I would have known. Death is kind of my thing," said Kassidy. "What I'm saying is, I couldn't sense *you*. The essence of you."

Kassidy shifted on the couch a bit and reached for Traci's hand. She sensed some hesitation in her, and then Traci drew her hand away completely. Strange. Traci craved Kassidy's touch. She'd told her as much.

"I told you about my empathic abilities," said Kassidy, finally able to hold Traci's hand.

"Yeah, I know. You sense everyone's emotions, often whether you want to or not."

"Right. So, with that ability comes a basic *sense*, for lack of a better word, for everyone. It's like an emotional fingerprint, or the way an animal might know someone from scent. Everyone has a baseline, or foundation, to which I connect. It's how I come to understand them. I can sense the emotions of virtually everyone, all mortals, at least, and most immortals, at least most of the ones I've encountered. But as I thought back to what happened earlier, your magical outburst, I realized that I could not sense you. There was a void where you were."

"And what about now?" asked Traci.

"Now, you're fine. Five by five, love. It's like any other day we're together. Except . . ."

"Except what?"

Kassidy let a few beats pass as she searched for the words to express what she sensed. She had no problem, of course, being straightforward. But given the fragility she recognized in Traci's emotional state, she wanted to be mindful of the words she used. She moved closer to Traci and, with her free hand, caressed her face while giving her hand gentle squeezes.

"Except," began Kassidy, "except you're . . . scared."

A pregnant and awkward pause filled the space between them. Kassidy couldn't sugarcoat it any more than that. She'd hoped that her comforting touch would ease things. Now, though, she sensed fear, anxiety, and some embarrassment. She certainly had not intended to make Traci feel bad. Perhaps it was the added vulnerability that existed when in a room with Kassidy. The few people that knew of her empathic ability always carried a certain anxiety in her presence. At least one person, her sister Sarah, commented that people who knew of Kassidy's abilities were always on their guard around her, emotionally. For one, they cared about her enough to try to avoid overwhelming her. But the other reason was not entirely altruistic. According to Sarah, people were afraid that their feelings weren't their own to experience. When Kassidy was in the room, they were forced to be open, whether they wanted to or not.

"It's human nature to want to keep things to yourself at times," Sarah had said. "But around you, nobody can do that."

So maybe that was the embarrassment Traci felt in this moment. She was going through something that was confusing and scary, and in the midst of a very new relationship. They'd joked about red flags before. Going through an uncontrollable magical crisis that resulted in physical damage and mental anguish was blood red.

"I don't know what to do," said Traci.

"You don't remember anything?"

"No. Nothing. I mean, I remember what happened before blacking out . . ."

Kassidy felt a slight tinge of happiness during Traci's apparent flashback. But it was quickly overshadowed by an oppressive weight. The darkness of uncertainty engulfed both of them.

"But after that, after you went into the kitchen, there was . . . nothing. At least nothing out of the ordinary. You went into the kitchen, and then the next thing I knew, you were coming out. And there was all . . . this," said Traci, gesturing to the mess on the floor. "God, we're never gonna get this place fixed up, are we?"

The words were delayed, but once they sank in, Kassidy started laughing. Traci followed. It was an apprehensive laugh, filled with hope, longing, sorrow, and regret. That combination, in Kassidy's experience, wasn't a good one. It only reinforced what she'd suspected. Traci was holding something back. She knew more than she was letting on. Kassidy wanted to press harder, but she wasn't sure what that would do. If Traci had the ability to unleash that incredible power and not be conscious of it, what could she do if provoked and fully in control? She'd once held a Wraith against a wall with an outstretched hand from four feet away. The Wraith was not only unable to move, but he was also unable to dematerialize. Wraiths weren't gods by any means, but they had a small fragment of god power. A gift from Azra-El when he created them. Even Reapers were unable to best

Wraiths. Kassidy was the only exception, and that ability only manifested in extreme circumstances. She wasn't even aware of what she'd done, or how she'd done it.

Not unlike Traci with recent events.

Kassidy pulled Traci to her, kissed her forehead, then wrapped both arms around her. She fell back, bringing Traci with her. Kassidy stroked Traci's hair after they'd both settled in.

"We'll get this place fixed up," said Kassidy. "And then I'm selling the shit out of it."

They both laughed again.

"Kass?"

"Yeah babe."

"I'm sorry."

Those words hit Kassidy like a dagger to the heart. It pained her to hear them because there was clear agony, regret, and fear that emanated from Traci. Kassidy needed to make it better. She needed to fix this . . . this . . . whatever it was.

"It's okay, love. It's not your fault. Something's going on, and we'll figure it out, and we'll fix it."

Traci did not respond verbally, but emotionally, and her unspoken words hit Kassidy almost as hard as the apology. Traci knew more than she was letting on. Maybe it wasn't a ripple effect of Anna's resurrection. Maybe it was something else. Kassidy wasn't sure but was determined to find out. Whether it was because of what she'd done for Anna or not, Traci likely wouldn't be experiencing anything like this had she never met Kassidy. And for that alone, Kassidy owed her the benefit of the doubt and a way out of the madness.

◆　　◆　　◆

In her mind, Hecate's laughter echoed. Everything happening now was a sheer delight. She had the Death God in the palm of her hand, using a simple spell to mask her emotions and allow Traci's to filter through without giving the young witch control. She would, of course, give control back. She wasn't quite at full power yet after all. But she would be, and soon.

For now, she would rest her head upon the Death God's chest and allow Kassidy to believe that her lover was tired yet comforted by her presence. She would allow Kassidy to believe that she was providing a place of safety for the young witch. She would allow them both to feel some hope for the present because it suited her. She would allow this until it was time to unleash.

And that moment was coming with each reddening of the moon.

CHAPTER TWELVE

KEIRON ENJOYED WALKING THROUGH THE CITY OF CHICAGO. HE'D thought about leaving soon, but he wanted to wrap up some of Octavia's affairs. Also, he needed to help Kassidy. He needed to get information on the broken seals. Walking downtown helped him reset and focus.

Right now, he also needed to stop the mugging taking place in the alley off Wabash.

Keiron ran directly toward two men attempting to wrestle a purse away from a woman. As the tug of war continued between the woman and the taller of the two men, the second man was pulling something from his coat. It looked like a cartridge from a distance, but as Keiron neared he saw that it was a switchblade. Bearing down on the scene, he saw that the two were just a couple of young teens.

"Get off me, punk!" screamed the woman as she continued to wrestle for her purse.

"Just let it go, and we won't hurt you," said the teen pulling the purse.

From Keiron's vantage, the kid didn't seem to need to steal. His coat was fitted and not cheap, by any means. He wore leather gloves, and though his jeans sagged a bit, they were rather expensive and tucked into Timberlands. The kid looked as if he lived a fairly good life, perhaps even a comfortable suburban life. His partner wore a skullcap with a marijuana leaf embroidered on it. He held his knife with little knowledge or technique and seemed to think it was his primary scare tactic.

"Kids," Keiron said under his breath.

The next thing he saw caught him off guard. The woman pulled her purse with great force bringing the young suburbanite toward her, and then she head-butted him, sending him backward where he tripped over his own feet. Now, fully in control of her purse, she turned her attention to the one with the switchblade.

"What are your plans with that?" she asked.

"I'm gonna fuckin' cut your throat if you don't—"

Switchblade's words were cut off as the flying purse knocked the blade from his hand. She then turned and sent a side kick directly to his chest sending him backward. He toppled over his friend. The woman slung the purse cross ways over her neck, then fished out a wallet. She opened it, showed the boys, and their eyes widened. Keiron was certain the Suburbanite was going to cry.

"I'm off duty," she said, "but if you two punks wanna run, I'll give you a five-minute head start before I come and bring hell into your worlds."

The pair scrambled, fumbling over each other before finally gaining traction and running away. Keiron was certain the suburban kid said something about getting his ass beat by a woman again. It was hard to make out as the El train overhead rumbled past. Keiron stepped up to the woman as she was picking up the blade from the ground.

"Are you al—"

Keiron's words were stopped as the woman turned, clearly startled, and thrust forward with the open switchblade. Keiron tried to block it, but somehow the woman anticipated his adjustment, moved with him, and the blade found a home in his palm.

Keiron didn't scream, to his credit, but he felt the sensation of open skin and blood flow down his palm. He also knew he'd recover fairly quickly from this. He was not just immortal, but the son of Cronus. Regeneration from this would happen as soon as he pulled the knife away.

"Who the hell are you?" asked the woman as she backed away and pulled another weapon from behind her.

"You stab me, then pull a gun?" asked Keiron.

"You part of the dynamic duo I just ran off?"

"They were anything but dynamic," said Keiron.

"No shit."

"I was coming to help, but as I got closer it was clear that you didn't need it," said Keiron.

"So . . . you're telling me you're not with them?"

Keiron nodded.

"I'm Detective Shay Walker, Chicago PD. I'm going to put my weapon away and cuff you to this bike rack while I look at your hand, okay?"

Keiron wanted to protest, but it would get him nowhere. He could pull the knife from his hand and run. But there was something about the detective that kept him where he was.

So, he nodded and allowed her to cuff him.

"I heard you say that you're off duty. I can simply take care of this myself," said Keiron. "No harm, no foul. I know what it's like to get caught up in the moment."

"Just be quiet and let me take a look," she said.

The knife had gone straight through and was, in fact, sticking out of the other side of his palm. He knew he had to go and take care of this on his own, yet he stayed. He couldn't quite put his finger on it, but there was some connection that kept him there.

"Shit," she said.

"What?"

"Well, you're going to be okay. You're just gonna have one hellava scar. And . . ."

"And?" asked Keiron.

"I'm gonna get my butt reamed for this."

Keiron felt some compassion, so he stifled a laugh.

"Look, this is fine. I'm going to be okay. I'm not going to report this, I promise," he said.

"Yeah, that's what they all say."

"They all? Do you stab people often? There are easier ways to meet people."

Keiron said it with a grin. When the detective looked at him, it was several beats before she too smiled, and eventually laughed.

"I am so sorry about this," she continued, as she took off her scarf. "How are you taking this so well? Here, let's wrap this around your hand and I'll pull—"

"I don't think that's the way it's supposed to be done," said Keiron.

In the back of his mind, a battle raged. He wanted to pull the knife out and just show her he'd be fine as they both watched it heal. On the flip side, he wanted to keep his nature secret. But again, something about this woman had him on edge. It wasn't danger he was sensing, it was kinship. Perhaps because they were both warriors of a sort. He wasn't certain, but something deep down told him it would be okay if she knew him.

The *real* him.

He made a fist with his cuffed hand and pulled down swiftly, breaking free.

"What the . . ."

As the detective unholstered her weapon again, Keiron pulled the knife from his hand and held his palm up. They both watched as the wound closed. He used her scarf to wipe the blood from his palm and wrist. In his mind, it was the least she could do.

"What the hell are you?"

He looked at Shay and saw something strange in her eyes. It wasn't fear, which should be the natural reaction when you see someone heal in seconds from a knife wound. Why wasn't it fear? Instead, it was . . . astonishment? No. Curiosity? No doubt. But there was something more, something like . . . validation?

"I'm complicated," he said. "Listen, my apartment is not far, how about we head there and get off the street so I can clean up."

Her eyes widened and her mouth opened as if she wanted to say something but just couldn't find the words. This area they were in was pretty silent at this time of night, but there were people a short distance away coming toward them. Keiron held out his hand and urged her to take it. If his eyes had voices, they'd be pleading with her to follow him. Her eyes were begging him to take her down the rabbit hole, but her brain was switched onto skeptic mode.

"Shay, people are coming. You need to decide now. Are you staying here or coming with me?"

She finally put her hand in his and they left the area.

As they rounded the corner, the detective's cell phone rang. Keiron stopped with her as she checked the caller ID. The look on her face sparked a dozen questions in Keiron's mind. The look spoke volumes.

"I need to take this," she said.

Keiron nodded.

"Walker," she said into the phone.

Keiron again watched her face. She closed her eyes and lowered her head as a voice spoke. Her shoulders dropped. She mouthed the words "Jesus Christ."

Duty had called.

"I'm on my way," she said.

CHAPTER THIRTEEN

KASSIDY FELT THE WEIGHT OF TRACI'S HEAD ON HER CHEST AND the even breathing as she fell into slumber. Much like the other night, Traci had fallen asleep after her supernatural event. Kassidy concluded that the amount of energy it took to manifest those acts must have been draining. Even if she was not aware of them happening.

Kassidy shimmered both their forms to the bedroom, then shimmered again, appearing in the master bathroom. She placed her hands on either side of the sink and just stared at her reflection. She didn't look old. In fact, she looked better than she had in years. As that thought crossed her mind, she gave herself an internal, "go 'head girl," along with a crooked smile. But that was the comic relief of a woman who was weary. She was doing her best to hang on, to do the things she needed to do to stay upright. She was throwing herself into her work, but the work of a Death God was never truly done. Kassidy could try to blend her immortal life and duty with the normal world, but there would never be true balance or cohesion.

And she would always second guess herself.

Her internal voice was turning against her. There was a great deal of bravado when she worked, when she went after vagrant souls, and wraiths, and supernatural baddies. But it was all an effort to keep them on their toes and to ensure that they knew she was the Alpha. She was the Death God, after all, so it stood to reason that she'd be seen that way. But when she pulled the curtain back on herself, there were still traces of doubt, and certainly exhaustion. The weight of her responsibility was formidable.

Kassidy splashed some water on her face then grabbed the hand towel on the side and patted herself dry. There was something about the smell of the towel that always calmed her. As she sat there for several beats, images of Traci flashed in her head.

The towel smelled like Traci.

Kassidy had associated that scent with her, which was nothing more than an off-brand laundry detergent. Traci used it because it had organic ingredients. Other detergents made her itch and break out, but this one was golden. So, to keep her from having a reaction, Kassidy began using it on the towels and bed linens. It was a small gesture, but something she could do to make Traci comfortable.

She thought back to that night at Mullen's when they'd first met. Then her thoughts moved to the next morning, waking up in Traci's bed after dispatching the murderous Wraith, Ethan, and escorting the soul of his victim to the Beyond. She thought about the time she welcomed her into the family home, and so many little moments in between. Kassidy found herself smiling.

Then she opened her eyes and that all went away.

Her reflection was gone. In its place a scene of fire and chaos. Buildings and vehicles burned turning the sky black. Smoke was thick, and through it she could see people frantically running. Most were just shadows through a haze. Others were vivid, bruised, bloodied. Ashen faces streaked with tears. Screams and sirens filled Kassidy's mind, and, in the distance, she saw four figures.

Four figures cloaked in shadow and a fifth hovering above them.

Four figures in command of the chaos.

Four figures in command of destruction.

Kassidy felt a hand on her shoulder, turned, and stared directly into a hooded figure. Its eyes glowed bright blue and in an instant, the figure enveloped her. Flailing her arms about, trying to get free, she fell back against the sink, the shock bringing her back to the present moment.

To her home.

Breathing hard, she glanced beyond the door and found Traci still asleep in bed. The towel she'd held had fallen on the floor. Other than that, nothing was amiss, except for her rapidly beating heart. Taking some time to compose herself, Kassidy splashed water on her face again and dried it, then hung the towel up. She left the bathroom, kissed Traci on the forehead and headed downstairs. Finding her cell phone, she scrolled through previous calls and pressed a name.

"Hey, it's me. You're still in town, right?" she asked.

"Yeah, I'm here."

"You okay? You sound a little shaky," said Kassidy.

"Yeah, I'm good. Just a weird night.

"Same. Can we meet? I could use your help. Or at least, a sounding board."

"Yeah. I thought I was going to be busy, but my new friend got called away. Meet me at Clark and Addison in, say, fifteen minutes?"

"See you there."

Kassidy hung up the phone, then grabbed her shoes and a jacket. After putting them on, she stared at her reflection again in the small mirror above the mantle. She could have sworn she had aged about ten years in the last ten minutes. She shook it off and prepared to leave. After two steps, she stopped.

"Clark and Addison?" she whispered. "What the fuck is he doing there?"

CHAPTER FOURTEEN

the leader was always a direct descendent of Hecate, goddess of witchcraft. Only those witches that demonstrated great proficiency in, and respect for the craft were invited. All swore to use their magic for the betterment of mankind. It was that connection to a common mission that kept them in tune with one another and with things that were amiss in the magical world.

As the leader, Mary Leeds was particularly in tune with what was happening. She and her bloodline, though diluted over the centuries, remained the most powerful of all mortal magic wielders. Their direct connection to the goddess made them formidable foes against evil entities. She hoped it would make them formidable foes against the strengthening forces coming now. Deep down, she knew they stood little chance. Of all the witches in her coven, she was the only one who knew what was coming, and possibly why.

"I know we're all concerned," began Mary, "but we can beat this."

"We don't even know what *this* is," said Kendall.

Kendall Jameson was around the same age as Mary and the two had grown up together in St. John. While they referred to all magic wielders as "sister," the term took on a special meaning for the two of them. They had supported one another through challenging times. Kendall's daughter had been among many young witches kidnapped and later rescued by a mysterious person with black eyes. Kendall's daughter suggested the girl may have been Hecate reborn, given what she'd done to that man.

The two witches stood side by side in Mary's living room, staring out the window and watching young neighborhood kids play. Mary was hit with memories of her own childhood, and a part of her wished she could go back to that time. Life was simpler then—at least in hindsight.

Because of their connection, Kendall was not one to readily disagree with Mary. Something Mary greatly appreciated. In fact, she supported Mary on virtually every issue because, as she once put it, "That's how deep my admiration, respect, and love for you goes, sister." But on this issue, Mary felt that Kendall may be questioning whether her optimism was misguided.

"That's true sister, we don't know exactly what it is. But with our combined strength and that of some other powerful magic wielders, I feel confident that we can see this through successfully."

"It's just . . ." began Kendall, trailing off.

"What?" asked Mary. "Please, tell me. We hold no secrets from one another."

The look of skepticism Mary received from her childhood friend struck hard. There was an awkward pause that seemed to last a lifetime. Mary felt some relief as Kendall opened her mouth to speak. She welcomed any noise to cut the tension, even if it was going to add to her angst.

"It's just that I feel there's something you're not telling us, sister. I've never felt this before, especially with you, and I feel silly for even bringing it up. One part of me thinks it's just fear. Fear of the unknown, of a pending doom that we're ill prepared for. But another part feels like there's something you're holding back. And if there is, I need you to know you can share it. You can trust me. You can trust *us*."

Mary let the words sink in, and she knew her pause was a giveaway. Silence was often the thing that felled many relationships. In this instance though, it wasn't just a damaged relationship that was at stake. Her silence could very well mean the end of the coven. But what was she to do? Choose between the coven and her daughter? For her, it was a lose-lose scenario.

Perhaps that's why I'm in this predicament now.

She walked away from Kendall and took a seat. She invited her lifelong friend to do the same. As Kendall found comfort in the old rocking chair, she spoke again.

"I always loved this chair."

"Oh, I know," said Mary through a chuckle. "I remember when we were super small, and we could both sit in that thing."

"Oh my god, and read books all night long," said Kendall.

"*Charlotte's Web.*"

"Oh, poor Charlotte," said Kendall. "What about the *Encyclopedia Brow*n books?"

"They were the *best* mysteries!"

"*Beezus and Ramona*!" they said in unison.

Mary laughed with Kendall. Hers was a deep laugh, and once again Mary's memories took her back to a time of fun, of innocence, of hope. She bathed in that feeling for a time. Then, the laughter subsided, and she was brought back to the present. The fun, the innocence, the hope . . . gone. Instead, the room caved in like a boobytrap, the walls spiked with dread and fear as the shadow of death floated overhead. What was she to do? She'd done everything in her power to avoid this, to ensure that Traci never found that damned girl. But fate was a fickle thing.

"Sister. Mary. Talk to me," said Kendall.

"I don't know where to begin," said Mary.

"Start at the beginning."

As Mary prepared to speak, the phone rang. Relieved, Mary read the name on the face. The relief vanished when she saw Traci's name.

"Excuse me, sister, I need to take this," said Mary as she quickly exited the room. Tempted to let it go, she thought better of it, and answered.

"Mom," said Traci, before Mary could even speak.

"I'm here."

"Mom, it's starting. I didn't think it would be like this. I didn't think it would be this bad. I . . . I—"

"I understand, Traci. Calm down. Tell me what's happening."

"You can . . . you can feel it, can't you? The imbalance? It's . . . growing."

"Yes, I know. What's worse is the sisters can feel it, too."

"What's worse? How is that worse? How is that worse than what's happening to me?"

"Traci, I—"

"No, Mom! This is the problem. This has always been the problem. You care more about the damned coven and your damned legacy than you do me."

"Well, I wouldn't have to, if you'd just . . ."

A beat passed.

"If I'd just what, Mom? Just listened to you? Just not read the book? I was too busy trying to measure up to you. Trying to measure up to your ideal. Trying to get you to not resent me."

"Resent you? Traci, you're my daughter. I could never—"

"Oh, but you could. And you did. I was an embarrassment to you. A direct descendant of the goddess, with no power. *Your* daughter. With no power. I wasn't going to inherit the mantle and keep things going the way you envisioned, and you hated me for that."

"Traci, I . . . I swear. I swear to you. I never felt that way," said Mary, pleading.

"You did, Mom. You did. You didn't say it. You didn't have to. I felt your disappointment every damned day. So . . . what was I supposed to do? I read that book for you. I tried to jump start my power for you. To make you proud."

"You read that damned book for you. And you alone!" said Mary in a harsh, but hushed tone.

Another few beats passed.

Cold, awkward pauses.

Moments Mary would never get back with her daughter.

"Well, you don't have to worry about me disappointing you anymore. The imbalance is growing. Her power is growing. She'll be here soon, and I'll be gone. Forever."

"Tra—"

The line went dead.

Mary stared at her phone, the look of pain and loss on her face.

"What has she done?" asked Kendall.

Startled, Mary looked over to find Kendall standing in the entryway. It didn't take a genius to read her friend's face. A combination of concern and anger practically filled the room. Mary's assertion that nothing was wrong, that everything would be okay, suddenly had the strength of a single strand of thread bearing the weight of an elephant.

"Traci . . . um . . ." began Mary, unable to finish.

She didn't know when it happened, but somehow, Kendall had crossed the room and wrapped her arms around her. Mary felt a gentle squeeze, and with it, the comfort of home. Her friend had waded through the clear and deliberate deception, and come to Mary with peace, love, and the promise of understanding. This friend. This unrelated sister. How had Mary failed to do the same for her own flesh and blood?

"I failed her," began Mary, "I . . . I failed my daughter."

Through her sobs, Mary felt pangs of loss. Only this time, it wasn't for the coven. Finally.

ᛏWENTY ᛃEARS AGO

St. John High School was a quiet, small-town institution that boasted no famous alumni, nor county, state, or nationally recognized sports team. It was, for all intents and purposes, just a building, with teachers, about one thousand students at any given time, and overactive involvement from the parents of the town. Nothing exciting ever happened in St. John.

Until that kidnapping and rescue.

There'd never been a need for specialized counseling sessions until that kidnapping and rescue.

And Traci Leeds had never been in a school fight until that kidnapping and rescue.

As Traci replayed the events of the past few months in her head, she wondered, like many victims of trauma, where she'd gone wrong. She blamed herself for the events that led to her, and her cousin, being taken by that man. The things he offered, though. He knew who they were. He knew *what* they were. He also seemed to know that their powers had not yet manifested. Traci and her cousin were offered a way to fix that problem. As the only two in their generation without active powers, they felt the sting of embarrassment and disappointment. It wasn't real, of course, but they felt like they were the odd ones in their family and coven. They studied, they absorbed the history, and they practiced. But in the end . . . nothing. So, when he came to them with the promise of a jump start, as he put it, the temptation was too great to turn from. They went, they were caged, and they were terrified.

Until she came.

That amazing, dark-haired warrior. Her power, her ferocity,

her confidence—it made Traci feel so many things all at once. She felt the fear, still. Anyone able to fight the monster that had taken them could be a greater threat in the long run. But she also felt hope. Hope that this would be the moment they'd all be saved. Twelve girls in all. Caged, taunted, fearful witches with latent abilities hiding just under the surface, saved by a girl, a peer, a power to be reckoned with.

The girl consumed Traci's thoughts. She had to find her. She had to know her. She had to thank her. She had to tell her about the spark, the tiny tingle she felt when she saw the girl move, fight, and win. The sensation she felt when she saw the girl's eyes, her true eyes, not the silver then black counterparts. Traci had found a way to locate her. But because the girl was supernatural, it would take a little extra power—power that was forbidden in her coven. So, Traci sulked, cried, and fought out of anger and frustration.

And now she found herself sitting in a counselor's office.

"So sorry I'm late," said a voice from behind.

Traci didn't bother to look up. Out of her peripheral vision, though, she saw a woman walk toward the small couch that was opposite the one she sat upon. She'd never been in a counselor's office before. This one was small, lined with shelves that held books and trinkets, a few photos, and those cute, but often annoying canvas prints with inspirational sayings. The office was longer than it was wide with the entry door on one end and a desk on the other. In the middle, were matching loveseats, separated by a brown coffee table with a dying plant upon it.

"You're . . . Traci, right?"

Traci nodded.

"And . . . you clearly don't want to be here," said the counselor. Traci inclined her head and raised an eyebrow—the international "no shit, Sherlock" non-verbal response.

"That's fine," the counselor began, "we can just sit here for forty-five minutes in silence. You'd be surprised at how well I can just sit in silence. I feel like I've done it for thousands of years. Well, until recently."

Traci let the words travel without allowing them to fully take root in her mind. She didn't care. It was true. She did not want to be in that office. She did not want to be in the school. She wanted to be anywhere else . . . everywhere else, doing everything she could to find the girl that saved her.

Traci dared to look up at the counselor sitting across from her. The woman seemed about average height. It was difficult to tell when she was sitting. Her skin was smooth, mocha-colored, that paired well with her dark hair and Mediterranean features. Her eyes, though, were magnificently hazel. They almost seemed unnatural. It gave her an exotic look. Her clothes screamed money. She wore a simple pantsuit, but it was designer, complete with designer heels. Traci's would-be counselor seemed more like a full-fledged diva than someone trained in psychology.

"What are you doing here?" asked Traci.

"I'm here to help," the counselor said.

"Why?"

"What do mean?"

"You look, I don't know, like we're not exactly your regular clientele. How does someone like you end up in St. John?"

"You make a lot of assumptions for a teenager," said the counselor.

"Not trying to be rude," began Traci, "but you just look like this town can't afford your services."

"Well, if we're being honest, which is what you seem to want, they can't."

The frankness took Traci aback, but she appreciated it. The

counselor smiled, Traci felt a smirk on her own face, and she let out the laugh she wanted to keep in. Some of the tension left her shoulders.

But she still didn't want to be there.

"I get the sense you haven't laughed in a while," said the counselor.

"Haven't had much reason to," said Traci.

"Understandable. I can empathize with what you're going through. I know, firsthand, what it's like to be locked away, helpless . . . hopeless, for a long time."

Traci's interest was piqued.

"When my captivity ended," began the counselor, "I spent a lot of time angry as well. I still am, in fact. But I also found a way to channel my anger, to direct my rage, by asking myself what I wanted and making a plan to go for it. So, instead of focusing on your feelings of being kidnapped and subsequently rescued, and instead of exploring your fear and anger, let's focus on one question, Traci. What is it that you want?"

A simple question, with a simple answer.

Or was it?

Traci knew she wanted to find and meet the girl who saved her. She wanted to talk to her, know her, be strong and confident like her. But . . . then what? Would that give Traci everything she wanted? Did she even know what she truly wanted?

"I want . . ."

Traci stopped and took a few more beats to consider her thoughts and feelings. And she lingered on one thought. Then what? What would she do if she met her savior? What could she actually bring to that friendship, or whatever it would become? She was a witch with no power in a world filled with strong and capable people.

"I want . . . to be worthy," said Traci.

"Interesting," said the counselor. "And for you, what does that mean?"

"It means to not be weak. To be able to stand up for myself and others. To be a protector and someone worthy of my legacy and . . . and . . ."

"And?"

"And a relationship, or a friendship, with someone who is already all of those things," said Traci.

"Like . . . the person you say rescued you."

Traci nodded.

"You have feelings for her?" asked the counselor.

"I don't know what I have. I just know that I want to be like that. Just . . . powerful. Safe and secure."

A beat passed. Traci felt her cheeks flush. She was slightly embarrassed. Seemingly gushing and fangirling over someone she didn't know. It seemed silly and juvenile. But she couldn't help it.

"You spoke of legacy, too. What did you mean by that?"

Shit.

Traci sat with that for a moment. She could tell the counselor and resident Diva that she was a descendant of a long line of witches. She could tell her that among all the witches in the coven, she and her family were the only direct blood descendants of Hecate, goddess of witchcraft. She could tell the counselor that not being able to wield magic, given that lineage, was a great disappointment for her, and even more so, she felt, for her mother. She could tell her that, but it probably wasn't wise. Then again, what did she have to lose?

So, she told her.

Everything.

She even talked about the book.

"I see," said the counselor.

That's it?

"So, what can you do to live up to this legacy?" asked the counselor.

"Wait," Traci began, confused, "you believe me?"

"Traci, in my field, it doesn't matter what I believe. Only what you believe matters. What you believe is most important. Because it is that belief that will drive you and sustain you."

"Well . . . shit," Traci said.

"And also . . ."

Traci watched as the counselor uncrossed her legs and leaned forward. She seemed hyper focused on the dying plant on the coffee table. As the counselor stretched out her arm and placed her open palm over the plant, Traci saw the hue of her hazel eyes change. It was faint at first, then strengthened, brightened, until they were a metallic blue. Traci's own eyes widened, but it was the new life that entered the plant on the coffee table that made her go slack jawed.

"This is also why I believe you," said the counselor.

"You're a . . . witch?"

"I'm a little more than that. It's complicated. But suffice it to say, I hear you, I understand you, and I want to help you achieve your goals, Traci."

"I . . . I . . ."

"I know it's a lot to take in, right now. So why don't we start slowly."

Traci nodded, excitedly.

"Maybe we can spend some school time practicing magic. You mentioned a book. It sounds a lot like the grimoire of Hecate," said the counselor.

"You know about the grimoire?" asked Traci, eyes wide.

"I do. I'm pretty familiar with it actually. In fact, I could help you with some things I remember from the book. Of course, at some point it would help to actually have it. But . . . we can work up to that. If you're comfortable, that is."

Traci felt goosebumps form on her forearm. Her heart raced. She noticed after a few seconds that her leg was shaking. Was this really happening? Her mother told her to wait and just let her powers manifest on their own. But she didn't want to wait. She couldn't wait.

She *wouldn't* wait.

"When can we start?"

"We still have fifteen minutes," said the counselor.

Traci smiled.

CHAPTER FIFTEEN

"How did you get in here?" asked Kassidy.

"I'm a master strategist and warrior," said Keiron. "I've been around for a while. Nothing is impenetrable for me."

"Hmm."

Kassidy settled into a seat and stared straight out. Parts of the infield were still snow covered, as was most of the outfield. But on this surprisingly warm winter night, Wrigley Field seemed to be preparing itself for the upcoming rigors of a full baseball season.

"How are you, Kass?"

"I'm good. I'm good. I mean, you know, still a lot to do out there. But the Wraiths are gone. Now it's just grabbing hold of these souls, man. Fucking Azra-El took on a lot to regenerate. Rounding them up has been a chore."

Kassidy said all of that without giving Keiron so much as a glance. She knew his eyes were on her. She knew there were more questions. She knew he was probing for more than cocky surface level fluff. So, she did what she does best.

She changed the subject.

"Are you bleeding?" she asked after glancing down at his hand.

It was difficult to see in the darkness of Wrigley Field, but the crimson stain on his cuff made a statement. It still looked wet, in fact. Like the injury had just happened.

"Um, no. Well, I was. But I healed up. Knife incident."

"Like, you caught one in your palm?"

"More like stabbed."

"What the hell?"

"By a cop."

"Dude!"

"After thinking I was going to help her with a couple of muggers."

The confusion on Kassidy's face could not have been lost on Keiron. There were more questions, but like her, he was trying to shift the conversation. She wasn't ready to talk about her feelings. She sensed that was what he wanted to discuss, but that wasn't why she reached out.

"Kass, look—"

So, she changed the subject again.

"Something's going on with Traci," she said.

"What do you mean?"

"Well, I don't know if it's a witch thing or something, but it's like, she has these moments where she's not herself. It's like she's there physically. But someone else is driving the boat."

"Possession?"

"That's the thing, I can't sense any other soul inside her. Traci's definitely in there. But at the same time, she's very much not."

"Is her power still present?" asked Keiron.

"Her power seems to be on overdrive in those moments. She caused a weather event in my living room and at the end of it, she looked at me like she had no clue it had happened. And the other night, she did some straight up Ghostbusters 'I'm gonna levitate and spin around above the bed' shit. And again, after it was over, had no idea what she'd done."

Kassidy made full eye contact with Keiron and hoped the

change in subject would be fruitful. It seemed to be working. She felt a lot of confusion within him. He certainly seemed to be pondering the dilemma with Traci. Underneath it all, she felt the same concern that had been present when she arrived. Now, though, with a side of frustration. She knew what it meant. He'd recognized the change in subject, and he was humoring her for now. He'd come back to trying to talk about her feelings, and that would be her cue to leave.

"Do you know what type of witch she is?" asked Keiron.

"Type? There are types? Oh, what the fuck, man."

The chuckle from Keiron was heartwarming. Her ignorance of the supernatural world was the root of a few jokes at her expense. Learning of vampires, like London, was the first exposure to a hidden world beyond Reapers. She'd been younger then, and while shocking, it did nothing to encourage her to explore the existence of other supernatural beings. She felt strange enough as it was. An empath, an actual, honest to goodness empath capable of feeling the emotions of others, who was also a Reaper? She'd been teased and physically assaulted all because she was strange. All because she was Krazy Kassie. Learning of other supernatural beings would have done nothing to help her feel less alone. So, she avoided digging deeper into that world.

But that world was coming for her.

"What do you know about the origins of her powers?"

"I know they manifested late. In fact, she was one of the girls I inadvertently rescued when I dispatched my first Wraith."

"From that house in St. John?"

"Yep."

"She was there?"

"Mm-hm."

"Fascinating," said Keiron. "And after all those years, you just happened to find each other again?"

Kassidy paused. The truth was really creepy on the surface. In certain novels and movies, it was romantic. In other novels and movies—and news reports—it was downright crazy. It took a little while for Kassidy to come around to the romance perspective. By the time she'd learned the truth, she was already falling for Traci, so that helped. Still, it was weird. She got the sense that Keiron felt the same after filling him in.

"So, her powers had not manifested, and when they did, after the kidnapping, as soon as she was strong enough, she used her powers to find you? That's . . . also fascinating."

"Dude, why are you stuck on that word?"

A beat passed.

"Well," began Keiron, "let's think about it. Shortly after that incident, you battled Azra-El."

"Yeah. And?"

"*And* you fled."

"You don't have to say it like that," said Kassidy.

"Okay. You relocated."

"Thank you."

"But, you relocated, and from that moment on wore an amulet that was warded with a spell blocking your presence from Reapers and Wraiths," said Keiron.

It was clear he was waiting for her to put the pieces together, but his point was escaping her. She had indeed wanted to vanish. She remembered the battle clearly and remembered the overwhelming desire to get away from possible retaliation. Keiron gifted her with an amulet that he said would shield her from detection. For maximum effect, she would have to leave the Chicagoland area. It was that moment that she left and traveled a bit before heading back to St. John, New York, where Keiron also lived. She made a life for herself for a long time. After almost twenty years in St. John, the train came off the tracks. But up until the point where her powers began growing out of control, that amulet worked. The magic held.

And then it clicked.

"So, how was she able to find me?"

Her question was met with a finger-pointing nod from Keiron.

"If she was using spells and such to try to find you, it's quite possible that her magic inadvertently degraded the integrity of the wards on your amulet. That, coupled with the increase of your powers, is likely how the Wraiths were able to find you."

"Son of a bitch!"

"Easy, Kass," said Keiron.

"Easy? Her magic fucked up my world," said Kassidy.

"No. Your *father* fucked up your world. *I* fucked up your world. Octavia, your mother, Azra-El—we all had a hand in creating events that brought us to this moment. Even you."

Months ago, Kassidy would have jumped all over that. She would have jumped all over Keiron. She'd swing, she'd kick, she'd curse, and she'd demand an apology for daring to say she was, in any way, responsible for the bad that had come to her life. Now, though, she was a little wiser and a little more tolerant. Now, she recognized her own culpability in certain events. She'd grown in some ways since her ascension. This new revelation, the new possibility, was a lot to take in, though. There was a fire brewing within her, and she was ready to pour bourbon on it. The desire to drink was strong, but she held it at bay.

For the moment.

"Ok," she began, "let's move past the notion that my current girlfriend is indirectly responsible for the death of my last girlfriend and my subsequent ascension to godhood. How could she have done that? She wasn't that strong. She said it herself. I mean . . . look how long it actually took for her to find me."

"Fair point," said Keiron. "Add to that the fact that the amulet was created by the most powerful witch in existence. For her to degrade that at all is a feat in and of itself. Unless . . ."

Kassidy became uncharacteristically uneasy as Keiron seemed to drift off into some wild tangential thought. She no longer felt confusion and frustration in him. Now . . . it was flat out concern.

And a hint of fear.

"What?" asked Kassidy, anxious for an answer. "Unless, what?"

"Unless . . . she's a descendent of the witch that created the amulet. If she's linked by blood to that witch, then she's linked to the power that amulet is imbued with. And if that's the case, she would have been able to degrade the warding. It would have happened slowly as her power grew. But it would have happened . . . eventually."

"Well . . . shit."

"There's more," said Keiron.

"Oh god, please no."

"I know. It's a lot."

"You have no idea," said Kassidy. "But go ahead."

"If she is, in fact, a blood relation to this witch, it could explain what's happening now."

"What do you mean?"

"The witch in question was powerful. Ancient. Strong enough to stand toe to toe with the most powerful of gods."

"How's that possible?" asked Kassidy.

"She was a god herself. She'd betrayed the Twelve and was sentenced to death. Before that, she vowed that she would return and take vengeance upon them."

"So, what? You think she's making good on that threat? Through Traci?"

"It's hard to say. The witch escaped after her sentence. She was wreaking havoc on the world for a bit until she was found by Zeus' bloodhound, a being known as the Tracker. After that, the sentence of death was carried out. There were always rumors that she'd done something to lay a foundation for her return, but no one really knew for sure. If those rumors are true, and if Traci is tied to her, it could open a doorway to her return."

Kassidy sat with those words for a moment and thought about how unfair it was that gods, goddesses, and other supernatural creatures, just couldn't seem to stay dead. First Jeremy Reins, then Azra-El, now, possibly, some all-powerful goddess. Meanwhile, her adoptive mother, Marlene, her biological mother, Allesandra, and her ex, Lynn, remained dead. She could bring them back if she wanted. She had the power. But it would upset the balance of the universe even further. And that wasn't fair.

"Who is this witch, or goddess?"

"Hecate, goddess of witchcraft," said Keiron.

"And she was one of the Twelve?"

"No. Hecate was a Titan."

Kassidy was not too keen on Titans. She needed a drink.

"And if she somehow returns, it sheds new light on the prophecy. And we could soon have hell on Earth."

Kassidy replayed the prophecy in her mind again. She'd done it often, but of late, it felt more like a mantra. The oracle, a man Keiron identified as Bobo, had recited the prophecy with his dying breath.

Death will change, and War will grow, his power veil soon shall cease. And when the sick and starving seek their vengeance, the Horsemen will be unleashed.

There was still some ambiguity in the prophecy. At least, that's what Kassidy felt. The part about Death changing could mean anything from the fact that she'd now assumed the mantle once held by her father, or it could mean that she herself would change. And the part about War growing. Was that about Jaxon? Or was it about the unrest increasing in the middle east and other areas around the globe? The prophecy was as much a riddle as warnings from Jacen Lucas.

"What makes you think she might be coming back?" asked Kassidy.

There was a long pause, and then Keiron took a deep breath. Kassidy didn't like that. She knew it meant something bad was coming. Well, maybe not bad, but certainly not something she wanted to hear.

"Did you feel the Pulse the other night?" he asked.

"The Pulse?" asked Kassidy.

"Yeah. An overwhelming pain throughout your body."

Kassidy stared at Keiron. She thought she was nodding, but his lack of response seemed to say he was waiting for acknowledgment.

"Uh … uh … yeah. Yeah, I felt like I was being ripped apart from the inside out. It's called the Pulse? That's a shitty name. Maybe call it the ass kicker. What the hell is it?"

"It happens when a major celestial event takes place. It can happen when a powerful deity dies. Sometimes when one is born. It can also happen when someone returns."

"Does this happen often?" she asked.

"No," began Keiron, "it's not a common occurrence. The last one happened about twenty years ago."

"What was it, then?"

"We still don't know," said Keiron.

"Wait," began Kassidy, "that was around the time I first battled Azra-El."

"Yes, but that wouldn't have been enough to cause a Pulse. He wasn't powerful enough. There had to be something else."

"So, something is out, or someone is dead," said Kassidy.

"I think more the former than the latter," said Keiron.

"You seem certain."

"I spoke with Jacen Lucas," said Keiron.

"And?"

"He didn't say much, but he did confirm that a seal had been broken."

"A seal? Shit. This is about the Four, isn't it?"

Keiron's silence answered the question for Kassidy. For the first time in a long time, Kassidy made a fist and squeezed tightly. The anxiety and fear were taking root and sprouting limbs within her.

She wanted a drink bad.

CHAPTER SIXTEEN

YOU'RE NOT GOING TO SURVIVE THIS. WHY ARE YOU FIGHTING SO HARD?

Traci ignored the voice, though she knew better than to think that ignoring it would make it go away.

Was she worth it? Was she worth damning your soul to hell?

Traci had been wandering the streets for quite some time and found herself asking that question herself. After waking up to find that Kassidy was gone, and after having a less than loving conversation with her mother, Traci needed to escape. She'd hoped to escape everything. She would have settled for escaping the voice inside.

Had Kassidy been worth it?

Were the few months she got with her worth the trade of her soul?

She stopped for a moment as the question rattled around in her head. As she looked around, trying to get her bearings, she saw that she was standing outside a funeral home.

"Perfect," she whispered to herself, defeated.

Mm, it is, isn't it.

It was the sinister laugh that disturbed Traci the most. She supposed that most people came to terms with their mortality at some point in their lives. Extending that further, she supposed that most of those who knew that death was around the corner came to terms with the fact that time was fleeting. She hadn't anticipated the level of malevolence she would have to experience on her journey to the other side. It was as if death were taunting her. Given her relationship status with a Death God, she knew that wasn't true, of course. But the being inside her, the one trying so desperately to break through, she was enjoying the pain and torture she was causing.

Traci felt some tears begin to well and fought hard against them. She took a few steps forward, away from the funeral home, and asked herself, "what would Kassidy do?" Traci stopped after only moving a few more feet and found herself standing outside a bar.

"Can't ask for a clearer sign than that," she said to herself.

Wiping the tears from her eyes, Traci walked in. There were tables and chairs scattered throughout the open-concept bar, with a sprinkling of them on what looked like a stage, or a potential stage, for performances. The bar was long, curving inward toward the middle, rounding at both ends. Traci grabbed a chair at the south end of the bar near the window, giving her a view of a quiet yet steady suburban intersection, the door, now to her right, and the rest of the bar, which included some dart boards at the north end. This place, Healy's, seemed pleasant. And they seemed to have enough alcohol to drown her sorrows.

And possibly drown the bitch talking in her mind.

"What can I get for ya?" asked the bartender.

"Um . . . good question. Let's start with a gin and tonic," said Traci.

"Any preference on gin?"

"No. Surprise me."

"You got it."

"Actually," began Traci, catching the bartender before he got too far away, "let's go with Tanqueray. Yeah, Tanqueray and tonic."

The bartender acknowledged her with a slight nod, and

Traci settled into her seat. The bar wasn't packed, but still lively. It was a weeknight, after all, so it made sense that things would be light. She noticed people were eating, and it reminded her that she'd not had any food all day. For a self-proclaimed foodie, that seemed odd. She typically noshed on things throughout the day. Mostly healthy things. Healthy eating and living didn't seem to matter anymore. The returning bartender kept her thoughts from drifting to that dark place.

"Thanks," said Traci, as he set the drink down. She pulled out cash to pay, then thought better of it. "Can I start a tab? I think I'm gonna add food, too."

"Yeah, no problem. I just need a credit card."

Traci pulled her bank card from her wallet and handed it over.

"Be right back with a menu."

"Oh, no need. I want that," said Traci, pointing to a guy with a burger and fries.

"Got it," said the bartender. "Cheese?"

"American. Oh, and with bacon."

"You got it. I'll put it in. If you need anything else, my name is Mike. Just give me a shout."

"Hey, Martin! Get over here!" yelled a pulsating voice from behind.

"And that," began Mike, "is my last name. And that'll be his last drink."

Traci laughed, gave him a head nod, then reached for her drink. The cold glass felt abnormally good. Maybe it was the shock of the cold reminding her that she was still alive and should try to enjoy as many moments as she could. Emotion, physical contact, love—all the things that were so inherently human, the basic building blocks of human existence, they weren't gone. If she could just find a way to—

Tick tock, my dear.

The voice spoke as she took her first sip. She almost choked but held on and tried her best to let the cold botanical notes settle on her tongue. There was no burn like Kassidy's various whiskeys. As a witch, with powers rooted in nature, Traci was brought closer to the energies of the earth through the notes of juniper and coriander. It had begun as justification for underage drinking, but as she aged, she truly felt it. Maybe this would be the way to drown out the voice.

I'm not going anywhere. But soon, you will be. I can make it easy for you. I can send you to the Beyond with no pain. Surely that's where you'll end up. No fear. Just a gentle transition to what comes next.

"No," whispered Traci, with her eyes closed after swallowing the cool combination of gin and tonic.

You won't have a choice little witch. I'm coming. Thanks to you. I'm coming. And there will be blood.

"No," said Traci to herself, this time, just above a whisper.

She grabbed her drink and took several more sips. The voice in her head continued its musings. Continued its maniacal laughter. The taunting was overwhelming. She thought back to Kassidy's stories of her childhood, and then the later struggles with her empathic powers. All the things that led to her drinking, all the things that led to her looking for a way to quell the pain. She was halfway through her drink when she decided to finish the glass. When she lowered it to the bar, it hit the wood surface harder than she'd intended. Eyes turned to her.

"Sorry," she said, embarrassed.

Traci pushed the glass to the edge of the bar. Her noise caught the attention of the bartender, who moved back to her quickly.

"I take it you liked that one?" asked Mike.

"*Needed*, more than liked," said Traci through a chuckle. "I'm sorry. I didn't mean to slam that down on the bar like that. Total accident."

"No worries," said Mike. "You want another drink?"

"Yeah, please."

"You got it. Your food should be up shortly, too."

"Thanks," said Traci.

Aw, you've made a new friend. Be a shame to have to kill him.

Traci felt her fists clench.

I'll tell you what. Let me have control now, and . . . I'll spare him. Deal?

Traci held fast to her emotions. She wanted to scream. She wanted to break things. Her anger was welling, but once she realized it was anger at herself, she put the emotion back in its compartment.

"Here you go," said Mike.

"Thanks. Again . . . sorry."

"It's all good," said Mike, holding his hands up. "I just took it as a hearty Viking nod of approval."

Traci laughed quietly, held up her drink, and toasted him. She took a healthy sip before placing her glass gently on the bar. Turning to her left, Traci looked out the window as cars passed and people crossed the street. As a man and woman walked hand in hand into the crosswalk, another man crossed paths with them and said something that must have been offensive. Both men squared off, and within seconds punches were thrown. The fight spilled over into the intersection where both of them were hit by a speeding car. Traci jumped back, as the screams from the people on the street made their way through the glass and into the bar. She turned to look away and noticed, in the reflection of the glass, that her eyes were blue, and pulsing with power.

Oh my. What a terrible accident. You'll need another drink, I think, to block out the shock.

"What's happening?" Traci whispered, turning her head away from the scene outside. And most importantly, from her reflection.

Nothing. Nothing at all. Just the power of the earth running through our veins.

"Our?" asked Traci.

You're right. I guess I should say "my" since this body will be all mine soon. You see, you feel a closeness to the earth when you drink this swill because of its ingredients. Well . . . so do I. Ironically, the other ingredients mitigate your ability to suppress me. It's just a glorious conundrum.

As onlookers moved closer to the window to gawk, Traci absently drank more.

Yes. More.

Traci stopped drinking, slammed the glass on the bar—this time intentionally, and she screamed. She screamed loudly. It was a desperate cry full of fury and rage that she didn't know she was capable of. It was in that moment that she realized . . . she wasn't capable of that. This wasn't her. At least, not all of it.

"Hecate?"

She said the name, but it didn't escape her lips. It was in her mind. Her shared mind. A shared mind, inside a body, that she no longer controlled.

◆　◆　◆

"That's better," said Hecate, pushing herself back from the bar. Standing up from her seat she turned to the crowd standing near the window. One man stared at her intently.

"Freak," he said.

Hecate walked up to him, grabbed his head, pulled it to hers, and she kissed him, deeply. There was little struggle in the young man. He even took liberties and pulled her closer, grabbing at her ass and attempting to grind against her, as some young men full of testosterone are prone to do.

Then, the struggle began.

Hecate kept kissing, deeper, harder, and began sucking on his tongue. When she bit down, the sound he made brought her great delight. He tried to push away, but her grip was firm. She bit down further, then pulled back. Blood gushed from his mouth. The young man clamped his mouth with both hands, stifling blood loss and the groans of shock and pain. Onlookers backed up. Some uncertain of what had happened, others, those closest to Hecate, seemingly at a loss for what they'd witnessed.

Certainty washed over all of them as Hecate spat out the bloody tongue.

"Perhaps that will teach you not to call people names," said Hecate with a blood-soaked smile.

The young man's friends gathered round to support him. Some took out their phones to capture the moment on film or video. Some took out their phones to call the authorities.

"Mike," began Hecate, "I wasn't satisfied with the service here, so I'm not going to pay my bill."

Hecate allowed power to build, she raised a hand and waved it from left to right across the bar. Cell phones, televisions, and registers, all exploded and were engulfed in flame. Screams filled the bar. Hecate walked outside and looked up. The moon was full, and its pinkish hue was darkening.

Hecate smiled.

Then she shimmered out of view.

CENTURIES AGO

"This is a travesty!" screamed Hecate.

She stood among the Olympians, alone, but continued on. She was older than the Twelve. If not for her, most of them would be in servitude to the Titans. Others would be dead for daring to stand up to Cronus. She joined them because they were supposed to be better, they promised they'd be better. She was disappointed to find that they were only carbon copies.

"You, all of you, know the truth, and you choose to look the other way," she said, pointing to the crowd. "You stand here, watching this farce, knowing that Hades had done wrong with the support of his brother, your king, Zeus. And not only did you allow it, but you entertain Hades' accusations that somehow I've done wrong? That I've manipulated and warped the thinking of Persephone?"

Whispers ran through the crowd. Above, the skies darkened, thunder rumbled, and lightning flashed. The whispers lessened. Hecate could sense the fear in the crowd. Deep down, she felt it, too. Her anger though, overshadowed her fear of the Thunder God. She'd stood in reverence of him for his skill, his leadership, and his cunning. She'd even appreciated his skill as a lover. But that adoration was quickly coming to an end. Hecate knew that, in many ways, her powers were greater than most of the Twelve. Her control of the elements, the very forces of nature, were stronger. She was born to it, she had mastery of it.

If she wanted, she could have mastery of *them*.

Staring directly at Zeus, Hecate gave a crooked smile, raised her hand to the heavens above, and without uttering a word, the thunder and lightning dissipated, the skies cleared, and the sun shone bright over the crowd. When he stood, she did not cower. When his eyes crackled with electricity, she did not flinch.

And when he hurled a thunderbolt at her, she caught it.

The crowd gasped again at her show of power and defiance.

"I do not fear you, Thunder God. I do not fear you, and I tire of you."

Hecate allowed energy to build until the thunderbolt in her hand changed from white to black. Taking it in both hands she squeezed until it became a ball of dark crackling energy. Whispering an ancient spell, Hecate thrust her arms forward sending the ball directly at Zeus. The Thunder God moved in the blink of an eye and the energy sailed through the space he'd been standing in. He reappeared behind Hecate and grabbed her, one arm around her waist and a hand on her throat.

"You will stop this madness now!" exclaimed Zeus. "We find you guilty of the accusations, there is no changing that. Stop this now and I will show you mercy."

Hecate simply laughed.

"Do not mock me, goddess."

Hecate spoke a silent spell, and out of nowhere and bolt of lightning crashed down upon them. The power of the bolt sent Zeus flying backward. The onlookers, shocked, stood still, their collective gazes traveling between the Titan and their king.

"You are all complicit in the duplicitous rule of this . . . this . . . man-child," said Hecate.

"Hold your tongue, goddess," said Zeus, getting to his feet.

"I heard what you said to Hades. It was you who allowed him to take Persephone, and you only allowed that sham of a trial to placate those that are angry. You had no intention of allowing him to be found guilty, to make him pay for his crime."

"You are mad. You are not in your right mind," said Zeus.

"Not in my right mind? Was I in my right mind when I fought alongside you? When I lay with you? Was I in my right mind when I secretly bore your child?"

Again, the gasps from the crowd filled the chamber. Even Zeus' eyes widened at the revelation. Hecate walked slowly toward him, taunting him with her smile. She did not have the power to kill him, but she could certainly injure him. She wanted neither. This was a power play.

She had it.

He didn't.

"You like to use us as pawns for your games. The same way you use mortals. Now is the time where you learn what that feels like."

Standing directly in front of the Thunder God, Hecate felt his power growing. She knew he wanted to strike. As he inched closer, she heard and felt crackles of energy around him. She did not move. As his eyes glowed brighter and the heavens reacted to his emotion and power, she stood strong.

"Touch me, and you'll never find your child," she said.

With those words, she turned and walked away. As she neared the chamber entrance the yell from Zeus shook the foundation. The fear she'd once felt was gone. Now, there was only contempt. She did not look back. Hecate continued forward and then shimmered out of view.

CHAPTER SEVENTEEN

"You sure? That's like, your fifth bourbon in the last hour."

"It's okay," began Kassidy, "I'm a god now. It takes a while for me to get drunk these days. Like . . . a while."

Kassidy met Kevin's gaze and for a moment considered calling upon her power. But a dramatic change in eye color would not endear her to the bartender—of that, she was certain. Besides, he didn't deserve anything like that. She'd come into this bar a few times since being introduced to him, and he'd been nothing but kind. At his core, Kevin Lowe was a good man, and the type of person that cared for everyone. He especially cared for family, friends, and friends of friends. As a friend of Herb Jones, Kassidy fell into that last category. As did most people in Chicago's near west suburbs.

"If it helps, I'll recite the alphabet. Backwards. In Russian."

"You speak Russian?" asked Kevin.

"Yep. Well, not exactly. You see, one of the perks of being me is that I understand all languages, and when I speak to people, they understand me in their native tongue. It's a pretty cool trick. I'm basically a walking human translator."

As Kassidy spoke, she realized that the words coming from her mouth did nothing to prove that she was not inebriated. Once upon a time, not getting her drink when she wanted it would anger her. She'd yell. She'd fight. She'd break things. All the things, really. From glasses to tables to bones. She was prone to lashing out. And if Greek mythology taught her anything, it was that gods were prone to lashing out, so now she could simply chalk it up to genetics. But Kassidy was tired.

She could tell that Kevin saw it now.

"Tell you what," he began, "I'll get you another bourbon with a side of water. Just do me a favor and drink both."

Kassidy's annoyed voice screamed in the back of her mind. Thankfully, it too was a bit weary. Not strong enough to take over. So, the scream wasn't loud. More like the last few waves of an echo that began minutes ago.

"You are going to get the biggest tip ever," said Kassidy.

As Kevin walked toward the other side of the bar, Kassidy saw him turn to acknowledge someone coming around the corner.

"What's up, Kev?"

Herb Jones walked to the bar and gave the bartender a fist bump. They exchanged pleasantries and something made them both laugh simultaneously. Kassidy couldn't hear it, but she wasn't paranoid enough to think they were talking about her. Not anymore. Years ago, that had not been the case. In the past, it seemed like everyone was talking about her, whispering about her, or plotting against her.

But that was a lifetime ago.

Herb eventually walked down to her end of the bar and sat next to her. He didn't say anything for a while. Just sat there and stared ahead. She turned her head to look at him. Then slowly, he turned his head to regard her. It was comical. It was hysterical. It made her laugh.

She needed that.

They embraced in a side hug after the laughter subsided.

She'd needed that, too. Kevin came back with her bourbon and a glass of water. He then set down a shot of Jameson for Herb and gave him water, too.

"That's all you're having?" asked Kassidy.

"Oh, hell no. There's a long island iced tea coming in a minute," said Herb.

"Nice," she responded with a head nod.

She grabbed her bourbon as he hoisted his shot of whiskey, and they toasted.

"So, what's going on, lady? How are things? You ever get that mess sorted out from when you were lookin' for Burke?"

The last time they'd spoken, Kassidy was on the hunt for Jaxon Burke. At the time, he'd had a run in with a Wraith, the first Wraith created by Azra-El. Burke was the key to locating the sinister creature. In the end, she not only found Burke, but discovered that he was, in fact, Ares, the War God, robbed of his identity by her father, Thanatos. The revelations from those events changed Kassidy's life. Somehow, she knew that life-changing events were going to be a regular thing for her.

She was weary of that, too.

"Yeah," she began, "I found him and got everything sorted."

She said it in a manner that was very much all business. She could sense both unease and curiosity in her friend. Kassidy wondered if he'd leave it or probe.

"Cool. So, what's next?"

Thank god.

"Um, I'm not sure. I thought I'd be out of here after the repairs to the house. But something has come up, and I think I may stay now. Like, maybe indefinitely."

"Moving back? Nice," said Herb, raising his just-delivered Long Island Iced Tea for a toast.

They both took sips and let a couple of beats pass.

"What's really goin' on, kiddo?" asked Herb.

"I don't even know where to begin," said Kassidy.

"You can try the beginning. Or we can just drink. It's still gonna be there, though. Whatever you're going through."

"Yeah, I know," said Kassidy. "It's just . . . a lot. And it's all quite weird."

"I can do weird," said Herb.

She laughed. But she also wondered whether or not he really could. Herb Jones was something of a neighborhood concierge. He seemed to know virtually everyone. He connected people, and he always seemed to know what was going on. When she was looking for Jaxon, he suggested she reach out to an investigator named Alex Frost. She'd already been connected with Frost through her friend, London, another investigator in Chicago. Frost was a wizard. Well, maybe not a wizard per se, but he was a manipulator of magic and had a remarkably long lifespan. She wondered how much of that Herb had already known. If he did know, and if he was able to deal with that kind of weird, maybe he could deal with hers, too.

"It's . . ." began Kassidy.

She let the word just hang there in the air for quite a while. She wanted to vomit this amazing and ridiculous word salad to someone other than Keiron. But she didn't know how far she should go.

Or if she should go there at all.

"You know, it's fine," she said. "It'll be fine. Everything will work out in the end. It always does."

"Well, if it doesn't, that just means it's not the end," said Herb.

"Amen, brother," said Kassidy.

They toasted again.

Their small revelry was interrupted by the sight of Traci walking into the bar. She was dressed as if she were going out to a club. In tow was some guy who looked like he should be studying for college exams instead of drinking pints of beer on a weeknight. Kassidy squeezed her glass so hard it shattered.

"Whoa," said Herb. "You okay?"

Kassidy said nothing. She got up and began walking toward her girlfriend who was now in a deep kiss with the college kid. She heard Herb's voice calling her name, but it was in the background and getting exponentially distant with each step. Anger and confusion also grew exponentially in those same steps. Standing in front of Traci and the frat boy now, Kassidy cleared her throat, loudly.

"Oh, hey, what's up," said Traci.

The response was a kick in the gut.

"What's up? What's up? Why don't you tell me?" said Kassidy.

"What's your deal, chick?" asked the frat boy.

Kassidy turned to him, allowed her power to build and allowed her eyes to change color. The metallic blue of the gods was intimidating. It was otherworldly. When they wanted to, they could make their eyes look like blue fire.

Kassidy wanted them to know.

And they did.

"What the . . ."

The frat boy removed his arm from around Traci's waist and backed up. He then quickly turned and walked away. She turned her gaze back to Traci who stared at her and smiled.

"Subtle," said Traci.

"I don't really give a fuck about being subtle right now," said Kassidy. "Now why don't you tell me what the fuck is going on."

"First of all, chill the fuck out. You don't own me. Hell, you're not even my girlfriend, right? I mean, what are we really doing anyway?"

Kassidy felt another punch to the gut.

"Where the hell is this coming from?" asked Kassidy.

As Traci opened her mouth to reply, a ripple of energy passed between them. It was invisible to others, but they both felt it. As it subsided, Traci began to shake, then fell to the floor. She convulsed, violently, causing everyone to stop and stare. Kassidy went to her knees to try and help but could do nothing. As the crowd gathered, she heard Kevin on the phone calling paramedics, and behind that, she heard Herb telling everyone to back away.

"Kass, what can we do?" he asked.

In an instant, the power went out. After a beat, it was back on. Traci lay on the floor, motionless. Kassidy shifted her vision to check her life sign. Even before she'd become a reaper, Kassidy had the ability to sense death. She could actually see a glow around an individual that told her whether or not someone was alive, near death, or dead. Blue auras signified life in mortals. Pink indicated they were near death. Red was the sign of death.

Traci's aura flickered between gold and pink.

"That's . . . not possible," Kassidy whispered.

Kassidy had only recently encountered the golden aura. It had surrounded Keiron and her aunt, Octavia Lord. The three of them had battled Wraiths, and all of them had been wounded. When Kassidy checked on her companions, she saw the golden glow. She later learned that it was the sign of an immortal. Traci's aura flickering was not uncommon. But the colors were. She was flickering between immortality and that of a mortal near death.

That shouldn't be a thing.

It wasn't a thing.

Yet here it was.

Kassidy was jolted from her thoughts as Traci began to stir. First, movement in her legs, then a flex in her hands, followed by a low moan. Traci opened her eyes next and there seemed to be some awareness.

"Babe?" whispered Traci.

"Can you hear me?"

Traci nodded.

Kassidy grabbed Traci's hand and held it close to her heart. Confusion was still present, but there was also relief. Strangely, it seemed to be coming from everyone except Traci. There was nothing coming from Traci. Once again, Kassidy could not sense her girlfriend's emotions.

"Babe," began Traci, "where are we? Why am I on the ground?"

Questions swirled in Kassidy's mind as the paramedics arrived.

What the hell is going on?

CHAPTER EIGHTEEN

"YOU KNOW THE OLD SAYING ABOUT THE ONLY ABSOLUTES IN LIFE being death and taxes, right?" asked Cyrus.

"I've heard it," said Ramsey.

"Well, we are not accountants."

Ramsey chuckled. It was the laugh of a new hire. Uncertain about how to engage, amenable to everything. Even tired old jokes about death and taxes. This was the life he'd chosen, or rather, the life that had chosen him. From either perspective, he was now one of an elite number. A group dedicated to helping maintain the balance between the dead and the living.

"Now," began Cyrus, "I want you to close your eyes, and I want you to focus."

"On what?"

"On energy. The energy surrounding you, the energy within you, the—"

"This sounds a lot like—"

"I know," said Cyrus. "Believe me, we've talked about it. Turns out, the former Primus was a fan of George Lucas and his first movie and casually bumped into the young director one day. They talked over many drinks, and the next thing you know, an ancient religion, yet somehow in the future, was born."

"That's—"

"Weird, I know. But you're now a supernatural being that escorts souls to the afterlife. So, weird has levels, wouldn't you agree?"

"Quality point," said Ramsey.

"Let's get back to it, we don't have much time. Close your eyes and concentrate."

Ramsey did as he was told. His mind swirled with thoughts. The past and present collided. Images of his old life, his mortal life, flashed through his brain as if on an 8mm reel-to-reel projector. The last frame, the night of his death, burst into flame and dissolved in a brilliant flash. For the next several moments there was nothing but darkness—cold, emotionless, bottomless. Ramsey felt fear, initially. But slowly, feelings of comfort crept in. Feelings of . . . belonging. A dim light came to life in this darkness and grew brighter and larger within seconds. Ramsey felt a flush of heat radiate through his body. It almost hummed with power. When he opened his eyes, he saw the world in a new light, a greenish-gray light. When he looked down, he saw the body of the woman he and Cyrus had come to transition. Her still form outlined in deep red.

"Welcome to the Nexus," said Cyrus, appearing next to him.

"This is where I was when *she* found me," said Ramsey.

"Yes. This is the place where we help souls move on."

Ramsey's body was vibrating as power ran through him. He'd only been a Reaper a few weeks, but in that time he'd not transitioned to the Nexus, nor had he attempted to manifest his weapon. He'd only followed and listened to Cyrus' stories. Now though, he was fully realized. He couldn't see them, but he knew that his eyes had transformed from their normal brown to silver. Looking down at his left hand, he took a deep breath, focused his thoughts, and watched as it became vapor, only to coalesce into a sickle.

"Whoa!" he exclaimed.

"What do you say we help this woman move on?" asked Cyrus.

Ramsey looked to his silver-eyed mentor and nodded.

"Do you remember what I told you?"

Ramsey nodded again.

"Proceed."

Ramsey's hand re-formed. He dropped to one knee and slowly allowed his hand to phase through the body of the dead woman.

"Good," said Cyrus.

Ramsey waited for the moment of connection, when the woman's soul would recognize the presence of a psychopomp, the being that would help it transition. He'd heard about the moment from Cyrus and other Reapers. They described it as a sort of ethereal click. One Reaper even said, "It's like when a seatbelt clicks in the thing."

But there was nothing.

Ramsey waited for several more moments before removing his hand and trying the process again. And then he tried again, and again, and again. Still . . . nothing.

"What am I doing wrong?" he asked.

"There is nothing wrong with your technique here, Ramsey. Let me try something," said Cyrus, gesturing Ramsey to step back. As Cyrus repeated the same actions, and saw the same results, their shared gaze spoke volumes.

"This shouldn't be happening," said Cyrus.

"What is it? Does she not have a soul? Has someone already been here?"

"No. Her soul is intact. But it's stuck. As if there's a barrier around it, restricting it, keeping it from crossing over."

"What causes that?" asked Ramsey.

"There is . . . nothing that I'm aware of that would cause that. I know of no force that can trap or manipulate a soul like this. I don't even believe a Death God can do it."

"Should we call her?"

"No. No, we don't have much time. We have to find a way to help this woman transition," said Cyrus. "If we don't act soon, the soul will most assuredly be trapped, and we'll be forced to dispatch it instead."

"What do we do?"

"Let's work together," said Cyrus.

Ramsey quickly moved to the other side, and with his mentor, phased his hand through the woman's body. He felt the energy radiated by Cyrus, and he felt . . . something else. There was a tingle, awareness, something that told him he was close. He felt resistance though. In looking at Cyrus, he could tell his mentor was feeling it, too. Ramsey felt an extra surge from Cyrus and with it, a sensation.

A click.

Together, Ramsey worked with Cyrus to help the soul rise from the body. Standing alongside the woman, all three looked at one another, then collectively, down.

"Oh my god," gasped the woman. "I'm . . ."

The silence that followed was heartbreaking. At the urging of Cyrus's nod, Ramsey explained the next steps to the woman, answered all her questions, and extended his hand. Several feet ahead, a swirling blue-white light formed.

"I . . . I feel it. Calling to me," said the woman.

"Go to it. It's time," said Ramsey.

The woman took a few steps and in a rush was pulled forward into the light source which quickly closed after she entered. Ramsey let out a breath.

"Why did that feel so wrong?" asked Ramsey.

"Because it was. It was very wrong."

"What do we do? Do we tell her? Do we tell Kassidy?"

"We do," began Cyrus. "We will. But first, we need to find out if this is isolated or more widespread."

"And if it is widespread?" asked Ramsey.

"If it is, then the balance between life and death is in danger. And if that is in danger, so is the very existence of the universe."

"Oh. Shit."

"Yeah," began Cyrus, "shit."

CHAPTER NINETEEN

"HERE," SAID KASSIDY, HANDING A DRINK TO TRACI.

"What is it?"

"Gin."

"Nope," said Traci, standing and backing away from the table.

"Listen, it's light, and it may take the edge off. I know it helps me."

Traci continued to shake her head and backed as far away from the table and Kassidy as she possibly could.

"Trace, it's just gin," said Kassidy.

There was concern in her voice. Traci could sense that much. But there was a hardness to her words and her demeanor. Traci was fearful that there was some tough love coming, especially after they talked about what happened at the bar. Once again, Traci had no memory of it. The last thing she remembered was being in another bar, waiting for food, and talking to a bartender named Mike Martin. Then the accident in the street.

The accident.

She caused the accident.

She killed those people.

That's right, little witch, you killed those people.

"No," said Traci, responding to Hecate.

"No, seriously, it's just gin," said Kassidy.

And I think I'm going to kill your little girlfriend here next.

"NOOOO!" screamed Traci.

The glass of gin flew off the table against the wall. Seconds later the cabinets began to shake. The dishes inside them rattled. The table and chairs began sliding along the floor, and an unearthly wind swirled in the kitchen. The lights flickered and there was a hollowness to the area. Traci wasn't sure what was happening, but she knew she was somehow responsible.

And she couldn't stop.

"Traci!"

Traci saw Kassidy's mouth move and heard her name on the swirling winds. She didn't know what to do with it. She wanted to run, to hide, to scream, to be anywhere but here answering for things she'd done, answering for the decisions she'd made that put all this in motion.

All for her.

"Fuck you!" screamed Traci, again. "Fuck you to hell! Get out!"

As the last words came out of her mouth, the wind died down, the rattling stopped, and everything was as it should be. Except Kassidy. Traci looked at her and saw something she'd only seen one time since they'd been together—her blue eyes, the eyes of a god. She'd seen eyes like that earlier in the evening, only they were her own. But at the same time, they were not. She knew they weren't hers, nor were they a sign of her power. She knew exactly who was using her as a vessel. She could tell Kassidy, and maybe get some help. She could at least tell Kassidy that she didn't mean what she'd just said. That she was responding to, well, something else. Somewhere deep down, though, Traci knew that Kassidy's help would more likely usher in Kassidy's death. And that just could not happen.

"Um, fuck me? Get out? This is my house! Who the hell are you to tell me what to do in my own house?!"

"Kass . . . I—"

"No, you need to tell me right the fuck now what's going on. When I found you the other night, I was terrified for you. After that shit went down in the living room, I was certain this was a punishment for something I'd done. But now, I'm not so sure. And I can't be sure until you tell me what the hell is happening with you!"

Traci recognized that she'd been holding her breath, exhaling only when Kassidy's eyes grew brighter.

Aw, poor little witch, began the voice inside. *Your little girlfriend thought you were talking to her. How sad. Looks like she's planning to kill you now. Look at those eyes. So much like her father.*

Traci froze at that. She knew who and what Kassidy was. But it felt strange to hear how much Kassidy was like her father from a disembodied voice that knew him. Maybe that was her way out. Maybe Thanatos could in fact help her through this. Kassidy's father was missing, though. For all they knew, he could be dead. If the original Death God could die, what chance did Kassidy have. She'd only ascended recently. She didn't have the experience or fully understand the depth and consequences of her abilities.

I can't wait to end her life.

Traci felt tears well.

"Jesus, Traci, just... talk to me," pleaded Kassidy as she walked toward her.

"No," said Traci, holding out her hand. "Don't come any closer."

Traci channeled some power through her body, causing an invisible barrier to manifest between her and Kassidy. As Kassidy pushed against it, a lump formed in Traci's throat followed by a bottomless ache in her gut.

"Take this damned thing down, Traci!" demanded Kassidy.

Traci was certain that once Kassidy knew the truth, she'd

stop at nothing to save her. But there was no coming back from this. Her mother knowing what Traci had done was bad enough. If Kassidy knew, if the sisters of the coven knew, they'd fight to save her. They'd fight to strip her of her powers, and she couldn't have that. Her powers, such as they were, gave her life meaning. Without them, she was nothing.

"Traci! Trace! Please!"

As Kassidy shimmered out of view, Traci quickly recited a spell that made the Death God reappear immediately.

"I'm sorry," said Traci, tracking the shock on Kassidy's face. "I'm not going to let you come near me. This is all your fault. I wouldn't be this fucked up if it weren't for you. Always so busy trying to save everyone. Why couldn't you just leave it."

She spoke the words with venom, or, at least tried to. She could tell from Kassidy's reaction that they had some effect. The eyes had powered down, and Kassidy staggered back.

"I'm leaving. Don't come looking for me."

The hollow feeling in her gut widened and deepened. Strength in her legs waned as her knees lost reliability. Mourning a loss that had yet to happen, Traci stared into Kassidy's eyes, whispered a spell to herself, and faded away.

CHAPTER TWENTY

"OKAY, WHAT THE FUCK WAS THAT?!"

Kassidy backed up against the countertop and stared at the empty space previously occupied by Traci. Her pulse was racing, and her skin was on fire. She could feel the energy she harnessed as the Death God just below the surface, ready to unleash, But, with no direction, it just pulsated. A low hum giving her goosebumps. A side of her, her celestial side, wanted to lash out, wanted to unleash power desperate for escape, desperate to destroy, to kill anything that stood before it. Kassidy had never before felt this combination of fury, fear, and confusion. Not even in her battles with Jeremy Reins, her attacker-turned-Wraith, or even with Azra-El during either of their epic battles. This was something altogether new.

Kassidy walked forward and stretched her arms out, looking for the invisible barrier she'd encountered before Traci vanished. There was nothing. Stepping closer to the spot Traci once stood, she closed her eyes and took a deep breath. She could still smell her. Traci's scent was intoxicating. As much as her eyes and her voice, her scent altogether calming, reassuring, and arousing. It was floral, with an underlying essence of the beach. It was sweet, light, and not overpowering.

It was ambrosia for the god within Kassidy.

But there was something else. Just under the surface. It wasn't a scent as much as it was a sensation. A byproduct of magic. Not

Traci's, though. No, it wasn't that. Kassidy had witnessed Traci's power before, and she knew that signature well. As she probed longer, she did, in fact, find some remnants of witchcraft. But there was more, decidedly more. The residue of power used only by gods. She knew it as surely as she knew her own name.

"Oh fuck. Traci . . . what's happened?"

The presence of god power was part of the reason she had powered up during Traci's magical tantrum. It wasn't that she was ready for attack. Despite everything, Kassidy felt confident that Traci would not intentionally try to hurt her. That god power triggered Kassidy's celestial impulses, though. It was no wonder Traci elected to exist stage left.

Kassidy thought back to her conversation with Keiron as they sat in Wrigley Field. She dwelled on the vagrant souls currently running amuck across the planet. Souls seeking shelter inside humans. Souls taking over the lives of people without their consent or knowledge of what was happening, or in most cases, *had* happened to them. And then she thought back to what Traci said. She said it was Kassidy's fault. Everything happening now was because of what she'd done.

"Anna," whispered Kassidy.

Kassidy made a fist in both hands and squeezed. Tighter. And tighter. And tighter. When it wasn't enough, she threw them into the walls. First a crack, causing paint chips to fall. Then the white powder of the drywall drifted to the floor, her knuckles coated in it. She spread her attack to various sections of the wall and did not stop, even when she found wooden studs.

They splintered under her power.

When she finally stopped, she took a deep breath to try and control her ragged breathing. Letting it out slowly she lowered her head and inspected her hands. They were bloodied, but the cuts were so superficial they were healing before her eyes. Then she gazed at her masterpiece of destruction.

"Damnit, Kassidy!" she said aloud.

She was at a loss for what to do. Nothing seemed to make sense.

She balled her right hand into a fist and squeezed again. As she did, she explored the possibilities at hand. She could try to make things right by killing Anna DeBartolo. She was supposed to die anyway. Perhaps doing it now could reset things. That's how it worked, right?

Stretching out her left hand, she called upon her power to summon the Scythe of Cronus. If nothing else, she could use the scythe to turn back time. It was dangerous, and could impact the natural order of the universe, but she could reset time to ensure that none of the activity subsequent to Anna's death had taken place. She could go back even further if she needed. She could stop Traci's kidnapping.

She could stop herself from ever becoming a Reaper.

The air around her hand crackled. Electricity danced around her fingertips. The strength and essence of death flowed through her, coursed through her as easily as her own blood.

But the scythe did not come.

She stared at her hand and opened it wider as if that would help. She gathered more energy, strengthening her call to the ancient weapon, but despite all her efforts, the scythe did not appear.

"Oh, no. No, no, no, no . . . NO!"

With one final attempt, Kassidy pulled in more energy. She channeled her rage. Purple streaks of lightning flickered in the air around her. It danced off the walls and the ceiling, shattering the lightbulbs, the only remaining light coming from her hand.

Slowly, a rift formed in the air. Tiny, struggling to take full shape, it widened.

Kassidy felt a tug.

Someone was calling her through the Nexus. She ignored it, focusing instead on the task of securing her weapon, her tool, her birthright. She felt a semblance of relief as the hardened wood of the staff touched her fingertips. She gripped it tightly once it reached her palm, and she pulled it toward her. There was resistance, but she soon wrestled it free. The blade caught the reflection of her eyes and was highlighted in blue.

"This can't be good," said Kassidy.

She felt that tug again.

She desperately wanted to ignore it. A large part of her was happy to. It was that same part that wanted to travel the planet to find Traci and somehow use her power and that of the scythe to save her. That's what Kassidy wanted, so that's what she was going to do.

The tug was stronger now.

With that added intensity came an overwhelming anxiety. Only part of it was hers. The heavy weight of it made her knees buckle. Using the countertop and the scythe to balance herself, the realization of what was happening struck her across the face.

"I shouldn't be able to feel that," she said.

The emotion was coming from a Reaper, through the Nexus.

Kassidy gripped the scythe harder with her left hand and made a fist with her other. She began tapping her fist against leg. She didn't want this. It was all too much. She needed to get out, to get away. Fury remained within her and spiraled. Thoughts of Traci ran through her mind, along with her adoptive parents, Dan and Marlene. Octavia's image passed through and lingered. As did Lynn Ambrose, her ex-girlfriend, killed at the hands of

Azra-El. All those images filled her mind. Images of the people she'd failed. Failed because of her actions, her inactions, her poor decisions.

Traci was going to be next.

The tug continued. Kassidy continued to ignore it. She was determined to escape, and so she did. She looked around at the damage in the kitchen of her family home and whispered, "I'm sorry."

Seconds later Kassidy shimmered away.

CHAPTER TWENTY-ONE

"DID YOU FEEL IT?" ASKED THE DIVA.

Jacen nodded.

"Wasn't it just exquisite?"

"I suppose that depends on a great many things," said Jacen.

Jacen Lucas allowed his mind to wander for the briefest of moments as he pondered just what the Pulse meant to the Diva. Nothing good. Of that, he was certain. The Pulse was the signal of something terrible coming. What scared him the most was the notion of the Diva getting ahold of the "something terrible" about to make its entrance.

As Advocates went, Jacen was still new to the game. He'd stepped into the order after a very frustrating life in social work, something he'd undertaken in an attempt to make amends for a dark life, a life that he'd returned to in an effort to save someone.

A life that got him killed.

When he was given the opportunity to do more, to be more, he jumped at the chance. He'd made a difference in the lives of many. Challenged people to think critically and view issues from multiple points of view. That was his life and had been for the last thirty years. Meeting the Diva over twenty years ago put things in a different perspective for him, though. He was forced to challenge his own way of thinking. Forced to grow quickly as an Advocate, tapping into abilities discouraged by those in the Advocate order.

It seemed to be a running theme with those he encountered.

After the Diva was released from her prison, she'd presented him with a proposition. His immediate reaction was to say no. In doing so, though, he knew he'd be leaving an almost unstoppable force free to roam the earth and cause havoc everywhere she went. So, he took a Dream Quest. He traveled through time and space to see how things might unfold if he did nothing. Once he realized that nothing good would come from him standing on the sidelines, he joined her and her pursuit—at least on the surface.

"You know, Advocate, sometimes I feel like you're not fully invested in this partnership. That vexes me," said the Diva.

"That's unfortunate. I would hate for you to continue to feel vexed. I'm certainly happy to move on," said Jacen.

The Diva was a ticking timebomb. He knew he was poking a sleeping bear when he said things like that. A sleeping bear with almost limitless power.

Almost limitless.

It was her rage that scared him the most. It was in those moments that her power was at its most lethal, as was her mind. She was prone to deadly outbursts when not happy. Century upon century of imprisonment had done nothing but augment her rage. Her reputation was one of playfulness and mischief. Being locked up had chipped away at the rational parts of her mind. Being locked away strengthened her resolve to get vengeance and build a new world with herself as absolute ruler. Jacen didn't fear her. His power was greater, and he was very careful not to reveal that, even allowing her to get the upper hand on him at times. It was because his power was greater that he carried the burden of watching over her. Under the guise of her ally, he could hopefully influence the outcome he'd foreseen.

"You're pretty shrewd, Advocate," said the Diva. "Not many

make the mistake of challenging me, even in a passive aggressive way. What is it that gives you the confidence to do so?"

Because I'm more of a god than you will ever be.

The thought ran through his mind. It was a challenging thought. A powerful thought. A very true thought. The Advocates possessed power that, if unchecked, could change the very fabric of reality. That's why they were so careful and intentional when choosing beings to join their ranks. It's why they had very specific rules about how to engage with beings, both human and supernatural. It's why he allowed the Diva to think of him as no more than a minion.

"I have power, just as you do," began Jacen, "and sometimes, it gets a little frustrating when you treat me as 'lesser than.'"

"If you want more, then ask. Take. I'm happy to share. Contrary to popular belief, I do play well with others."

She said it in that seductive tone as she stepped forward and gently touched his chest. The Diva was playful all the time. She was the personification of the Id, ruled by pleasure, desire, and the constant search for power and control. She weaponized her sexuality as much as she used her own powers to confuse, maim, and destroy. Jacen was careful not to succumb.

But the temptation was always great.

"I'm sure you do," said Jacen. "And we would, no doubt, have wonderful adventures. I think we've discussed that before. But we've also discussed the importance of not mixing business with pleasure."

Jacen removed her hand and stepped around her, heading toward the edge of the rooftop. He loved his city. Born and raised in Chicago, he loved every nook and cranny. While other Advocates lived in earthly versions of heaven, like Hawaii, the Caribbean, or some remote Mediterranean island, he chose to remain in the Windy City. He would venture away at times during the brutal winters, but he always returned. Because Chicago was beautiful.

Even when it wasn't.

"Have you had any luck finding Burke?" asked the Diva.

She was walking toward him. He wasn't concerned about having his back to her though, despite just rebuking her obvious advances. She needed him. He knew that. No matter how angry she might be, and no matter how she may choose to demonstrate that anger, she'd always have to come back to him.

"Burke is, quite literally, off the grid," said Jacen.

"The world thought that before, yet he was hiding in plain sight. And they say I'm a trickster. Thanatos may have pulled the ultimate jest with that maneuver."

"Sending Ares to the future was indeed … inspired. Stripping him of his memories, brilliant. Cruel. But brilliant," said Jacen.

"We have to find him," said the Diva. "If we cannot, then we will need another War God, and the only other god I know will not be easily persuaded or coerced."

"And you thought Burke would easily be coerced to joining you?" asked Jacen.

"He's a hot head. He lacks the drive and discipline of his sister."

"Sadly, some siblings are not influenced by each other. Such a loss to a potential harmonious household and existence."

Jacen knew he'd poked the bear one too many times with that statement. So, it came as no surprise when he felt his body flying through the air after being struck in the back by a blast of energy from the Diva. He felt a sting in his back, but no permanent damage. He crossed his arms over his chest, closed his eyes, and willed himself back to the rooftop, where he took form next to the Diva.

"Something I said?"

The Diva stepped to the side and squared up to Jacen, her blue eyes pulsing with power. She was angry. He could feel it. Jacen wanted to needle further, but the consequences of such an act could be catastrophic. Her desire for revenge was already great and it was laying the foundation for the apocalypse. He saw no sense in speeding up the process.

So he apologized.

"I am sorry if you took offense to my statement. I meant no disrespect."

This time, Jacen walked up to her. He reached out, moved hair from her face, and in doing so, brushed her cheek slightly. It caused her bright eyes to dim, then flicker, then return to their normal hazel. His hand lingered on her face for several beats as their eyes whispered to one another. Eventually, she pushed his hand away and walked away from him.

"We need to find the War God," she said. "And don't ever touch me like that again."

Jacen turned to respond, but the Diva was shimmering away. With a wry smile, he did the same, returning to a sanctuary in the Pacific Northwest that few knew of. In this cabin, he could have that sense of safety and he could take moments he needed for himself. The two-story wood cabin had a wraparound porch. On the second story, a balcony led out to an amazing view of the lake, rarely used and seemingly forgotten. Jacen walked in, looking for the cabin's current guest. When he didn't find him, Jacen continued through the cabin, toward the back, where he exited and found his houseguest practicing Tai Chi in the field beyond. Jacen walked slowly, quietly, so as not to disturb the man too much.

"When you try to be quiet, you're actually more distracting," said the man, stopping midform to look back over his shoulder.

Jacen grinned.

"My apologies, Mr. Burke. I didn't want to disturb you. I just came to check in," said Jacen.

"You can call me, Jaxon. Or Jax. I think I prefer either to Ares at this point. Definitely prefer it to 'Mr.' Burke."

"Jax it is," said Jacen, acknowledging the War God with a nod.

"Is it time?" asked Jaxon.

"We're getting there," said Jacen. "We're getting there."

CHAPTER TWENTY-TWO

AS CRIME SCENES WENT, THE ONE IN FRONT OF SHAY WALKER WAS pretty tame. There had certainly been worse in the city. More bloody, more chaotic, and barbaric scenes were rare, but not entirely uncommon. It wasn't really the blood and gore that made this particular scene problematic. It was the fact that there had been an increasing number of them in the last couple of months. Crime scenes involving bodies that were clearly dumped, poorly staged, but done so in such a chaotic fashion that it made clue development difficult even for the best Evidence Technician on the force. With the techs working overtime to sort out the mess, detectives focused their efforts toward developing a viable psychological profile to at least identify some characteristics of the person or persons involved with the body-dumping.

Shay had been tapped to sit in on the unofficial task force created to investigate the case. She was fairly new to the area having just moved to Chicago eight months prior. Out of college she'd gone directly into graduate work in the field of psychology. Her instructors noticed that she seemed particularly intuitive when it came to the criminal mind. She excelled at thinking in the abstract and demonstrated an uncanny ability to put herself in the mind of a psychopath. She was encouraged to focus on forensic psychology, and within six months it became her passion. Shay had been courted by many law enforcement agencies across the globe, including the FBI and Scotland Yard.

She sat down for a cup of coffee with a few intelligence agencies, too. Ultimately, she chose the FBI's Behavioral Analysis Unit.

For five years she helped track down some of the most notorious criminals in the nation, but in the end, it wasn't enough. Shay had a wanderlust. She craved a life of law, justice, and travel. She craved a world that was better and wanted to do what she could to assist that endeavor. With the help of one of her instructors, she was introduced to a senior leader of Interpol. Following a thirty-minute conversation, she was hooked and spent the next fifteen years traveling the world as a special consultant. In the last few years though, several cases in some very remote areas of the world had caught her eye. Strangely, these weren't criminal cases, though they were centered around death. On the surface, they were crimes against humanity—cases involving sickness and death resulting from famine and ongoing war, either locally, or from nearby neighbors. It was happening in strange areas, but areas that, upon further research, were strategic hotbeds for certain countries in power. Those cases, along with reports of sudden unrelated and unexplainable deaths in the United States, shifted her focus.

She left Interpol to pursue leads, and they led her to Chicago. For her, there was no better way to get to the heart of things than as a police officer. A few calls and several meetings led her to receiving a detective's star for the police department of the nation's third largest city. A city that had been knee-deep in death over the last couple of months.

"Thanks for coming, Shay," said a voice from behind.

She didn't need to turn around to know who it was. Shay knew that voice intimately. She'd been assigned to work with Detective Simms often. She later heard a rumor that the assignments had been special requests by a cop who'd had some clout in the department. Shay was both annoyed and intrigued when she discovered Simms was that cop. Over time, she found herself enjoying those consults more and more. Eventually, those consult meetings became meetings over drinks after work and then dinner. Detective Simms was a tall, athletic, blond, blue-eyed charmer who got by on great looks then stunned people with an equally sharp mind. Shay had initially tried to resist mixing business with pleasure. She soon realized that it was a futile battle.

"No thanks needed, Matt," Shay said as she turned around. "What have we got this time?"

The two stared at one another, their respective gazes having a conversation that no one would ever hear. Shay saw a man who could have been the love of her life. It was still strange to think that way. She'd spent most of her life alone. There had been some relationships here and there, but nothing ever lasted. Shay was not one to just be attracted to beauty, intellect, and charm. There had to be that intangible, unexplainable spark. She needed a connection that went deeper than surface-level nuances. Something had awakened inside of her when they'd first met, and it wasn't too long ago that the little spark grew to full on wildfire. Even now, after everything that had happened between them, Shay still felt that pull toward him. It was hard to resist, and she was fairly certain Matt could sense that.

"Something similar to our other body dumps," said Matt. "Like the others, this body is decayed for what looks like decades."

"But?" asked Shay.

"But there's identification on the body, a driver's license, for a woman named Sophia Clark."

"And how old is Miss Clark?"

"Thirty-three," said Simms.

"No other physical evidence here?" asked Shay.

"No, it's pretty clean."

Shay looked around the area for a sign of anything out of the ordinary, something perhaps the uniformed officers may have missed.

"This is a pretty strange spot to dump a body," said Shay. "It's not that hidden. Who called it in?"

"Anonymous," said Simms. "Call was traced to that payphone over there."

"Payphone? We still have those?"

"There are a few here and there in the city," said Simms with a chuckle.

Shay hated that chuckle. She hated it because she liked it so much. She liked the sound and the way he grinned. It was playful and warm. When she heard it, her mind made the leap toward thoughts of a future between them.

"Detectives?" yelled a voice near the body.

Shay and Simms walked together toward the examiner who'd taken the call. The building they were in was across from Navy Pier. A run-down, abandoned office with a lot for parking. It was no doubt a squatter's haven during the harsh months. There were scorch marks on the concrete where fires had burned through makeshift grills and traps. Stepping up to the body, Shay noticed that the clothes on the expired woman looked brand new. They weren't expensive, but they were definitely not cheap.

"What's up, Johnny?" asked Simms.

"Hey, guys. Just wanted to point out what appears to be a stamp on the left hand of this woman. It's hard to tell through the decayed flesh, but there's black ink there and, at first glance, it appears to be a bumblebee."

"Queen Bee's," said Shay and Simms in unison.

Ignoring protocol, Shay reached down to touch the woman's

hand to get a closer look at the stamp. The hand was cold and felt brittle. Like an aged wooden box that had been sitting for far too long.

Then the woman's eyes popped open.

Simms and Johnny jumped backward, while the sudden movement sent Shay to the ground.

The presumed-dead Sophia Clark was moving, and she was moaning. Her head shifted slowly from side to side. Her fingers extended and contracted. In a strained whisper, she spoke.

"Freeeeee meeeee."

Shay wasn't sure what to think. She'd never seen anything like this before. Sophia Clark was not only alive but clinging to that life. She seemed to be in great pain. When the head turned to look at Shay, there was life despite the vacant eyes. Desperate life.

Shay watched as the body convulsed, then arched at the midsection. A primal wail escaped Sophia Clark's mouth as if she were expelling the pain and agony within. After several seconds, the body stopped moving altogether. The head flopped to the side, and once again it seemed that the woman was dead.

Shay, Simms, and Johnny all looked at each other. Several other officers stared, dumbfounded.

"What . . . the fuck . . . just happened?" asked Simms.

"I . . . I . . . I," stammered Johnny.

Shay said nothing.

She couldn't say anything.

Her body would not allow her.

She was no longer in control.

"I . . . um . . . need a minute," she said.

Only, it wasn't her. The words came out of Shay's mouth, but it wasn't her who spoke them. She felt her body rise, and she felt it walk away.

"Shay?" asked Simms with concern.

"It's okay. I'll be fine. Just . . . give me a minute."

Shay felt one foot move after the other. She could see where her body was going. As it crossed the street and made its way to Navy Pier, she could hear the faint sounds of the lake's waves. It took several minutes, but she'd soon reached the end of the pier. Her body stopped and looked at its reflection in the window of a restaurant. The face that stared back was hers, but the thing in charge was not, and that thing screamed.

"What's happened to me?!"

Shay felt her arms move and her hands searched her body as if it were foreign. Her right hand found her service weapon, unholstered it, gripped it, and fired into the glass.

Neither Shay, nor the thing controlling her body were prepared for the resulting explosion.

CHAPTER TWENTY-THREE

KASSIDY TOOK A FINAL DRINK THEN TOSSED THE BOTTLE OVER HER shoulder. It took several beats for her to realize that it did not make a sound. She closed her eyes, stretched out with her senses, and felt nothing. There was an emptiness, a void, just a space of nothingness. Around it, life happened, life thrived, life wanted nothing more than to keep going—the antithesis of her current desire. But in that space, that space where she'd tossed that bottle and eight others before it . . . there was nothing.

"That you, Lucas?"

"Guess again," said a soft voice.

That voice brought Kassidy both the sensation of safety and embarrassment. There was so much comfort in those words, and with the person who spoke them. But there was dread in being seen like this. As a lost, fractured, insecure, and uncertain being of unfathomable power. Her natural defense was to push away, to make herself utterly unlikable, and tragically unapproachable. But those who knew her well were not swayed so easily.

London Jaymes was someone who knew Kassidy well.

"How did you find me?" asked Kassidy.

"Seriously?"

Kassidy nodded sheepishly in agreement with how silly that sounded. Like her, London was a private investigator. Like her, London's specialty was locating people, especially people who did not want to be found. It was, in fact, at London's request, that Kassidy had taken on a case leading to the discovery that Reapers were ingesting souls of the dead instead of ushering them to the afterlife. Eventually, she learned they were doing this to energize Azra-El. Those events led to her eventual ascension to godhood.

Those events led to her current misery.

"Still the best, eh?" asked Kassidy.

"The best? Maybe. Determined to find my friend when I know she's not well? Absolutely."

"Not well? That's an understatement," said Kassidy.

She reached into a bag and pulled out another bottle of beer. Being a bourbon lover, beer was a bit of harm reduction for Kassidy. It was doing nothing for her. Since her ascension she could enjoy the taste of alcohol longer and not worry so much about the shitty physical effects the next day. Today she was actually craving the shitty physical effects the next day. She wanted that misery because, in that space, she'd have an excuse to curl up and hide from everything.

"Tell you what," began London, "before you open that nonsense, how about we open this."

Kassidy turned her head to regard London for the first time since her arrival. She looked just as amazing as she always had. Her dark hair was longer and now had hints of crimson, though, it could have been an illusion of shadow, light, and reflection. Chicago nights, near Lake Michigan, against the backdrop of downtown illumination, caused many illusions.

It certainly wasn't the beer causing it.

"Is that . . . ?"

"Mm-hmm," said London.

As London walked toward her, Kassidy felt that void move with her. Kassidy felt no emotion from the woman. And it wasn't that London was emotionless. It was because of *what* she was rather than *who* she was. Kassidy found comfort with the woman. She found safety in the silence. She found she could just be herself.

"So, you're drinking bourbon now?" asked Kassidy.

"I'm drinking *this* bourbon," replied London as she lowered herself to sit next to Kassidy.

Kassidy took the bottle from London and examined it. It was called Brother's Bond. London pulled two whiskey glasses from the bag she had with her, and gave the international gesture toward Kassidy that said, "open it."

She did.

The aroma was fabulous. She smelled a subtle spice, enveloped in a sweetness that told her this would go down well with almost anything. She poured some into each glass, capped the bottle, and sat it between them. London gestured for a toast, and they did. Kassidy sipped, breathing in the aroma.

"My god, that's good," she said.

"Right?!"

"I can see why you're drinking this," said Kassidy.

"Yeah, it's so good. But, full disclosure, I only bought it because it's the brand of the guys from the vampire show. And . . . you know . . ."

It was a few moments before awareness washed over Kassidy. The bourbon. The vampire show. London's subsequent attraction to both.

"Well, I'm sure they would be delighted to know that an actual vampire enjoys their creation," said Kassidy.

"Oh, she very much does. I'm glad my limited diet doesn't exclude alcohol. I've gone through several bottles already. Channeling my inner Kassidy Simmons."

"I wouldn't do that if I were you."

"Why not? She's pretty badass," said London.

"Because people die. That's all that happens around me."

"I mean . . . you are the Death God. Also, I'm a vampire. I'm pretty familiar with death, too," London quipped.

Kassidy looked at London who stared back, and in seconds they both erupted in laughter. Kassidy had a dark sense of humor. London was one of the few people who could not only take Kassidy's humor and sarcasm but match it. She was never offended, and in return, Kassidy was never offended by hers. Right now, it was just what she needed. She needed that laugh. She needed that bellyaching, tear-forming, laugh that resulted in a fit of coughing.

And she needed it to turn into a bout of crying, too.

"Shit gets real when the laughs turn to ugly crying, babe. Tell me what's happening."

She did.

She continued to cry.

And London cried with her.

"Well . . . fuck," said London.

"Yeah . . . fuck," replied Kassidy.

"And there's nothing you can do to fix this?"

"I wouldn't even know how," said Kassidy. "When I was a girl, I thought Reapers would be the strangest thing I'd ever see in life. Then I became one. Then came the Wraiths. Then I met a vampire. Then I learned about gods. Now I am one. And now I've got to deal with witches and shit."

"Witches and shit sucks, girl. But that's just the tip of the iceberg," said London.

"Oh, god, don't say that."

"Listen, the supernatural world, the world of gods and monsters, is big. Huge, actually. But just like the real world, it has rules, and most of all it has balance. Whatever Traci is experiencing right now has an opposite. There is a way to balance what she's done. I don't know that it'll save her in the end, but that balance could be what saves us all from what she may become."

"What do you think she's becoming?" asked Kassidy.

"I don't know," said London. "But if it's the result of some dark magic rooted in retribution, it ain't good."

"Where the fuck is Glinda when you need her?"

"Right? Fucking magic wielders, man. Selfish sons of bitches," said London.

They toasted.

They laughed.

"I just ..."

"Just what, babe?" asked London.

"I just want to be happy. For once. I want people around me to be safe. Thriving. Not constantly in danger because of who and what I am."

"Unfortunately, you aren't in control of that," said London. "Death God, Reaper, empath, or investigator, there's only so much you can do. You have responsibilities, you have skills, and you have heart. Sadly, we live in a world where some of those qualities and skills need to be used at the expense of the others for the greater good."

"It's not fair."

"Agreed. But it, whatever *it* is, doesn't care about being fair."

Kassidy nodded. Then she sipped. Then she nodded again. She wasn't necessarily feeling any better, but she was getting to a point where she was closer to accepting the current reality. Deep down, she already knew the things London was saying. The fact that London was saying them was validating. But she felt others wouldn't understand or accept the inevitable choices she would make. The choices she'd *have* to make. Her current fears weren't rooted in failure and loss. They were rooted in the knowledge that she couldn't save everyone, and that those she *could* save would never forgive her.

"I'm going to lose her," said Kassidy. "Like my dad, my mom, Octavia . . . Lynn."

"You don't know that. You're a Death God, not a seer."

"Jesus, I forgot they're real, too. Ugh."

London's chuckle made Kassidy smile. She needed it. Just as she'd needed that laugh earlier. She let her senses go again and fell into the emptiness in the space where London sat. She allowed the comfort of feeling no one else's emotions but her own wrap itself around her like the arms of a lover. Then she felt the actual arms of a former lover envelop her. Tears flowed, but not in an uncontrollable way.

"How did you know I needed help?" asked Kassidy.

"I always know, love. Remember, we share more than memories and intimacy."

Kassidy's eyes widened.

"Oh my god, New Orleans," she said.

"Mm-hmm," said London.

"Even now, that I'm a . . . god?"

"Actually, it's stronger now that you're a god. It's like, I can feel you anywhere."

"Wow," began Kassidy, "that's so fucking cool."

"Yeah girl. It's pretty fucking cool."

With her head on London's shoulder, and the vampire's arm around her, Kassidy sank into the blanket of security, while on the other side of the lake, life happened. Life thrived. Life kept going.

At least until the sky lit up over Navy Pier from the explosion.

CHAPTER TWENTY-FOUR

JACEN LUCAS ENJOYED THE VIEW OF CHICAGO FROM THE OBSERVATION deck of the Willis Tower. He was, of course, an old school Chicagoan, so naturally it was always the Sears Tower for him. Just as the Sox stadium would forever be Comiskey Park. He had no such allegiance to the venue for the Chicago Bulls. He'd had occasion to visit the old Chicago Stadium, their former home, when he was a child. But those memories did not grant favor for the old building. And as he stood on the observation level of the tower, looking out at the city, the notion of allegiances played and replayed in his mind.

"What the hell am I doing?" he whispered to himself.

As the energy of the Chicago nightlife took form on the streets, Jacen stared out, wondering if his actions and inactions would ultimately end the beauty that existed in the urban jungle below. He had taken a huge risk siding with the Diva all those years ago. Well, seemingly siding with her. Some days, especially recently, he wasn't sure what side he was on.

Actually, that wasn't true. For as long as Jacen could remember, he was on the side of humanity. In his former life, his mortal life, he'd been a champion of civil rights and social justice. He'd marched with Dr. King *and* listened fervently when Malcolm X spoke. He protested America's involvement in many wars and international skirmishes, urging those in power to focus on the people of the nation, on the young soldiers sent to fight a battle over the ideals of the rich. Jacen Lucas was, and remained, on the side of the people—all people.

Even when he was silent.

His love of humanity was ever present. But as an Advocate he could not interfere with the course of their history. It was all very "prime directive" like. Actually, it was more of an urging than a rule. So, since it was not a rule, he wasn't bound to it. Hardcore advocates, traditionalists, lived the lives of quiet observers, engaging only occasionally, only when challenges faced by humanity seemed imbalanced. Jacen felt that it was often too late at that point. He also felt that such lack of action assumed a hierarchy that was unfair. Advocates were beings of great power, and Jacen felt strongly that the power should not be squandered or withheld. It should be used to help and further humanity—propel them to a future of wonder, exploration, and fellowship.

And that was why he experienced such dissonance in his work with the Diva.

He rationalized it as best he could. He reminded himself regularly that he was playing the long game. But all of the things that had to happen for the outcome he hoped for weighed heavily on him. The lives lost. The souls in turmoil. The war, the disease, the escalation of hatred across the planet—it was all so tragic, so sad, so ... painful. At times, Jacen felt like a puppet master using people for his own purposes. But the purpose, in the end, was a stronger, unified world. "You have to crack a few eggs to make an omelet"—his grandfather's favorite metaphor.

"I'm making one big-ass omelet, granddad," he said to himself.

Jacen walked to the eastern side of the tower and looked upon the city. During the day, it was one of his favorite views of

Chicago. Michigan Avenue, Grant Park, Buckingham Fountain, Navy Pier, the Museum Campus, all bordering the magnificent lake, that, in a few months, would be full of boats and people enjoying life, completely oblivious to the dangers lurking in the shadows. Or maybe, living life fully aware of the dangers lurking in the shadows. It was Chicago, after all. The city was not the safest, yet its citizens persevered because even when it was ugly, it was absolutely beautiful.

"The ability to have your 'office' be anywhere in the world is one of the best perks of this job, isn't it?"

Jacen turned slightly to acknowledge the voice behind him. He grinned, as was his habit when something pleasant occurred during his moments of deep introspection. The arrival of a fellow Advocate, of *this* fellow Advocate, was pleasant.

"Though, why you choose this place as your headquarters is beyond me."

"Easy there, pal. This city is amazing," said Jacen.

"You said the same of London, Prague, Budapest, and Sydney."

"Yeah, well . . . those places were amazing, too."

"Hmm, methinks for other reasons."

Jacen laughed, turned, and moved to embrace his comrade.

"It's good to see you, Malcolm," said Jacen.

"And you, brother," said Malcolm.

"What brings you my way?"

It wasn't the silence that answered the question, it was the non-verbal reply. One that Jacen had grown accustomed to over the years. Malcolm was not just a good friend, he was also the one who had recruited Jacen into the order. He was a mentor and a confidant. While he was of the old guard, the collection of Advocates who were traditionally hands-off in the affairs of humans, he was also a visionary, a progressive of sorts. He'd told Jacen, in no uncertain terms, that the reason he'd recruited him was because the order, the world, needed a kick in the ass.

The term he'd used at the time was "supernatural enema".

"Yeah, I recognize that look," said Jacen.

"Do you still think you have things under control?" asked Malcolm.

"Look, I never said I had things under control."

"You said, and I quote, 'Mal, don't worry. Everything is playing out as it's supposed to for the greater good.' Right? That's what you said."

"And it is," said Jacen.

A beat passed.

"It mostly is," said Jacen.

Another beat.

"It's gonna course correct," said Jacen.

Jacen's shoulders slumped as he said it. He wasn't sure he believed those words, but he'd gone too far to not support and follow the path he saw two decades ago.

"When you first encountered the Diva, after she'd escaped Pandora's box, you feared for the world. You feared what could happen. You see what's happening out there. Your fears are coming to life," said Malcolm.

"Yes, but there is renewed hope."

"In this girl? This . . . Simmons?"

Jacen nodded.

"Why are you so sure? How can you place all your faith in an alcoholic fledgling god?"

"Because I've seen what she can do. I know what she's capable of."

"Then why not ally yourself with her? Why do you continue to entertain the Diva?" asked Malcolm.

"Because if I don't, if I don't have a way of keeping tabs, I can't influence that course correction I alluded to."

The two stood in silence for a while. When Malcolm moved over to the window, Jacen followed. They stared at the city, watched the lights of the cars racing along Lake Shore Drive, the slower cars in stop-and-go traffic along Michigan Avenue.

"Something big happening in town tonight?" asked Malcolm.

"Obama," said Jacen.

"Nice. You know, I almost recruited him."

"Get out! Seriously?"

"Yep."

"Why didn't you?"

"Because, while contemplating it, something kept gnawing at me about him. I made a point of bumping into him outside the library when he was at Columbia University. We chatted for exactly six minutes and thirty-seven seconds."

A beat passed as Jacen gave a quizzical glance to his friend.

"I know," began Malcom, "weird. But it was the most profound amount of time I'd ever spent with anyone in my four hundred years of life."

"And because of that, you left it alone?"

"Oh, no. That conversation made me even more determined to make him an Advocate," said Malcolm.

"So, why didn't you?"

"I took a Dream Quest."

Those words froze Jacen. The Dream Quest was one of the most powerful tools in the arsenal of an Advocate. It was a magic that sent their consciousness into the past or future, to see multiple possibilities. That knowledge could lead an Advocate to act, or not. Because there was often too much temptation to act, the practice was highly discouraged. Advocates of course, still practiced. But no one ever admitted it. Jacen most assuredly did not admit it when he'd done it after meeting the Diva following her release from the box. So he was most certainly shocked with Malcolm's revelation now.

"That's a bold admission, brother," said Jacen.

"It is. But I wouldn't do it if I didn't trust you."

Jacen turned to his mentor, placed his hand over his heart, and inclined his head.

"So, what did you learn?" asked Jacen.

"What I learned was, making him an Advocate would have robbed the world of two people destined to impact it in the best ways possible."

"Two people?"

"Yes," began Malcolm, "you see if I'd made him an Advocate, he never would have gone on to do the things he did as a speaker, politician, teacher, and most importantly, father and grandfather. His descendants do some amazing things for this world. As an Advocate, that would never happen."

"Interesting," said Jacen, looking off into the distance, curious about what was to come. "And what about this second person."

"Ah, yes. Well, if I'd made Obama an Advocate, I would not have encountered the man I eventually recruited," said Malcom, turning to Jacen. "That recruit, will go on to have a significant impact on the course of this world's history as well."

As awareness trickled into Jacen's mind, he felt the weight of recent decisions bear down on him.

"Me?"

Malcolm nodded.

"I ask questions of you about the Diva, not because I don't trust you, but because I want to make sure you are still grounded and resolute in your decision-making. I trust you, brother. I want to make sure you trust yourself. Your path to becoming an Advocate was winding, and it took a lot to get the buy-in from the others, given your . . . colorful past. But I would do it again in a heartbeat," said Malcolm.

Jacen was overwhelmed with emotion, and he did not fight it. Feeling emotions helped him stay rooted. Great power accompanied the mantle of Advocate. He was determined to make certain that the power did not overshadow his humanity.

"I uh . . . I'm shocked. I had no idea."

"Well, seemed the right time to share. I sense you're a bit conflicted," said Malcolm.

"Maybe a bit."

"It happens. And it's usually in those moments that you need to reach out to an ally."

"Well, I have you, so I will most certainly—"

"Oh no, not me, brother," said Malcolm. "Don't get me wrong, you can always reach out, and I will always be there. But in this instance, I'm thinking of another ally."

Jacen pondered that for a moment. As the images of all the current players in this game came to mind, one stood out. He looked to his mentor, who stared back with a raised eyebrow.

"I've already reached out to her. Many times," said Jacen.

"Yes, but as an Advocate, no?"

Jacen shrugged.

"Hmm. Perhaps it's time to reach out as Jacen Lucas," suggested Malcolm. "Let her know you are indeed an ally, and not some seemingly omnipotent being passing through with enigmatic warnings."

"You've been watching?" asked Jacen with a wry smile.

"No," began Malcolm, "I just know you. And I know you well enough to know that this is the time to take that next step. For her peace of mind, and also for yours."

Jacen allowed those words to sink in, and at once felt some of the load he carried lighten. The mere prospect of opening up, even a little, sparked more hope. He hadn't seen this in his own Dream Quest, but that didn't mean it wasn't the right thing to do. Kassidy needed to trust him, to believe in him, because in doing so, it would help her believe in herself. And that was ultimately the key to everything that was about to happen.

"Thank you, my friend," said Jacen, extending his hand.

"Be well," said Malcolm, extending his own hand.

As Malcolm shimmered away during their handshake, Jacen once again looked out toward his city. It was indeed beautiful. Even when it wasn't.

The explosion at Navy Pier did not fall in the category of beautiful.

CHAPTER TWENTY-FIVE

KASSIDY MATERIALIZED IN A DARKENED CORNER NEAR THE FERRIS wheel at Navy Pier to avoid anyone seeing her. Peering out, she saw smoke and fire emanating from a structure near the end of the pier. There was no movement, but across the street she saw a number of officers rushing toward the pier in response to the explosion.

"Good! They can handle this," she muttered to herself. Kassidy prepared to leave until she felt a tingle in the back of her mind. There was a vagrant soul at the end of the pier. Could that soul have been the cause? Quickly weighing her options, Kassidy shimmered to a spot farther down the pier. With all the chaos of the explosion, if anyone took notice of her sudden appearance, they could chalk it up to adrenalin-fueled hallucination.

She reappeared just past the Billy Goat Tavern and Grill and Riva Crabhouse. Both were ablaze as fire spread. On her right, toward the lake, were the docking ports for the Spirit of Chicago and the Sea Dog speedboat. Ahead, she saw a figure that she suspected was the person hosting the vagrant soul. Kassidy kept a steady pace so as not to spook the spirit. Her gait became even more casual when she saw the person, a woman, take a seat on the edge of the pier just beyond the Aon Grand Ballroom.

As she closed in, the link became stronger. She also heard sounds. No, not just sounds, but speech. The figure was talking to herself. Or perhaps, talking to the spirit dwelling within her.

"Get out of my head!"

Kassidy saw the woman holding her head, rocking back and forth.

"Look, it'll be fine. Don't do anything stupid."

That also came from the woman, but the voice was decidedly not hers. It was deeper and the cadence was remarkably east coast. New York definitely. Brooklyn, maybe. Kassidy quickly got the sense that the woman and the soul within were at odds. Perhaps over who should be in control of the body?

"I can't live like this," said the woman. "I *won't* live like this!"

Kassidy watched as Shay turned to face the waters of Lake Michigan.

"Whoa there, sweetheart, what are you doin?"

"I'm ending it," said the woman.

"You can't swim!" cried the soul through its host.

"Exactly!" she shouted as she pushed herself from the pier into the cold water below.

Kassidy moved quickly.

She shimmered from where she was, reappearing as vapor just below the jumper. Enveloping the fractured woman, Kassidy moved them both to a safe space on the pier. Kassidy shifted to solid form, saw emergency services arriving, and quickly transported them both inside the grand ballroom near the pier's very edge, to give her privacy and time to help the woman while the first responders worked on the fire at the pier.

"What the—" began the woman.

"Fuck!" finished the soul inside her.

The duality was curious to Kassidy. Thus far she'd not encountered a situation in which a human shared control with the spirit inhabiting it. To date, the primary soul was silenced, dormant, leaving the possessed individual with no memory of ever being suppressed. This was something altogether different. Perhaps it was because of the woman? Or maybe it's another byproduct of what she'd done for Anna.

"Who are you," asked the woman, staring at Kassidy.

"Oh shit," began the vagrant soul, "it's you!"

Kassidy gave a slight bow. The woman's eyes widened as the words were spoken, clearly indicating that the vagrant soul was in charge of the whole body in that moment. When the woman's eyes softened, the body posture shifted as well. Clear signs that control had shifted. Kassidy wondered how physically taxing that was for the body itself. The woman began to contort. She was pleading for something to stop.

"No, damn you! No!" she yelled.

Kassidy watched the scene play out, fascinated and sympathetic. This woman was putting up one hell of a struggle against the vagrant soul inside. Finally, Kassidy reached out, put her hand on the woman's forehead and concentrated. She felt the soul inside. She was tempted to simply pull it from the woman, but something about this whole situation seemed, odd. Instead, Kassidy sent a command for the soul to quiet down, to aid the woman's attempts to control her own body outright.

"Are you, like, a witch or something?" asked the woman.

"Curious that you would ask that," began Kassidy, "do you have experience with witches?"

"No," said the woman. "Just seemed like . . . magic. All of this seems like magic."

Kassidy regarded the woman. She had short hair, a pixie cut, her skin announcing a decidedly mixed heritage, though Kassidy wasn't certain of the lineage. The badge around the woman's neck answered at least one question.

"Well, it is a type of magic. And no, I'm not a witch. My

girlfriend is. She can't do cool stuff like that, though. At least, I don't think."

A pregnant pause took up space between the two women.

"Your girlfriend is a witch?"

Kassidy nodded.

"I mean, yeah, why not. It's certainly not the strangest thing that's happened to me tonight."

"One of those nights, eh?" asked Kassidy.

"To say the least."

"Why don't you tell me what's going on. Let's start with your name, officer . . . ?"

"Detective. Detective Shay Walker."

"Nice to meet you, detective," said Kassidy. "Um, listen, I'm here to help and to get you out of this mess. But we won't have much time before your compadres find us. So, maybe fill me in with the quick version so I can deal with the thing inside you."

"So you *do* know what's going on with me?"

Kassidy nodded.

"And you can help me?"

Kassidy nodded again. "Let me ask you a question," she began. "Do *you* know what's happening to you?"

"Only what Dom's told me," said Shay.

"Dom?"

"Yeah. He's in here," said Shay, tapping at her head.

"How long has he been in there?" asked Kassidy.

Shay relayed the story of the dead woman and how emaciated she was. She went on to explain how she seemed to come to life when Shay touched her, only to allow time for the vagrant soul to leave that body and enter Shay's.

"He takes control sometimes. He can't seem to stay, but he also can't seem to shut up. At least, he couldn't until you touched me. He did say that he wasn't sure why he wasn't able to control me longer. He said I was different somehow."

Shay's emotions hit Kassidy like a bowling ball, almost knocking her over.

"Are you okay?" asked Shay.

"Yeah. Yeah, I'm okay. I just . . . uh . . . you know what, never mind. I'm good. I'm good."

"Can you really help me?"

"I absolutely can. Tell me, did Dom tell you anything else?"

"Nothing that made sense. He just kept telling me to let it happen, and that we could be a great team. And . . ."

"And what?" asked Kassidy.

"Right now he's begging me to get away from you. Says you're no good and that you're going to hurt us."

Kassidy gave a slight chuckle. "I'm not a threat to *you*, detective. To him, though—"

"He says you're death."

"First thing he's told you that's accurate. Souls are my domain, especially these vagrants popping from body to body like this Dom," said Kassidy, before deciding to take a moment and slow down. It was clear the detective was overwhelmed. "Listen, Shay, my name is Kassidy. I'm here to help. This soul inside you is Dominick Santorini. He's . . . not led a stellar life."

"Great! I've got a killer inside. Wait, how do you know who he is?"

"It's part of the power I possess. The same power that let me save you and transport us here. And Dom is not a killer. His crimes were less capital, but definitely felonious."

"How do we fix this? How can *you* fix this?" asked Shay.

"I've got a few tricks up my sleeve," said Kassidy as she allowed her power to build. She felt her eyes shift and saw the shock in Shay. The detective was clearly shaken, but she stood her ground as Kassidy stepped back, and stretched out her arm. Allowing her power to build, she called to the soul of Dominick Santorini. She felt resistance at first, then a slight release. That was quickly followed by more resistance. It wasn't that the soul was particularly strong, it was just increasingly difficult to separate.

"What the fuck is happening," Kassidy said to herself.

She concentrated harder, channeled more energy, and focused, desperate to separate the soul from the detective. It was Shay's scream that broke Kassidy's concentration. As Shay went to the ground, in pain, Kassidy followed, out of breath, to check on her.

"I'm so sorry," said Kassidy. "I don't know what happened. Are you okay?"

"Felt like I was being ripped apart," said Shay, through tears.

"It's not supposed to happen that way," said Kassidy.

Competing thoughts filled her mind. She ran through all the possible scenarios, but always came back to one inevitable truth. She never should have agreed to bring Anna back. No matter the debt owed to Jaxon, she should have stood her ground as Death God and protected the natural order.

"Looks like I'm stickin' around, eh?"

The vagrant soul had returned.

"Wait'll the others hear about this. The freakin' Death God is losin' her mojo."

The statement was followed by a fake laugh. A laugh quickly stifled when Shay regained control.

"Death God?" asked Shay.

Kassidy nodded.

"Like . . . the Devil? You're the Devil?"

Shay said it in a rushed, desperate voice, and attempted to scurry back, only to fall again on the concrete.

"No," began Kassidy, "definitely not the Devil. Different guy. In fact, I don't even know if he's real."

"Holy shit. This . . . this . . . this can't be happening. I gotta be losing my mind. First a guy's hand heals when I pull a knife out, then I bring back a dead woman only to get possessed, and now . . . a freakin' Death God."

Kassidy stood, held her hand out, and offered it to Shay. She felt the fear and apprehension. She felt the anxiety. This woman had been through a lot in recent weeks, and it was culminating into something terrifying.

"I promise, I'm here to help," said Kassidy. "And did you say you pulled a knife out of a guy?"

Shay nodded.

"You're the one."

"Pardon?"

"That guy you met, his name is Keiron. He's a friend," said Kassidy.

She felt some tension subside, then felt Shay's hand in hers. There was a clear shift in her mood when she mentioned Keiron. That too was interesting. Kassidy helped the woman to her feet, waited a beat, and decided to call upon the scythe. She prayed she wouldn't have the same problem she had earlier. As electricity and light crackled in the air, Kassidy saw Shay's eyes widen as the weapon appeared in Kassidy's hands.

And then the detective fainted.

"Probably for the best," said Kassidy.

Kassidy took a step back and stretched out both arms toward Shay. She shifted to the Nexus, allowing both the power of the Scythe of Cronus and the supplemental realm to augment her own. Kassidy felt the soul pull away. There was some resistance, like before, but Kassidy concentrated further, and with a final burst of energy, liberated Dominick Santorini from Shay.

"Oh, come on. Can't you just give me a pass? I promise I won't cause problems," said Dom.

"That's not how this works," said Kassidy. "You die, you go to the other side."

With those words, Kassidy *saw* more than *felt* fear swell within the soul before her.

"It's just . . ." said Dominick, letting his words trail off.

Kassidy knew what was on his mind. Dominick knew where he'd likely end up. There would be no trip to the Beyond for him, considering the life he'd led. It was straight to the Void. Straight to nothingness.

"Is there just a way I can maybe . . . I don't know—"

"Get a do-over?" asked Kassidy.

"Yeah, something like that. I mean, I learned some lessons and all, I just . . ."

This entire fiasco was unlike anything she had ever encountered. In all her years as a Reaper, she'd never encountered a soul filled with fear and remorse to this degree. Even as the Death God, there was nothing she could do. And quite frankly, she wasn't sure Dominick even deserved a do-over, despite his remorse.

"I'm sorry, Dom. This is the way it is."

Kassidy reached out and contacted two Reapers. After quickly bringing them up to speed, the first Reaper was instructed to escort Dom to the next plane. The second transitioned back to the real world with Kassidy.

"Stef, right? Stef Kemp?" asked Kassidy.

The Reaper nodded.

"This woman," began Kassidy, directing her gaze to Shay, "has had one hell of night."

"How can I help?" asked Stef.

"I need you to get her home, and then I need you to sit with her until she awakens and explain what happened."

The shock in the Reaper's face was what Kassidy expected. As a rule, Reapers didn't interact with humans until they were dead. They certainly didn't explain the finer points of death, the afterlife, and soul possession.

"I know, it's unorthodox," said Kassidy. "But she deserves the truth. Also . . . I think there's something special about this one."

"Special?" asked Stef.

"Yeah. I can't quite put my finger on it, but there's something there."

The Reaper looked even more confused, and Kassidy couldn't blame her, she was just as confused by it all, too. There was god power within Shay Walker. She wasn't a god, that much was certain, but there was something inside her that was decidedly celestial.

Despite the apprehension, the Reaper proceeded to do as she was told. Transitioning to vapor, the Reaper secured the body of Shay Walker, and flew off into the night. Kassidy followed their flight pattern and stopped after catching sight of the moon in the sky. It wasn't quite full, but soon would be. That eerie pinkish tint was now darker and spreading across the orb.

"Why do I get the feeling that's a bad thing," Kassidy said to herself. "God I need a drink," she said softly, her hands clenched. She realized that she still held the Scythe of Cronus in one hand. She sent it back to its resting place, just inside an adjacent dimension that only she could access. And then she shimmered out of view.

Seconds later, she found herself hurled back down to the ground on the same spot she had just stood. She winced at the shock, and then curled up in a ball as intense pain engulfed her abdomen. She'd felt it before. The other night, after the Pulse.

As Kassidy screamed in agony, the skies darkened, and the moon's hue intensified. She felt hands on her shoulders. Through the pain, they seemed distant, but somehow they provided hope. She looked up to see who was with her. Shock ran through her as the pain continued.

"We need to get you out of here," said Jacen.

Kassidy felt herself transported away from the pier and found herself home.

CHAPTER TWENTY-SIX

EACH MORNING MARY LEEDS GOT OUT OF BED, SHE FOLLOWED A very specific ritual. It was not the result of obsessive-compulsive disorder. It was not the result of psychological, neurological, or superstitious impulses that demanded to maintain a routine for maximum effectiveness in the world at large. For Mary Leeds, her routine was the result of genuine, honest, heartfelt gratitude for life and good health. She was a witch, sure, and as such felt a particular closeness to the earth, the heavens, and the forces that kept them together. Certainly, some of that gratitude was the result of years of training and practice of her beliefs. But she felt every bit of it. She had many friends who practiced different religions yet lacked the faith they claimed to live by. These people believed in a higher power "just in case" there was one. If heaven was real, they wanted to arrive with their membership cards intact and all the boxes checked on the admission form. Mary, though, knew from a young age that she was a believer. She believed in and loved the goddess and her sisters in the coven. So, there was no shock when her daughter revealed the true nature of her new girlfriend. There was no shock when her daughter confirmed that gods indeed walked among humans. The only shock was the knowledge that her daughter was going to die soon.

Shock, and heartache.

As Mary made her way downstairs to her meditation room,

she thought of her daughter, Traci, and wondered what she was experiencing. She was angry. Angry at Traci's decision-making all those years ago, her hubris, her belief that some stories were simply that . . . stories. She was angry that her daughter chose to spend her final days with Kassidy instead of her coven. Instead of her mother. In the end, she was angry at herself. For not being a better teacher of the arts and waiting so long to teach Traci at all simply because it seemed her powers would never manifest. Even if Traci was not destined to be a practitioner, she could have trained and taught others. There was value in that. Perhaps more than any other aspect of the practice. Yet she had not seen it, or she had not acknowledged it. She was embarrassed that her daughter—a direct descendent of the goddess—had shown no proficiency in the arts. And when she finally did, she wanted nothing to do with her mother. Traci had found comfort and guidance from another, and that was what led her down the path to death.

In more ways than one.

Mary sat cross-legged in her meditation room. It also doubled as a library and meeting room for her sisters when the weather did not permit them to practice outdoors. Rows of books, some ancient, lined the north and west walls. She faced the east when she meditated as it was toward the home of the goddess. Her curtains provided privacy as she recited the same words she'd uttered every morning for as long as she could remember.

"Beloved goddess, mother, and sister, I thank you. I thank you for the love, the compassion, the—"

Mary's recitation was ended by a violent flash of pain in her head. Falling to the side, she clutched her skull and cried out in agony. Through the syncopated throbbing, she heard a ringing in her ears, and then the images filled her mind.

Mary saw a figure in black wielding a weapon, swinging with precision and speed at her daughter. The weapon, a scythe, cut through Traci's midsection, dissecting her. The figure then stretched out a hand, and within seconds, Traci's body was engulfed in blue flame.

In another vision, Mary looked down on the bodies of her coven sisters, dead, burned, maimed, at their sacred meeting place. Visions collided as images of soldiers battling filled her mind. First swordplay, then guns, then hand-to-hand combat, all ending in a bloodbath from which no one survived.

Until they did.

Mary moved one hand to her stomach as it twisted in knots. The pulsing in her head continued as she watched the bodies of dead soldiers, of men, women, and children, rise from grave to wander and roam in search of sustenance. Above them, the sky was red, the result of a blood moon. The heavens rained down washing the crimson life force of the undead over cracked, black asphalt. In the distance, the dark figure with the scythe stood next to a cloaked figure with a sword, and two others, one with a staff, the other with daggers. Floating down from the sky, a fifth figure, a woman, with . . . a familiar face.

"Noooooo!" Mary screamed, in pain, in agony, in regret.

Mary continued to writhe on the floor.

"Mary!" she heard in the distance.

Beneath her name she heard inaudible words. They too were in the distance, but as the storm in her mind subsided, the words became clearer and drew nearer to her.

"Sister!" said a voice, closer now.

The throbbing in her mind slowed to a steady hum, the knot in her stomach unraveled, and Mary felt her body still with each word uttered in her mind. Clearer and clearer it became, until she recognized it. A soothing spell. A spell designed to ease the pain of the body and mind when one was in turmoil. The voice became louder; no longer did she hear it over the sounds of wind and rain.

"M-M-Myra?" whispered Mary.

"Yes, Mary. It's me."

Mary felt Myra's hands upon her. One on her forehead, the other on her chest. Myra Hutchens was ten years older than Traci and among the most accomplished healers Mary had ever encountered. She was relieved by her presence. The spell brought calm to Mary's mind and body, though the fear of the images she saw was just below the surface.

"What are you doing here?" asked Mary.

"I honestly don't know," said Myra. "I was leaving my house and heading to an appointment when I felt an overwhelming pull to come here. I was hoping you could tell me. When I got here, I knocked, and I was about to leave when you didn't come. And then I heard your scream, and I felt the pain in my temple. I was able to use a spell to unlock your door, and I found you here."

Mary finally lay completely still. She felt no tremor in her arms and legs. Her breathing was beginning to slow. Her eyesight focused. The worst had passed, at least externally. The images though. Traci. The four beings.

The fifth floating from the sky.

Her.

That woman.

The one who provided guidance to Traci.

"Myra...I...I think we're in trouble. I think...I think the end is nearer than we realize."

"What are you saying, Mary? What happened?"

"I came down to meditate, and then I was struck with a vision."

"Of what?"

"Of the past. Of the present. Of the future. A future where . . . where . . ."

Mary couldn't bring herself to utter the words. They formed in her mind, and they sat there, taunting her, frightening her, but most of all . . . promising her. Promising her that everything she saw was going to come true.

"Tell me," begged Myra, as she helped Mary, who was struggling to sit up. "What is happening."

"We need to get the others," said Mary, still trying to catch her breath. "We need to get the others, and we need to act now."

"Act on what? What do we need to do? Mary, you're not making any sense."

"We need to meet, and we need to get Traci here as soon as possible," said Mary.

"I'll call her now and—"

"No!" shouted Mary. "We can't call her to us yet. We have to gather, we have to combine our strength, and we have to stop her."

"Stop her? Stop Traci? Mary you're not making any sense. Why?"

"We have to get to Traci now. To protect her. To save her. To save us all."

"What?" asked Myra.

"We need to bind her powers," said Mary.

"Mary . . . no. We can't. That's—"

"We have to! We have no choice."

"But . . . why?"

"Because the Four are coming. And it starts with her."

CHAPTER TWENTY-SEVEN

"PLEASE TELL ME THAT YOU'RE HERE TO HELP ME?" ASKED KASSIDY.

"I am," began Jacen, "as much as I can."

"Dude?!"

Kassidy let out her anger on a tree as she stood in a forest preserve with her least favorite Denzel Washington lookalike. When she'd first met him, she had the briefest suspicion that he might be her father. Even after he'd told her Thanatos was missing, she let the thought linger a bit. He was an Advocate. That's all he told her, all she knew about him. That, and the fact that somehow he knew things. Somehow, he was intimately involved with everything currently happening in her life, and yet, he provided nothing but riddles and half-assed clues. Some things helped . . . eventually. If not for him, she likely would not have been able to secure the Scythe of Cronus from Azra-El. But most of his musings were cryptic. Perhaps if she sat down and pieced together every seemingly ridiculous thing he'd said over the last few months, she'd have some answers. But there was never time. Only one crisis after another.

"Kassidy, I'm . . . sorry," he said.

"Sorry? Sorry for what? You've done nothing. Like . . . literally."

She meant it as a jab, and she was pretty sure he felt it. Unlike many other people, mortal and immortal, she could not sense his emotions. That only told her that whatever he was, whatever an

Advocate was . . . he was powerful. He alluded to being part of a group, a collective of sorts. She often wondered how many and if they could potentially be threats. She supposed time would tell.

"That's fair," he said.

Kassidy moved to stand against the tree she'd just punched.

"A part of me gets it, Lucas. A part of me gets the fact that you've got rules. Supernatural beings all have their place, their duty, I get it. But you can't keep popping in and out and giving us more puzzle pieces. I mean . . . how the fuck am I supposed to know if you're really helping us or just steering down a creepy road to death and destruction."

Silence filled the air. Again, it was nothing Kassidy hadn't become accustomed to when he was around. She stared up at the sky, then back down at him, and sighed.

"You know what, I'm just gonna—"

"The devil left the keys to hell on his kitchen table, so, of course, I used them to escape," he said.

"What?" asked Kassidy. "Great, more metaphors."

"Oh no, this is no metaphor. Well, not entirely. When I tell you I escaped hell, it's not a euphemism for graduating college, getting divorced, moving out of my parents' home, or leaving prison. Well, maybe closer to the prison thing. Hell is very much a prison—of the mind, of the soul. It is the absence of hope, of all things good, of all things possible."

"You've been to hell? The Underworld?"

Jacen nodded. "It's as if you have to create your own bit of hope—but imagine trying to do that in a place that was unforgiving, a place in which there was no recompense for the thought or desire of redemption, a place where all thought and desire went unheard."

"How long were you there?"

"A while. It's not unlike the Nexus. Time works very differently there."

"Really? It's not my domain, so I know nothing about it. Is it empty? Like the Void?"

"No. Nothing like that. At least, not that I'd imagine. It's separate from the Beyond or the Void. Souls with a clear-cut path after death are greeted by you, or your Reapers. Souls with a more ambiguous path, enter Hell, or the Underworld, as your kinfolk refer to it. In the Underworld, souls are given a chance to atone. They won't see the Beyond, but instead, Elysium—and that was only *if* they've atoned."

"And Hades determines that?"

Jacen nodded.

"How did you manage?" asked Kassidy, intrigued at the rare vulnerability.

"I tried my best to fight through it all, to find some bit of hope to cling to. I'd heard stories of men and women who'd been given a second chance and replayed them in my head each day—only with me as the one to receive the pardon. Truthfully, I had no clue how many times I played those thoughts in my head. All I know is, the opportunity presented itself, and I had just enough strength to take it. So, I did."

"How?"

"Every place has a way out. As you found in the Void. If you can get in a place, no matter the spell or type of magic used, you can get out."

Kassidy suspected there was a lesson in there. She made a mental note only because she knew, if she pressed, she'd get nothing. At this point, she was just fascinated that he was sharing anything. Through it all, she wondered what he'd done to be sent to hell. Didn't quite give her hope that he was on her side.

"After I made it out, things went well, for the most part. Despite being a man out of time, I'd managed to acclimate to my new environment, the real world, relatively quickly. How I managed to not get caught and sent back was anyone's guess, particularly because I was so naïve to the ways of the modern world and in the third largest city in the United States—a brutal, deadly, and ridiculously beautiful city. It was remarkable that I'd avoided dangerous situations in Chicago for as long as I did. At least, until that day. The day my number was up."

Kassidy had never so desperately wished for her empathic powers to manifest. She wanted badly to understand what he was feeling as he relayed his story. Jacen, when not being a smart ass, was somehow even more difficult to read.

"I'd been found, and I thought I was headed back to the depths," he began, "but instead, I was offered an extraordinary chance to remain in the land of the living. As with all things, though, there was a catch. I should have known there would be. Considering what I'd done to earn my place in the Underworld, those things don't just get wiped clean."

"So, what was the deal?" asked Kassidy.

"It was a simple deal. Remain on Earth, in Chicago, be hunted, and if captured, be sent back to the Underworld where new forms of torture would be defined with me as the subject. Or return to the Underworld willingly, retrieve a box, and hand it over to my benefactor."

"And?"

"And . . . I made my way back to hell," he said with a shoulder shrug.

"And why are you telling me this now?" asked Kassidy.

"I don't know. Maybe because it's time."

"The time for us to be all chummy was a couple of months

ago when the Angel of Death was gunning for me."

"And yet you sorted that out just fine."

"Or perhaps when the rogue Wraith teamed up with the War God."

"Again, you made it through just fine. With a little flair, I might add," said Jacen.

"Fine. Tell me, why is it so important now for you to open up?"

"It's not," began Jacen, "but I think some elements of my story may help with what's to come."

"And just which element is that?" asked Kassidy.

"The fact that hell is not a final destination. People can escape."

"Yeah, well, considering all the vagrant souls I'm encountering, I'd say that tracks."

"I'm not talking about souls, Kassidy. I'm talking about people."

"Any particular people on your mind, Lucas?"

Several beats passed and Kassidy's frustration grew.

"I hate you," she said.

"For now," replied Jacen.

In a blink, he was gone. Kassidy was no closer to the truth of what was happening than she had been before his arrival. It was interesting though, him telling her he escaped hell. Perhaps it was some supernatural foreshadowing. Perhaps a warning. Maybe even a lesson that no door stays locked.

Kassidy felt the pull of another errant soul. "Fuck! I don't have time for this!"

With a sigh, she shimmered away.

CHAPTER TWENTY-EIGHT

THE LAST THING BEN SPADA REMEMBERED WAS THE SENSATION OF his life force being drained from him by some old bum with boney hands, black eyes, and a bloody mouth. Now, he found himself sitting in a bar, with a beer in front of him, staring back at a face that was not his. It was a pleasant face. The guy at the bar called him John. And so, Ben Spada sat, inexplicably, in a bar drinking beer, inside the body of some pleasant-faced man named John.

"What the hell, man?"

He thought he'd whispered that. The look on the face of the bartender pouring a beer from the tap opposite him told him that he in fact, did not use his library voice.

"You all right, John?" asked the bartender.

Ben said nothing.

"John?"

Ben continued to stare in the mirror.

"Hey! Johnny!" said the bartender, much louder.

Ben snapped to attention and looked up. Dazed and confused he sought direction on how to move forward with this. He was a Marine, or had been in another body. Another . . . life? He'd been an elite warrior, trained for virtually anything. A man who was taught every way to adapt to the unknown, to overcome the challenges he might face in battle.

But this was not battle.

This was Ben, trying to figure out what to say to a bartender while trapped in the body of a pleasant-faced man named John.

"Uh . . . yeah?"

"Dude? What's wrong. That's only your second. You good?" asked the bartender.

"I'm . . . good. Yeah, I'm okay. Just . . . trying to sort some things out. Sorry, man."

The face wasn't his. The body wasn't his. The voice wasn't his. Yet here he sat. He ruminated on the stories he'd heard about reincarnation, but that seemed like a stupid thing to do given the circumstances. So instead, he grabbed the beer in front of him, and he drank. He saw a menu out of the corner of his eye and reached for it. Seemed like typical bar food. Wings. Fries. Onion rings. Mozzarella sticks. Basically, a cornucopia of fried treats. His body wasn't hungry, but his mind definitely was. So, he ordered a few things.

"You want what?" asked the bartender.

"An order of wings. Lemon pepper. As many flats as you can give me. And some of those mozzarella sticks."

Ben looked into the eyes of the perplexed bartender. He speculated on what he'd done wrong. Maybe his voice, his true voice was breaking through. Maybe . . .

"Man, are you sure you're okay?"

"Yeah. Yeah. Look, I'm fine. Just . . . a little hungry. Told you, I'm distracted."

"So distracted that you forgot you're a vegetarian?"

Oh boy.

"Uh . . ."

"I think the latest ad campaign he was working on got the better of him," said a soft voice from behind.

Ben checked the mirror and was shocked to see a dark-haired

woman standing behind him. Not shocked at her beauty, or the fact that she seemed to know him. He was seemingly hitching a ride in someone else's body after all. The shock came at the fact that he seemed to know her. He couldn't exactly place the face. He certainly couldn't recall a name. But there was something about her that screamed familiarity.

"Talk about taking your work home with you," said the bartender.

Ben watched as his order, scribbled down illegibly on a napkin, was taken to the back. He looked up into the mirror and watched the mystery woman move to his right and take the seat next to him. She wore black jeans, black boots, and a gray T-shirt with the graphic, "Dear bourbon, I love you" on it in white lettering. Her hair fell past her shoulders. In her eyes, Ben saw awareness. Awareness from her, and some semblance of it within himself.

"Do you know who I am?" she asked.

Ben shook his head.

"Feel like you should?" she asked.

Ben nodded.

"That's good. That's something."

"You, um . . . you know me?"

The dark-haired woman nodded.

"Are you like, my girlfriend? Or . . ."

Ben let the words linger and trail off. He wasn't fully invested in the question. He wasn't even necessarily hopeful for an affirmative answer. He just wanted to know what the hell was happening to him.

"I am definitely not your girlfriend, Ben," she said after a low chuckle.

"Oh. Okay. Well then . . . wait . . . what did you call me?"

"I called you Ben. That's your name, right? Ben Spada?"

A chill ran through him. His heart, or rather, John's heart, seemed to speed up and beat with authority. He was afraid he'd cause the man to have a heart attack. He closed his eyes to try and calm himself. He felt a soft hand on his arm and, within seconds, felt a warmth radiate through him. Not just warmth, but comfort, as if he were being enveloped in a warm, compassionate embrace by someone who loved him unconditionally. He saw the image of his fiancée. He was taken back to the last time he saw her. The last time he hugged her. She was his safe space, his sanctuary, his center, and he felt her now as sure as she'd been standing next to him.

"What is happening to me?" he asked.

Opening his eyes, he looked down to find the hand of the mystery woman on his arm. He sensed an energy around it. There was heat, but not so much that it felt uncomfortable. There was no fear of burning, just . . . peace.

"My name is Kassidy, Ben. I'm here to help."

"Help how? How do you know me? I mean . . . this isn't even me," said Ben, looking at their reflections in the mirror.

"You died, Ben. You know that don't you?" she asked.

Ben nodded.

"Good. That's good."

"How is that good?"

"Well . . . yeah . . . okay. Not so good that you died, but good that you know it. It shows awareness and makes the rest of this easier."

"The rest of what?"

"The rest of what I'm going to tell you."

For the next few minutes, Ben listened to Kassidy explain how he died, and why he was back. In the back of his mind, he'd hoped that he was dreaming or tripping on some wild hallucinogenic back at the base. Maybe he was a part of an experiment. He was the type to volunteer for anything. Maybe he'd forgotten that he'd volunteered for an experiment that he was now trying to come out of. It was certainly more plausible than the notion that he'd been killed by something called a Wraith and his soul absorbed by a man named Azra-El. It was absolutely more plausible than thinking his soul was released upon Azra-El's demise and now resting in a stranger's body.

The body of a pleasant-faced man named John.

"It's hard to take. I get it. Believe me I do," said Kassidy.

"Yeah. Yeah, just a bit."

"The important thing is, I can make this all go away."

"Go away? What? How?"

"I can make sure your soul gets to where it needs to be."

Ben stared ahead again. He weighed those words. Contemplated what they really meant. He didn't like it. Fear crept in again as he recalled the moment that boney hand phased through his chest. The immediate cold. The electricity. The feeling of his energy slowly being drained from him. He began shaking his head vigorously, saying the word no over and over again.

"Ben. Ben. It's okay," began Kassidy, "it's not going to be like last time. I promise you. I need you to calm down, and I need you to trust me."

"Why? Why should I trust you?"

Ben turned to look at Kassidy. It was the first time he'd made direct eye contact with her since she arrived. As he looked at her, he saw the color of her eyes transition, then saw them brighten. Before long, they glowed bright and blue, and realization washed over him.

"I know who you are," he whispered.

"Good," said Kassidy.

"What do I need to do?" asked Ben.

"You've been out there floating around for a while," said Kassidy.

Ben shrugged.

"This is your first body, right?"

"I . . . I . . . guess so," he said.

"No memories of being anywhere else since the night you died?"

Ben shook his head.

"Well then, we don't have much time."

"Before what?"

"Before your soul begins to fight for permanence, or seemingly dissipates into nothing."

"That doesn't sound pleasant."

"No, no it does not. If I don't get you out of this body, you'll either take it over or jump from it. And if you jump, you'll die a true and final death. No afterlife. No nothing. And . . ."

"And?"

"And the soul that truly owns the body you're in will be tainted. It'll whither. And the guy, John, will be nothing more than a vegetable. We are nothing without balance of the mind, body, and soul."

Ben did not like the implications of that. Once again, he was faced with the prospect of saving someone. This was going to cost him, again. But as always, it was what he did. Always faithful to the mission of protecting lives.

"All right," began Ben, "let's go. Let's do this."

As Ben rose from his seat, the bartender returned and placed some napkins and a plate in front of him.

"Your order will be up in a couple of minutes," he told Ben.

Ben looked from the bartender to the plate to Kassidy. He inclined his head as if to ask if he could stay. He heard a slight chuckle from Kassidy, then watched as she shook her head in comic disbelief.

"The power of wings, man," she said.

As Ben awaited an answer, he watched Kassidy, the woman he finally recognized as the Death God, fly back through the air as if pulled by something. He leapt back off his stool, readying himself for anything. Kassidy was now pinned to the back wall by some force. Ben watched as she struggled. Her head moved side to side as if punched by invisible fists. Her body contorted in the middle as if she'd taken a punch to the gut. Ben looked around for help, but everyone was just as shocked and frightened as he was.

Except for one woman.

The woman walked toward Kassidy with an outstretched arm, her face obscured by an oversized hood. As she got closer, she used her free hand to reveal her face, and Ben saw shock in the face of the Death God still pinned high against the back wall.

"Traci?" said Kassidy.

◆　　◆　　◆

"NO!"

Traci's screams seemed to echo as if she were trapped in a cavern, a cavern of her own mind. She could only watch as Hecate attacked Kassidy. She tried hard to wrestle back control of her body, but Hecate's strength was growing, and with each darkening of the moon, it was becoming harder and harder for Traci to return, even when Hecate slept.

Calm down, little witch, I'll be done shortly.

"No! You have to stop this! You can't—"

I will do as I please! And you will learn your place, little witch.

Traci felt a weight on top of her. An overwhelming force bearing down, pressing upon her, suffocating her. As she seemingly drowned, while being pulled down into nothing, she watched as a man was flung through a window while trying to help Kassidy. She was helpless as Kassidy grasped at invisible hands clamped around her throat. She'd pass out soon, and then she'd be at Hecate's mercy.

"I'm . . . so sorry, Kass."

Traci felt the weight continue to press on her consciousness. Fear surrounded her. So, she did what she was taught. Clearing her mind, she focused and spoke the word to relax her spirit.

"Calm. Calm. Calm."

She repeated it. As she did, she felt an external shift. Hecate's power faltered. Long enough to allow Kassidy to shift to mist and re-appear next to her. Traci felt fortunate that she could not feel the physical assault her girlfriend initiated. Under the circumstances, she hoped Kassidy would come out on top.

Traci continued her calming techniques.

Stop! Stop!

The plea was not to Kassidy. It was to Traci. Realization set in as the Titan continued to beg. The calming technique was having an effect on Traci's body. It was becoming too relaxed, and Hecate was unable to maintain control and focus her power.

All of a sudden, Traci felt herself flying through the air. She was regaining some semblance of control as Hecate slowly began to fade in the background.

You want control, little witch? Fine! I'll sit back and watch and watch the Death God beat you into submission. And then I'll return when you're bruised and broken.

Traci felt Hecate retreat just as Kassidy pounced and

straddled her. She saw Kassidy pull back to deliver a knockout punch. In control, she opened her eyes wide, covered her face, and screamed, "No, Kass! No!"

When the blow didn't come, she lowered her arms and stared into the bright blue eyes of her lover. Kassidy was as confused as she was angry. There was no mistaking that. In the next instant, Traci found herself on the floor of Kassidy's living room. She'd transported them home.

"Talk!" demanded Kassidy.

CHAPTER TWENTY-NINE

DESPITE EVERYTHING, TRACI WASN'T PARTICULARLY INTERESTED IN talking, but she was smart enough to know that you can only go so long ignoring a major, life-changing, and relationship-ending event before you had to stare it in the face. There was no fixing what was going to happen. There was no reprieve in the eleventh hour. And as powerful as Kassidy was now, there was no way for her to solve *this* problem. Traci also got the feeling that the elephant in the room needing to be strangled was her.

"Can we just keep avoiding it and maybe cuddle and watch a movie?" asked Traci, playfully.

"Enough with the cute shit, Trace! Dammit! My girlfriend is having magical outbursts and then forgetting about it. So, no! We can't fucking cuddle. I'd really rather know why this is happening so we can maybe get ahead of it. I don't know, probably a silly idea, huh?"

Traci felt the bite in Kassidy's sarcasm, and, of course, it stung. She had every right to be mad considering everything that had happened thus far. In many ways—well, in every way—Kassidy deserved an explanation. It was the very least Traci could do. She just hoped that it would go better than the conversation about her being a witch and the related revelation that Traci was one of the young women that Kassidy had rescued when she killed her first Wraith.

"I'm not trying to be a bitch," said Kassidy. "But something is happening here and keeping me in the fucking dark is the absolute wrong move. I want to help, and I probably can. But I can't do that if you don't talk to me."

"I know, Kass. I understand where you're coming from. But I also know you're up to your neck in Reaper stuff and lost souls and all that. Adding this to your plate is not fair."

"Why don't you tell me what *this* is, and then *I* will determine if it should be on my plate."

"Fair enough," said Traci.

Traci walked to the mini bar and grabbed a couple of bottles and two glasses, then made her way to the couch.

"Shit," began Kassidy, "this is an alcohol conversation?"

"Don't most of your conversations involve alcohol?"

The silence was deafening. Traci's hand was still on one of the bottles, and as soon as the last word came out of her mouth, she regretted it.

"So, we're going there?" asked Kassidy.

"Kass, I—"

"No, no. It's all good. Truly. Whether you meant it or not, it's out there. No need to feel bad. I'm not the only one dealing with shit, so it's not fair to make this all about me."

Traci expected so much worse. She suspected that Kassidy felt the relief in her as well. That was confirmed when Kassidy walked over to sit next to her. She gave Traci a side hug. It was a little cold and mechanical, but the effort had been made. For that, Traci was grateful.

She still needed the gin, though. And she didn't much care about the consequences this time. She poured a drink for herself, then poured bourbon for Kassidy. Both glasses just sat on the coffee table. Both women stared at the glasses, anticipating what was coming next.

"I can feel your fear and apprehension, Trace. I can understand where it comes from. Can we please just talk it out and get it on the table. If I can help, I want to. If this is a magic thing, I mean, I've got magic, too. Maybe we can pool some shit together and—"

"Magic won't fix this, babe. It can fix a lot and has fixed a lot. But, not this," said Traci.

A beat passed.

"Wait, it's not the magic stuff you're worried about. There's something else."

Traci gave a halfhearted nod and took several sips of her gin. The truth had to come out. She imagined her mother, the only other person who knew what she'd done, telling Kassidy the truth. She knew the story would manifest as an accusatory rant, and that wouldn't be good for anyone. She realized that her best chance of getting through this was to control how the story was told.

"So, this goes back to the first time I saw you," said Traci.

"In the basement when I fought the Wraith," said Kassidy.

Traci nodded.

"Did something else happen? Did the Wraith—"

"No, it has nothing to do with anything he did or didn't do. It's about the things that happened after that."

Traci took more sips and in doing so, made note of the fact that Kassidy had, thus far, not had a single drop of her bourbon. She wasn't quite sure how to read that. Part of her told her not to try to read it at all. But she was all over the place, both emotionally and psychologically. At some point, through all the rambling in her mind, she felt Kassidy's hand on top of hers. She looked down, smiled, and her eyes began to tear up. She held them back and pressed on.

"So, after we were all freed, I went through this whole thing where I felt like a failure. I felt like I failed as a witch because my powers had not manifested, and if they had, I could have saved everyone. So, I failed them, I failed my mother, and . . . just . . . I don't know."

"All understandable," said Kassidy.

"And then, there was this . . . lingering feeling inside," said Traci.

"About what?"

"You."

Traci shifted on the couch. She took another sip, much bigger this time, then sat up straight and prepared to press on. This was the part where everything could go south really quickly if she wasn't careful.

"Back then, I couldn't even begin to define what I was feeling. I just knew that for so many reasons I couldn't get you out of my mind."

"Yeah, I know, babe. We talked about this."

"I know. I know. But . . . there's more to it," said Traci.

"More to it than you using magic to find me?"

Traci nodded, took another sip, then just decided to finish the glass. As she poured more gin, she continued.

"My magic started to manifest slowly after you rescued us. I could do small things. Parlor tricks really, but nothing large or even sustainable. Certainly no big life-altering spells like trying to find a magical being."

She noticed Kassidy's grip tighten on bourbon glass. It seemed clear to Traci, that even though Kassidy had said she'd let it go, some part of that story still bothered her.

"Teenagers, by nature, can be very impatient. So, you can imagine, a young witch, the daughter of a coven leader no less, would be exceptionally impatient in waiting for her powers to manifest."

Another sip.

This time, Kassidy took one, too.

"Well, I eventually found this book that had a bunch of high-level spells in it. Like, high level," Traci emphasized with her hand. "They were all centered around activating latent powers or augmenting existing powers."

When Kassidy drank more, Traci took notice. But still, she pressed on.

"So, I started reading it, and I started practicing it. I was advancing pretty well until my mother found out, and she shut it all down. She took the book, yelled at me for what seemed like a week, and forbade any talk or further practice with any spells I may have perfected or remembered from it."

"Why? What was up with the book? Was it, like, black magic or something?" asked Kassidy.

"Something like that," said Traci. "We don't call it black magic. That's some movie and TV shit. We call it what it is. Forbidden magic."

"So, let me guess, you continued practicing?"

"I did," said Traci. "And then I went further."

Traci heard a light, continuous tap, and realized it was Kassidy. Her leg was shaking. It was a common occurrence when she was mad, anxious, or desperate for a drink. Most times, it was the result of other people's emotions. Sometimes it was a combination of her emotions and others. The leg tapping was a sign that Kassidy was struggling with control.

"How much further?"

"Well," began Traci, "around this same time, I met a woman, a counselor at school, who turned out to be a witch. She recognized what I was and before I knew it, she was becoming something of a mentor. She knew about the book. She knew about the spells.

And when I told her what I wanted, she encouraged me to go for it. She said she could teach me ways to keep the magic in check, so it didn't cause a ripple effect."

"A ripple effect?"

"Yeah. So, magic, in any form, is always about balance. When you do too much of one thing, something else has to happen to balance things out. So, like, if I cast a spell to be rich, someone out there is going to be poor. If I were powerful enough to bring back a life, someone would have to die."

Traci noticed Kassidy stiffen up at that last statement. Maybe talking about resurrection spells with the Death God was a no-no. She didn't know if that was a fact, but something seemed to add to the tension.

"What was that? Why did you tense up there?" asked Traci.

"What you said, about bringing someone back to life . . . I've done it."

"Oh my god," Traci began, "you can do that?"

"I can. Whether I should or not is a totally different story."

"Have you felt or seen any repercussions from it?" asked Traci.

"Well, I don't know. That's what I was assuming was happening here," said Kassidy.

"You mean, with what's happening with me?"

"Yeah."

"Well, I can pretty much assure you that this is the result of me continuing the practice of forbidden magic. The time has come to pay the bill on that," said Traci.

"How do we stop it?"

Traci hesitated. Now, knowing more about Kassidy's concerns, she wasn't sure how much more she should tell her. She didn't want to add to her guilt. She also didn't want to add to any anger or frustration.

"I just . . ."

"What?" asked Kassidy.

"I don't know that we can. The blood moon is coming. Once it's here, she can't be stopped," said Traci.

"What? Who? Is someone causing this?"

"Please, just let it go. I'll deal with it."

"So, we're just supposed to live with random acts of witchcraft and you blacking out when it happens? No, dammit! I don't accept that. What aren't you telling me?"

Now it was Traci's leg shaking uncontrollably. Much like Kassidy, it was due to discomfort and anxiety. Unlike Kassidy, the discomfort came from the fact that an ancient deity was occupying her body, and at times taking over. She wondered if Kassidy could sense the duality but felt pretty confident that she'd hear about it if she could.

"That's really it, babe. I just kept messing around with the magic without fully accepting the consequences. I guess . . . I guess I just thought the warnings were old stories, legends, cautionary tales, you know. Things people say to scare you. I never imagined that—"

"There's more," said Kassidy with certainty.

"Kass—"

"Dammit," began Kassidy, slamming her glass on the table, "I'm here to help. I'm here to help because I love you. But I can't do that if you don't tell me the truth!"

"There's nothing else to—"

"You're lying!"

"I swear, there's nothing more!" Traci exclaimed, standing up.

She watched as Kassidy stood and, in that moment, she recognized that neither of them was shaking anymore.

She knows you're lying. Tell her everything. Go ahead.

"Traci, you can tell me now, or I'll start digging around."

She's going to tell your coven.

"And if I have to do all that and then find out the truth, I'll never be able to trust you again."

They'll strip you of your powers and then you'll be nothing!

"Nooooooo!" screamed Traci.

Extended her arm, Traci used her power to push Kassidy back against the wall with great force. Knocking the wind out of her, she flung the coffee table out of the way and pressed on. She generated balls of energy and flung them at Kassidy. One from her right hand, then her left, alternating back and forth to keep the Death God down.

"You can't tell them. You can't let them bind my powers. I can't let you!" Traci screamed.

Traci stretched out her hand and watched as Kassidy rose in the air. With another hand she created a pool of energy in the ground. It crackled with black and purple electricity.

"Traci," pleaded Kassidy, seemingly shocked, "don't do this."

With a last pulse of energy, Traci brought her hand down, and Kassidy dropped into the pool of energy . . . and vanished.

In the back of her mind, Traci heard sinister laughter. It was cold. It was angry. But it was satisfied.

"What have I done?"

Well done, little witch. Well done.

Traci dropped to her knees and felt her mind swirl. Her vision blurred. The room seemed to spin, and she tipped forward, hitting the floor—but she felt as if she were falling. Endlessly.

I'll take it from here.

As darkness enveloped Traci, her heart sank. The end was coming. And there was nothing she'd be able to do about it.

CHAPTER THIRTY

TRACI AWOKE TO THE SOUND OF BIRDS CHIRPING AND THE FEEL OF wet grass against her skin. On her leg, she felt the sensation of something moving, slowly, then . . . digging? No, it was biting. She moved quickly, twisting, turning, and swatting at her legs, then rubbing her arms and brushing off her clothes lest any other bugs thought they had refuge.

She stood, ran her fingers through her hair and continued to brush off her clothes as she looked around. Nothing looked familiar. She was in a grassy area with scattered trees and saw nothing that sparked a single memory as to where she was or how she'd arrived. The last thing she fully remembered was . . .

"Kassidy," she whispered.

She'd had another episode, and Kassidy had found her in a bar. Kassidy had taken her home. They talked, or at least, tried to. Then all hell broke loose.

"God, I hate this," she said to herself.

She was wearing clothes that she didn't recognize. Dark jeans, ripped, with ankle high boots with a small heel. Nothing she wore screamed "hey, let's go out to the woods," yet here she was. Looking around, she saw a trail of footprints. They were light, but the wet grass and intermittent patches of mud gave her a direction to follow. Leaving the clearing, Traci found herself in a heavily wooded area. In the distance she thought she could hear vehicles traveling swiftly. A highway, or something, was near, so she continued on, if for no other reason than to flag someone down for help.

As she walked, flashes of memory ran through her mind. She'd gone into a store, a department store, and tried on clothing. Looking down, she realized she was wearing everything in that memory. She'd tried it on, and she'd run.

"Dammit," said Traci, stopped midstride. "I stole these fucking clothes."

The memories continued as she resumed her walk along the path of footprints.

At some point, images of a nightclub emerged. As did images of her dancing and drinking, and eventually leaving with some strange man. Concentrating further, she settled in on his face. He was black, bald, with a goatee, and he wore a single diamond stud in his left ear. The man was fit, fashionable, and wildly flirtatious. Images were fuzzy beyond that, except for the car, a silver Tesla.

As Traci got closer to the sound of cars, she saw a shape against a tree ahead. A human shape. Her adrenaline spiked, and the part of her that told her to run in the opposite direction was overridden by the part of her that was curious and wondering if the person needed help. As she neared the tree, she saw that it was definitely a human, a man . . . with familiar clothing.

"Oh my god!" she said as she got closer.

The clothes were the same, the face a bit bruised, but the goatee and the diamond stud confirmed her memory flash as fact. The only thing different about the man from last night and the one currently lying dead against the tree, was the burn in the middle of his chest. It was as if a burst of electricity or some other form of energy hit him, center mass, and killed him instantly.

"Hecate," said Traci.

She knew this was not her. She knew it as surely as she knew the theft of clothing wasn't her doing either. Her lost time, while not entirely recovered, was starting to come back in stages. Her mind, the mind of the voice within, was starting to merge with Traci's. Soon, it would be the dominant essence, and Traci would be nothing but someone else's memory.

"I'm sorry," Traci said to the man before her.

After a few moments, she continued on the path out of the wooded area. Getting closer to the edge, she saw a car parked on the side of the road. It was a silver Tesla. The sight of it sparked another memory. She'd begged the driver to pull over. *She* had. Traci. In one of the few moments in which she was back in control of her body. Once they were off to the side of the road Traci immediately left the car and ran off into the woods. He'd followed her, foolishly, only to be confronted by *her*—by Hecate. Traci's mind replayed the moment the ball of energy left her hands, hurled into the body of an innocent man who'd been left dead in a wooded area off a busy highway.

She felt tears well up, but she held them at bay. She needed to get out of the area, away from people. But she needed to find out where she was.

Traci raced to the driver's side of the car, only to find it was locked. She had no key. Whispering a simple spell, the door unlocked, and she slid into the vehicle as cars and semis sped past. Traci pressed her foot against the break and pushed the start button bringing the car to life. As the electronics sprang up, she pressed the navigation button on the touch screen control pad. A map appeared showing her exactly where she was.

"How in the hell did I get to France?"

The shock of her current circumstances was overridden by a pull. Some . . . thing, some force, urged her to put the car in gear.

She wondered if it was another witch because the sensation was most certainly external. Perhaps another member of the Hekatos reaching out to her. She hoped that's what it was. The pull was strong, compelling her to follow.

So, she did.

✦   ✦   ✦

After a couple of hours of travel through small towns and villages, and a few twists and turns up a hill, Traci found herself pulling into the gravel driveway of a cottage. It was modest, but clearly some money had been spent to build and maintain it—its rustic exterior betrayed by the solar panels that adorned the roof, and the satellite dish on its side. As Traci exited the car, the front door opened. She blinked rapidly, as the late morning mist made it difficult to see. Her eyes saw a familiar face, but her mind told her it was impossible. Traci continued forward as the woman from the cottage descended the stairs. Even as she closed in, Traci could not believe her eyes.

"H-h-how are you here?" asked Traci.

"Well, hello to you, too."

"Um . . . sorry," began Traci, "hi . . . hi. I just . . . I can't—"

"Believe I'm here?"

"I can't even believe I'm here," said Traci continuing to shake her head in astonishment.

"The life of a witch is nothing short of astonishing. Remember when I told you that?"

"Yes. I absolutely do, Miss Donegan."

"Oh . . . no. Traci, the time for formalities is long gone. Besides, I never liked being called Miss Donegan anyway. These days, I've decided that I rather like the nickname my old friends gave me. At one time, it was pretentious. But in the age of social media and reality TV, I think the name Diva fits right in. Besides, it's Latin for goddess. Who wouldn't want to be a goddess, right?"

"Well then, hello, Diva," said Traci.

"It's good to see you, Traci. Please, come in. You no doubt need to rest and likely have questions."

Traci, overcome with emotion, felt a pang in her stomach. This woman had been a great help to her as a teenager. She'd given her hope and guidance in place of a mother who'd done nothing but question, control, and judge. To find her here, now, with all the chaos going on around her, Traci felt a sense of comfort. Something she'd previously only felt with Kassidy, though, in a very different way. She felt the tension leave her shoulders. As soon as it did, so too did the will to keep from crying. Traci quickly stepped up to the Diva and embraced her, letting all of her emotion pour forth. The Diva's returned embrace felt like home.

"It's going to be all right, Traci," said the Diva. "Let's go inside and talk."

The two women turned and walked toward the cottage. As they did, the late morning mist intensified, engulfing the wooden home as soon as the door closed.

CHAPTER THIRTY-ONE

THUD!

Kassidy landed hard, face down, on a jagged stone surface. Prickles of pain raced through her forehead, nose, and chin.

"What . . . the . . . fuck?" she said, with heavy emphasis on the last word.

The ground was cool but did nothing to relieve the heat she felt in her face. She took a moment to collect herself, then slowly rolled over to her back. Her midsection was sore, and she felt some stiffness and every bit of the pain coursing through her in that moment.

Kassidy opened her eyes as she felt droplets of water fall onto her face. The water provided a cool contrast and soothed the heat expanding on her face and knees. She could already feel her body repairing itself, and there was some relief in that. Anxiety shot through her, though, as she began to take in her surroundings. Looking up, she saw a brownish green sky. Clouds moved swiftly, as if the entire atmosphere were on fast-forward. Looking to her left, she saw a large river of red water with streaks of black. It was filled with debris and smelled of sulfur. In the center was a large rock that appeared to be . . . bleeding black blood.

Lifting her head slightly, she saw several other rocks in the river in the same state. All had onyx liquid sliding down the sharp edges and into the river, leaving dark streaks in an otherwise crimson liquid thoroughfare.

"Ow! Fuck!" she yelped after a failed attempt to rest on her elbows and look around further. The surface she'd fallen on was hard stone, maybe granite, with uneven edges and shards of various length. She pulled one such shard out of her forearm and threw it do the ground with disdain.

"Fuck this! I'm outta here!"

Kassidy shimmered from her sitting position then re-formed standing.

"What the hell?"

She tried to shimmer out again, only to find herself right back where she was. Her breathing increased and her hands balled into fists. She tried once more and failed once more.

"Dammit!" she screamed.

On the bright side, her pain was gone. She'd recently realized that when she shimmered after some injury, particularly a serious one, somehow, her healing sped up even more. It was as if her body re-formed to its memory of its healthiest state. Didn't seem to help after the Pulse, but that was an entirely different kind of pain. Now, the only thing she felt was confusion. Confusion as to her present location. Confusion as to why she could not escape her present location. And beyond that, confusion over the event that led to her arrival to the place.

The anger and the venom Traci had spat was not only uncharacteristic, but otherworldly. All the strange things that had been happening to Traci up to the point, the mood swings, the lost time, the supernatural phenomena, left Kassidy feeling very uncertain about her own abilities. She was a god. Why was she so uncertain about what was happening to her girlfriend?

"What did she do to me?" Kassidy asked herself, spinning around again, trying to catch her bearings.

Kassidy took in the scenery, hoping to glean some sense of where she was. This place, this realm, seemed like somewhere she should be aware of. She felt a deep sense of dread all around her. Unlike the Nexus, where everything existed in a world of greenish gray, this place was vibrant with color, though most of it foreboding. The skies above, the black-streaked crimson river, the granite ground and rock formations, all screamed pain and suffering. To the right of her, a bit in the distance, she could see a structure that appeared old and decayed. She turned toward it, concentrated, and vanished. When she reappeared, she was standing in front of the crumbling wall.

"Well, if I can't get out of here, at least I can save some steps."

She stretched out and ran her hand along the wall. She felt a strange tingle in her fingers and quickly pulled back. The tingle was not of electricity or shock, but of awareness. There was something familiar about the structure. She touched it again and this time held firm. Feeling the wall vibrate beneath her hand, Kassidy closed her eyes and let the sensation wash over her. She was, at once, connected to the structure, to the ground, to the sky, and the river. The vibration turned to a low rumble and instinctively she spoke.

"Aperta."

Slowly a three-foot by six-foot rectangle appeared in the stone where her hand had been. It retracted from the rest of the wall and then slid to one side. The rumble stopped, and Kassidy looked into the opening, into the darkness.

"I'm in the freakin' Underworld. This is Hades," she whispered. "Damn you, Traci!"

She didn't know how she knew it, but there was no doubt in her mind as to her location. Her connection to the place was unmistakable, no doubt due to her station as Death God. With nowhere else to go, Kassidy stepped forward, into the opening. Once inside, the rumbling resumed, and the wall closed behind her. Engulfed in darkness, Kassidy stretched out with her senses, hoping that intuition would return.

Kassidy recalled an almost forgotten power. She hadn't practiced it much since her ascension, but her thoughts traveled back to the first time she had used it. The night Jeremy Reins had attacked her in Potter's Field. After Azra-El changed her, after she'd returned to the park, she'd placed her hand on the ground, and the events of that night that she'd forgotten flooded back into her mind. That must have been what happened when she touched the stone.

Hoping for an encore, Kassidy knelt and placed her hand on the ground. It was smooth like glass, perhaps marble. It was cold to the touch. After a beat, she felt that tingle once again, and in her mind a word formed.

"Illumine," she said softly.

On her left and her right, torches lit. All the way down the stretch of the hallway. Kassidy smiled, though remained wary. She stood and cautiously walked the path. The ground was indeed marble. Smooth and reflective. On either side of her, the torches had a mirror image below them. On guard, Kassidy allowed vapor to engulf her as she walked. In seconds she was no longer wearing the ripped jeans and a T-shirt, but instead the black leather pants, boots, and tank that were a staple of her work as a Reaper, and now, as Death.

"God, how dramatic am I?" she said, poking fun at herself.

Despite the heel on her boots, there was no sound as she walked along the marble surface. After finally reaching the end of the long hallway, she could clearly see openings for two cavernous paths ahead, one to the left, and the one to the right. There was no light in either. She spoke the word again, hoping it would light the paths.

"Illumine," she shouted.

But nothing happened.

She knelt again, touched the ground, and attempted to discern the hazards and pitfalls of each path. When nothing happened, she realized that she had to choose which path to walk before the magic would take hold. Impatient, she attempted to shimmer beyond both paths, but an invisible barrier countered her, and she was flung back to the ground.

"Dammit!"

Kassidy sat for a moment and thought about her predicament. She was in the Underworld, and she couldn't leave. She had to choose a path with the hope of finding something or someone that could help her escape. She still had some power, though with apparent limitations. Invulnerability was at least there, so besides pain, what was the worst that could happen if she chose poorly?

"Fine, I'll go left," she said aloud, as if proclaiming it would make it easier.

Kassidy stood and stepped forward toward the path on the left.

"Illumine!"

A beat passed, and then two blood red orbs appeared in the darkness. Seconds later, two more appeared just to the right, with another two orbs appearing to the left. The six red orbs moved up and down, side to side, each pair together. Stepping forward, Kassidy hoped the rest of the path would light up.

She was met with a low growl.

Then a second growl overlapping the first.

Then a third.

The six orbs started to move toward her, and that cautious step she'd initially taken was retracted. Kassidy continued her slow retreat as she felt the growls vibrate through the marble floor.

Coming through the darkness was a tall beast with the blackest hair. It walked on four legs, and it had three heads, each with a mouth full of the sharpest fangs she'd ever seen. Each head growled, each head snarled, and each head drooled a thick, foul-smelling liquid the color of blood. It stepped closer. Inching toward Kassidy, stalking toward its prey. Kassidy was nothing more than a meal for the beast carefully guarding its master's home. It took several moments more for Kassidy to realize who the beast was. She'd read about her, seen her in countless movies and television shows. She was guardian of the Underworld, loyal servant to its lord, Hades.

"Cerberus," she whispered.

The three heads of the beast howled in unison.

CHAPTER THIRTY-TWO

"HOW ARE YOU HERE? HELL … HOW AM I HERE?" ASKED TRACI.

Her question was met with a chuckle, as her host, her former guidance counselor and magical mentor, settled into a plush couch after stoking the fire. The crackling flames sparked a memory of her on the couch with Kassidy shortly after some construction had been finished on the Simmons home. Kassidy was nestled against her, exhausted, grief-stricken, yet strangely hopeful. She'd lost her aunt, a woman she'd only recently met, and in the same night had come to recognize and appreciate herself, her power, and her role as Death God.

God, Kas. What have I done? I'm so sorry.

She'd done something that would not be easy to come back from. It was unforgiveable. At least, she'd never be able to forgive herself.

"You are of the Hekatos, Traci. Your strength is such that any magic wielder knows when you're near."

"Yeah, I get that. But I was hours from here. That just doesn't seem possible."

"It is possible, when your power is growing the way yours is," said the Diva.

Traci sat with that for a moment. Growing? Her power wasn't growing. Hecate's was. That's what her mentor was feeling. And that simply meant she did not have much time left. She was supposed to have thirty days, but things were escalating so much faster. She didn't quite understand why, though.

"That's just it," began Traci, "it's not *my* power. The spell, the book, it . . . everything they said was true. I'm dying."

It dawned on Traci that she'd never said those words aloud before. In her mind they bounced around almost every minute, but the words had never escaped her lips. It was both chilling, and strangely liberating. Knowing the time of one's death was an insight not available to most. Her original plan had been to enjoy every minute of her last days. To spend time traveling and loving Kassidy until her last breath. She had not counted on her final days being so angry, so . . . violent.

"Perhaps it's not so much death as it is re-birth? Shifting our perspective on things can often make the seemingly unpleasant permanently palatable."

"As much as I appreciate alliteration, there is nothing pleasant or palatable about what's happening to me. She's in me. She's taking over. This isn't a re-birth for me. It's a coming out party for the goddess. Hecate is coming, and she's pissed."

The slight smirk on the Diva's face was concerning, to say the least. Traci got the distinct impression that her mentor was happy. Happy with her death? With the return of Hecate? With the destruction that would likely follow?

No, that couldn't be.

Could it?

"Tell me what you know of the goddess," said Traci."

"I know that she was formidable," said the Diva. "She was a Titan, powerful, so very powerful. In fact, aside from Nyx, she was the only goddess that Zeus feared."

"Why?"

"As you know, the power of a witch is rooted in two things— their emotions and their ability to manipulate the energies that exist all around us. This is also how gods utilize their own power, but for Hecate, her connection to the earth and sky, to the sea and below, was exponentially stronger. Her connection to all four planes not only gave her access to them but the ability to wield their energies to stand against the god, or gods, who held dominion over them."

"So, you're saying she could battle Zeus and win?" asked Traci.

"Probably. It never actually came to that. But conceivably, using energies of the sea or the underworld, planes where he was still powerful but held no true dominion, Hecate would be a challenge."

"Why is she so angry? She talks of betrayal. Who turned against her?"

"You speak to her?" asked the Diva, leaning forward with an uncomfortable eagerness.

Traci nodded, noting the not-so-subtle excitement in her mentor's tone.

"In the final days of her life, she was betrayed. Made the scapegoat for the misdeeds of Hades. She was hunted, imprisoned, and eventually destroyed."

"I was told … well, all the Hekatos are told … that the goddess elected to end her life and dispersed her power among her progenies."

"Well, of course they said that" said the Diva. "They said that because it's much easier to believe that the goddess was full of love and light and the advancement of peace and fellowship. Now, don't get me wrong, she was, in many ways, all those things. But toward the end, she wanted more. She demanded more. And for that, she was sentenced to die."

Traci felt uneasy for many reasons. She felt lied to. Betrayed. Gullible. All of the things her mother and the Hekatos taught, for centuries, was a lie. Underneath it all, she felt uneasy about the Diva, too. This woman was not Hekatos, and in that Traci felt uncomfortable, and a little scared.

"You know, you never actually told me what type of witch you are. I mean, we're all descended from the goddess, but you're not Hekatos," said Traci.

"No, I'm not Hekatos," said the Diva. "And, truth be told, I'm not a witch."

Traci's felt the hair on her arms rise. That feeling of pain in her chest from the power of swift heartbeats. The dread in her stomach causing bile to rise.

"Wh . . . what are you?"

Traci's question was met with glowing blue eyes. Like those she'd seen in her own reflection when Hecate took control. Like Kassidy's. Glowing blue eyes were the mark of a god.

"No. No. No, no, no, no."

"Oh yes, my dear. I'm afraid so."

"Why? Why would you lie to me?"

"Ultimately, because it's what I do," said the Diva.

"Why, though? Why . . . me?"

"You are a direct descendant of the goddess," said the Diva, standing and walking toward Traci. "As such, you are the perfect vessel for her rebirth. I mean, I couldn't use your mother. She was too smart, too wise, and quite frankly, too old. I needed someone young. Someone desperate. You were so anxious to find your savior, so caught up in the romance of falling for the mysterious stranger who rescued you and vanished. I couldn't have asked for a better partner in bringing back the goddess."

"Partner?! I'm no partner! You used me!" screamed Traci, as she rose from her chair.

"Yes. I lie. I cheat. I deceive. It's . . . my thing," said the Diva.

As fear turned to anger, Traci felt the room begin to shake.

The couch, the chairs, the table all vibrated against the hard-wood floor. Glasses shattered as they crashed to the floor. Windows cracked, and the small one above the kitchen sink blew out completely. Winds swept through the cabin, and Traci's power rose. In her right hand a ball of energy formed. It crackled with electricity. She drew her arm back and threw it toward the Diva with added magical force. Her heart sank when her target caught the energy and easily simply absorbed it.

"You know," began the Diva, "I'm starting to think we're not friends anymore."

Traci screamed and lunged at the goddess. She whispered a spell to augment her strength. With added power, she threw a punch to the Diva's abdomen. As the woman bent over from the blow, Traci brought her knee up, connecting with the Diva's jaw. Catching her off guard, Traci sent a barrage of blows to the woman's face. One punch after another, backing the goddess up. Traci funneled her power into one final blow, and it spun the Diva around and sent her crashing into the wooden wall behind her.

Traci felt the temporary power fade. She backed up and created another ball of energy, then a second. She hurled the first, and the Diva dropped to the ground. Traci then hurled the second, and the Diva curled up to protect herself.

The swirling winds stopped. The only sound now was Traci's breathing. The temptation to launch another barrage of energy at the lifeless goddess was strong, but she held back, choosing instead to turn and escape. As she grabbed the handle to the door, she heard laughter. Mocking. Sinister. Deadly.

"Impressive, young one," said the Diva. "Very impressive. But you forget your place."

Traci turned to find the Diva standing, eyes aglow, and her body was pulled across the room toward the Diva's open hand.

Seconds later she was lifted off the ground, held from the neck by the Diva's powerful grip. As she struggled, a surge of electricity ran through her body.

"I tire of you, Traci Leeds. You were put into play for two reasons. To weaken Kassidy Simmons, and to serve as a vessel for Hecate. I'm done with the games. It's time to get to work."

As the electricity surged through her, fear and sadness overwhelmed her. Moments of her life flashed in her mind. And then, she heard her.

I think it's about time you set me free, little witch.

Traci felt the tears escape and the pain intensified. She wanted it all to end. She wanted to feel nothing . . . ever again. She let her mind slip away, allowing Hecate to take control. The last thing she saw was the reflection of her own eyes, now blue, in the Diva's. The last thing she heard was the Diva's voice.

"Welcome back."

◆　◆　◆

"Where have you been?" demanded Hecate.

The Diva raised an eyebrow, gave a signature smirk, and moved back to the couch. Taking a seat, she crossed one leg over the other and spread her arms across the back of the couch.

"It's good to see you, too," said the Diva.

"You promised me you'd come for me! You promised you'd free me!"

"And it seems I have."

"Centuries too late!" screamed Hecate.

Outside, thunder and lightning took the stage. Rain fell in torrents, crashing against the cracked windows and soaking the kitchen sink and floor through the broken window. The Diva's eyes raised as she heard it, and again, she smiled.

"You'd think you'd be a little more grateful."

"Grateful? Grateful!"

As the unnatural storm raged outside, Hecate created a ball of fiery energy, and was fully prepared to launch it at the Diva. The Diva sent a gentle wind from her lips, dousing the flame, then rose, stretched out a hand, and lifted Hecate into the air.

"I'm going to need you to calm down. You're not at full power. You're trapped in the body of a mortal. I could end this rebirth with a thought. Now, are you willing to calm down and listen? Or do you wish to die? Because I need you. And you, my dear, most assuredly need me."

The rain outside slowed. The thunder was silenced. A few flashes of lightning continued, but Hecate was otherwise calm under the circumstances. The Diva lowered the deity, walked up to her, and gave her a hug.

"As I was saying," began the Diva, "it's good to see you again."

"I'm . . . sorry," said Hecate. "I'm just—"

"I know. Believe me, I know."

"What happened?"

"Not long after the Twelve passed sentence on you, I was captured and imprisoned."

"How?"

"My brother."

"No," said Hecate with a gasp.

"I was placed in the box."

"Pandora's?"

The Diva nodded.

"How did you escape?"

"Luck," said the Diva. "Dumb luck. A couple of students inadvertently set me free when they found the box and translated the inscription. I have no idea how they found the box in the first place. Thankfully, they had no idea what they'd done, until it was too late."

"And I suspect they regretted it . . . with their dying breaths."

"Indeed."

"Please accept my apologies again," said Hecate. "I can only imagine the hell you've been through."

"The apology isn't needed. The execution of our plan is. It's taken almost two decades to line everything up. Your return is one of the final nails in the coffin."

"The daughter of Thanatos has grown strong," said Hecate.

"Yes, but she's still young in her role. She has no idea how to use the power she has. She certainly has no idea how to battle you. And with you in that body, she'll be no trouble."

Hecate's laugh brought a light to the Diva that she'd not felt since her release. The end was in sight. Finally.

"What do we need to do next?" asked Hecate.

"The only other potential obstacles are—"

"The Hekatos."

The Diva nodded.

"Women of my blood. My witches. My sisters."

"Your sisters have long held the magic that is rightfully yours. It's time to take it back," said the Diva.

"It will kill them."

"For the greater good."

Silence took up space between the deities. The Diva sensed some sentimentality from Hecate for her witches. That was unchanged over the millennia. She needed to ensure that the goddess would hold up her end of their covenant.

"The witch you inhabit, Traci, is at odds with her mother and the coven. I believe they intend to do her harm. They suspect she is tied to the rise in famine, violence, and war happening in the world today. I thought you taught your witches to support each other? No matter what."

The blue glow in Hecate's eyes told the Diva that she'd hit the right series of triggers within the goddess.

"I need to get to them," said Hecate.

"Indeed."

"Any suggestions?"

"Perhaps we resurrect more than you," began the Diva. "Perhaps we resurrect that wily old fool, Odysseus. Or at least his plan to breach the walls of Troy."

"Ever the trickster," said Hecate.

The two deities walked to kitchen of the cabin and stood on either side of the island. Using their combined power, they repaired the broken glass and windows, then used Traci's cell phone to contact her mother, Mary Leeds.

"Um, mom? It's me. Um, something's happening. I don't know how to fix this. I don't know how to control this. I need help. I'm . . . I'm coming home. Please. Help me."

The Diva laughed after Hecate ended the call.

"Perfect," she said. "What mother can resist a plea from her child."

"I'll need to let the girl take control," said Hecate.

"Will you be able to return?"

"It's getting easier. It may take some time, but I think my return shouldn't be too difficult to manage. I'll need help getting there, though. I don't know that I have enough power. I think I used a great deal of it to get here. And . . . to send the Death God on a bit of a journey."

"Wait. What? What journey?"

"I sent her away. She was getting too close, and I needed her away so I could get a greater hold on the girl," said Hecate.

"Where. Did. You. Send. Her."

CHAPTER THIRTY-THREE

A BURST OF FLAME ESCAPED THE RIGHT HEAD OF THE MASSIVE BEAST. Kassidy dove to the left, feeling the oppressive heat even though the flame had not touched her.

"That uhhh . . . was not in the books, my friend," she said, standing again, but slowly backing down the hallway from which she'd come. Thinking back to what she'd read of Cerberus, she was at a loss for how to defeat her. According to legend, only Heracles had ever bested the creature, and even in that story all he did was capture her. She'd clearly managed to return on her own.

On all fours, Cerberus stood at a height of at least ten feet, and she was no less wide. The creature was solid, and hell-bent it seemed on doing her job—protecting the gates of Hades. As the beast bounded forward, Kassidy caught a glimpse of a shadow off to the side of the four-legged sentry. It was fleeting, though, likely a trick of the limited light and flickering torches.

"Listen, girl, I just need to find a way out of here," said Kassidy in a fairly calm voice. "I've got no beef with you or anyone down here. I'm not here to take anything. I just want to move on."

Her hand extended, Kassidy did what anyone does when meeting a new dog—she tried to give her the chance to do a sniff test. Stopping to allow the beast closer, Kassidy stood opposite the center head.

"That's it, girl. Yeah . . . I'm not here to hurt you."

As most dogs did, Cerberus sniffed Kassidy's hand, even allowed a light petting. Kassidy smiled, feeling that perhaps, all those years walking dogs and pet sitting had helped. At least until Cerberus reared up and attempted to stomp her.

Kassidy fell back and rolled from one side to the other as each head tried to do its worst. Finally, she shimmered out of view and reappeared closer to the two paths Cerberus was guarding. She thought about running, and with her speed she might be okay, in most circumstances. None of this was *most* circumstances. She thought perhaps she could lure the creature back into the entryway it had exited and bring down a stone to trap her. But that would then block her path, too. And what she needed was down there, she was certain of it.

That shadow reappeared then vanished again behind Cerberus.

"What the hell is that?" she whispered.

Cerberus crouched down, preparing to strike. As she did, Kassidy willed her hands to become sickles. In most battles, even in her early days as a Reaper, Kassidy was certain of her skill and her ability to win. Even when she battled Azra-El decades ago, a small part of her felt some semblance of confidence and dared to think she could win. This though, was something else entirely.

"I guess we're doing this," she said.

Both she and Cerberus bounded toward each other. Nearing the creature, Kassidy leapt in the air, preparing to come down on the center head with both sickles, only to be struck by some invisible force. It was not a barrier like the one she'd encountered before. It was as if a giant, invisible fist hit her, center mass, sending her flying backward through the air.

Once again, she landed hard on the ground. Her hands reformed, she managed to get them down to push herself up while trying to catch her breath. When she looked over, Cerberus had stopped moving, though each head was snarling, growling, and anxious to pounce.

The shadow then returned.

First, she saw it to the left of the beast before it vanished and reappeared on the right. With each movement it seemed to come closer to Kassidy until it was upon her. By the time she realized exactly where the shadow was, she felt a kick to her midsection that sent her flying to the wall behind her.

When she landed on the ground, she felt shards of stone embedded in her skin. Every part of her body screamed in pain. Tears welled in her eyes from the intensity of the impact. Pulling herself to her hands and knees again, she looked around for the apparition. Cerberus was unmoved, and the shadow seemed to have retreated.

"Show yourself, coward!" she screamed.

Straining with every movement, Kassidy stood. Once again, she willed her hands to transform into sickles. Taking a defensive stance, she closed her eyes, and stretched out with her senses, hoping to capture a small glimpse of her attacker's emotions. Anything that would betray his or her location or approach. She felt the vibration of Cerberus' growl through the ground. She heard the crackle of flame from the torches down the hall, but all she felt was cold. A cavernous expanse of nothing.

Crack!

Until the sting of a punch to the face interrupted her.

Followed by what felt like a knee to the midsection.

"Ahhhhhhh!" screamed Kassidy, swinging her sickles wildly hoping to connect with whatever was out there.

"You dare come here, Reaper!"

The voice was disembodied and echoed through the chamber. It was ominous, threatening, frightening.

"You do not belong here, Reaper!"

A kick to the side of her knee sent Kassidy to the ground with a yelp. The shock again caused her hands to re-form. Just in time to brace her fall. She felt another kick, then a punch, and all she could do was cover her head and cower as she took the barrage.

Reaper? she thought to herself.

Whatever was attacking her thought she was a Reaper. Kassidy soon realized that everything she'd done up to that moment was very much the act of someone who did not possess the power she did. The power of a god. The power of Death.

The ground beneath Kassidy began to rumble. She no longer heard the growls of Cerberus. Now, the creature whimpered. Uncertain of what was to come.

Kassidy called upon her power, allowing it to fill her. As the walls trembled, she rose, curled in on herself as if in a cocoon, then unfurled, holding her arms wide. Cuts and bruises healed instantly. Bones mended, and she opened her eyes allowing the metallic blue orbs to announce her station as a god. Kassidy released a pulse of energy that sent Cerberus flying backward. It also sent her invisible attacker flying against the wall behind her.

Clang!

Kassidy looked down and saw a helmet roll beneath her. She lowered herself, picked it up, and turned toward its origin. Slumped on the ground was a man. His black hair obscured his face. He was shirtless, wearing only leather pants and boots. Throwing the helmet to the side, Kassidy walked toward him, grabbed him by the throat, lifted him in the air, and stepped forward to press him against the cold hard stone wall.

"You're no Reaper," he said.

"No. I'm pissed, is what I am."

His face was revealed. He was handsome. Chiseled. He wore

a light beard and his eyes, like hers, were a metallic blue—the mark of a god. Kassidy again called upon her power and summoned the Scythe of Cronus from its resting place just beyond this plane. Given the trouble she had trying to leave the Underworld, and the trouble she had when she last called for it, she was relieved when the scythe appeared in her hand and came to life—crackling and humming with power.

"You . . . you . . . can't have that," said her captive.

"Oh, but I can," said Kassidy.

"That's not possible. Unless . . ."

Kassidy lowered the god to the ground, gripped the scythe with both hands and pulled back, ready to strike.

"No!" said a new voice.

From her left, Kassidy saw a woman step closer. Her olive skin seemed bronze against her dirty blond tresses. She wore sandals, and a dark blue dress that came together around a gold ring in the center of her stomach.

"Please don't kill him," said the woman. "You could destroy everything around us if you do."

"Who are you?" Kassidy backed from both, securing the scythe close to her.

"Persephone," said the woman.

Kassidy looked from her to the god, now standing away from the wall. She looked back at Cerberus, then returned her gaze to the couple. Awareness trickled over her. The helmet of invisibility.

Of course.

"Hades," said Kassidy.

He inclined his head to acknowledge her.

"How did you come by that weapon?" asked Persephone, eyes trained of the scythe.

"Not easily."
"We should talk," said Hades.
"Yeah. I think you're right," said Kassidy.

CHAPTER THIRTY-FOUR

"MOM?"

Traci called for her mother after closing the door. She was prepared for the multiple questions that would arise. At least, she thought she was. She hadn't expected to wake up in a hotel room back in St. John with no recollection of how she got there. But that seemed to be the new normal. She knew it had to be Hecate, but the things she could recall and the things she could not were disturbing.

"Mom? You here?" she called.

Traci continued farther into the house but saw no sign that her mother was home. She walked into the meditation room, the space her mother had entered the first thing every morning since she was a girl. She felt a strange energy within. Something cold, dangerous. Something so disconnected from the energy of the coven and her mother that Traci was afraid something terrible had happened. Something . . . lethal.

Oh my god! Did I do something?

Traci fell to her knees, distraught, hands in her lap, and she just stared ahead.

"Traci?"

Startled, Traci fell forward as she turned her head to look behind her.

"Mom?"

Jumping to her feet, Traci ran to embrace her mother.

"Goodness, girl," began Mary, "what's gotten into you? What's wrong? And how are you here? I just spoke to you last night about coming home."

Traci heard the questions. She was prepared for the questions. But for the moment she chose to ignore them.

"Traci . . . ?"

Traci held on tight as she felt her mother attempt to pull away.

"Traci."

She buried her head into her mother, secretly praying she could make all this madness go away.

"Traci!" her mother yelled, pulling away and holding Traci by her arms. "Girl. Stop. Now tell me what's happening."

Traci only made eye contact with her mother briefly before looking away. She couldn't face her. She'd been feeling her mother's disapproval for decades. The only thing keeping them together was the fact that the end result of her spell had not taken hold. Now, though, not only was the end result coming to fruition, so too was the end of the world.

"Traci, look at me, please," said Mary.

Slowly, Traci moved her head and met her mother's gaze. In those eyes she saw judgment, she saw fear and anger, but underneath it all, there was love. Still. Traci wanted to embrace her again. She wanted to know everything was going to be okay.

She wanted to be forgiven.

"Sweetheart, how did you get here so fast?"

"I . . . I . . . I don't know."

"You . . . don't . . ."

Traci searched for a stronger response, but nothing came to the surface. She could lie, but at this point, being less than truthful served no purpose. Her fate was sealed. At best, she could work with her mother to stop the goddess from taking over. But her days were short.

"She's . . . in me, Mom."

"What? Who?"

"The goddess. She's inside me. The curse, the legends, they were all true. She's coming back, and she's using me to do it."

"Are you sure it's not just—"

"Mom! No! It's nothing else but the legend coming true. Just like you warned all those years ago."

"Because of that girl. Because of Kassidy."

"Jesus! No mom. Because of me. Because of genetics and fucking witchcraft," said Traci.

"Watch your language!"

"Or what?" said Traci with a chuckle. "I'm going to die soon. You think you can do something worse to me than that because I'm fucking cursing in your house. Fuck! Fuck, fuck, fuck. Shit. Damn. Fuck. Now send me to my room with no dinner."

Traci stepped back, shaking her head, throwing her hands up in exasperation, uncertain of what to do next . . . if anything. She'd spent the better part of two decades looking for a loophole. When she thought she'd found one, a way out of the curse, that was the moment she found Kassidy. The moment she found her heart's desire.

The moment that signaled the beginning of her end.

"I'm . . . sorry," began Mary. "I know this is difficult for you."

"Difficult? Difficult?! I spent my childhood living in the shadow of great magic wielders and never living up to your legacy, or grandma's. I found love, I found my power, and it all came with a price. I'm the happiest I've ever been in my life, but I have to give it all up because I'm the descendant of an angry goddess who was fucked-over centuries ago. So yeah, this is a little more than difficult."

As she finished speaking, she felt a sharp pain in her temple. The pain intensified, turning to a low hum, then a violent throb. She touched the side of her head and doubled over, screaming in agony.

"Traci!" said Mary, rushing to her daughter's aid. "What is it? What can I do?"

There was an increase in the energy permeating the room. Traci could feel it as easily as she felt her mother's hand trying to comfort her. Heat blossomed in her abdomen. The tips of her fingers tingled. The echo of her rapid breathing bounced inside her ears. Through it all, she managed to look up, once again meeting her mother's gaze. She sought comfort and safety, and instead watched in horror as her mother gasped and began backing up.

"Mom?" said Traci softly, regaining strength and cautiously standing up straight. Traci felt the throbbing subside back to a hum, and she spoke again—only now, the voice was not hers.

"I am here now," she said.

"Who are you?" asked Mary.

Mom?

"You know exactly who I am."

Mom, it's not me!

"You are . . . the goddess," said Mary.

"I am your salvation. And your destruction."

Within the body of Traci Leeds, the young witch screamed, but no sound escaped. The being in control turned to look into a mirror that hung upon the wall. Her metallic blue eyes glowed bright, as did the sinister smile on her face.

◆　　◆　　◆

Mary was a true believer in all that she and her sisters practiced. So, when she'd found Traci reading the forbidden magic when she was a teen, her beliefs told her something terrible would happen. As coven leader, Mary was certain that Traci's actions would lead to the return of Hecate. As a mother, she held out hope that she was wrong.

She was not wrong.

Mary watched the body that she gave birth to walk around her meditation room, and she felt empty. She wondered what she'd feel when Traci died, but this certainly was not it. She'd anticipated sadness at the loss. Having lost loved ones before, she knew there would be gut-wrenching emotional pain that would last, well, as long as it needed to. It was the thought of never seeing her daughter again that weighed so heavily upon her. A hollowness filled her stomach. A part of her soul was missing. Her daughter was gone, but her body remained. Was she dead? Mary didn't know. The only thing she knew for sure, was that Traci's body was now occupied by another.

Occupied by Hecate.

"Why—" Mary stopped that sentence as Hecate swiftly turned to face her, blue eyes ablaze. "Pardon me, goddess. I meant, how . . . how can I serve you?"

Mary's question was met with laughter. It was condescending. Not evil, but certainly not offered with any element of good. Certainly no compassion. There was anger in the laugh. Centuries of anger.

"You wish to know what's happened to your daughter, yes?" asked Hecate.

Mary nodded, hesitantly.

"She's still here, witch. She's fighting. Right now, she's screaming, begging for me to let her out again. She wants her freedom. Freedom from me, from you. She only wants her love. Her dear, sweet, Kassidy."

The laughter stopped, but the smile. Maniacal. Even though the body was Traci's, the voice, the words, the mannerisms, the intent in her movements, none of it belonged to her daughter. The pit in her stomach grew. In seconds she ran through all the moments she'd been angry or less than loving with Traci. Regret filled her mind and heart. Tears welled in the corners of her eyes as she realized she'd likely never get to tell her how sorry she was.

"Aww, are you going to cry? Would you like me to let her out? Maybe just for a second?"

Hecate bent slightly to whisper that last part in her ear. Mary felt her anger rise. For the first time in her entire life, Mary hated the goddess. The being she'd been taught to respect, the mother of her bloodline, and the matron of all witches, was an absolute bitch.

Mary held her anger in. She stifled the frustration she felt and responded with a simple, "If . . . if I may, goddess. Just to say goodbye."

"That is so incredibly sweet. I'll tell you what, I'll pass on the message," said Hecate.

Mary watched as the goddess closed her eyes and seemed to go into some trance. She looked quickly left to right for anything she might use as a weapon. Thoughts of causing harm to Traci overrode any serious moves.

So did realization that Hecate was now staring at her.

"Looking for something?" asked the goddess.

"Um, no. I was, um—"

"Maybe looking for this?" asked Hecate as a dagger flew from the wall above Mary's altar to her hand.

Hecate ran the tip of the blade along Mary's neck and up her cheek, and a shiver ran through the witch. She felt the warmth of the goddess's breath against her ear as she came close again.

"Your daughter. Is not welcomed. Back. Now, you can either work with me, or you can work against me. The latter results in this dagger entering your abdomen and moving upward as I slice up to your mouth so I can pull out your spine."

Mary shook at the statement. She tried hard to maintain her resolve. But it was hard. She wanted her daughter. She wanted to reach out to her, to connect with her to—

"Agh!" screamed the goddess.

Mary stepped back as the goddess doubled over, dropping the dagger. Mary kicked it away.

"No!" said Hecate, holding her head.

Mary watched the brightness in the eyes of the goddess dim. Could it be?

"Mom?" whispered the goddess, looking up at Mary. "Mom, I'm here. Help me."

"Traci?"

"Nooooo!" screamed the goddess. "You will not come out!"

Mary's thoughts focused on her daughter again. She tried hard to sense her, to connect with her. The currents of connection ebbed and flowed. Finally, she was able to latch on to a strong impulse from her daughter. She felt Traci as clearly as she had before Hecate's possession.

"Traci, I can sense you. Take hold of my power. Use it to fight back."

"Mom! I'm here. I feel it!"

Mary felt the connection strengthen. She felt her daughter's return. She also felt Hecate fighting back, but the power was fading. She reached out, grabbed Traci's hand, and concentrated solely on her child. Feeling the energy leave her and enter Traci's body, she recited a spell in a low whisper that willed the goddess to fall back so that Traci could emerge. As she spoke the words, soft at first, then louder, she heard them echoed. Traci, regaining some strength and standing tall, recited the words along with Mary, using what little power she had as she siphoned strength from her mother.

"Traci?" asked Mary, catching the collapsing form of her daughter.

"Yeah . . . I'm here," said Traci.

"My god, girl."

"Yeah . . . I know," said Traci as she lowered herself to the floor.

"This is what you've been dealing with?"

"Yeah."

"Okay. Okay," said Mary, trying to regroup. "Okay, we can do something. We can try, at least. When I gave you power, you were able to strengthen yours and fight her, right?"

"It was hard, but yes."

"Okay . . . that's good. We just need to get you boosted."

"How do we do that?" asked Traci.

"We call in the sisters," said Mary. "That's what family's for."

CHAPTER THIRTY-FIVE

FEW THINGS IN THE WORLD BROUGHT BOTH COMFORT AND TERROR to Traci Leeds. As in tune with nature as she was, spiders were a source of wonder and dread. Love was most certainly another. She'd never felt completely whole. She'd always had an idea of what love was, but the practice of it frightened her. The fear of pain, deep-rooted emotional pain, the pain of betrayal—that downright terrified her.

Traci followed her mother into the basement of their family home. Together they recited an incantation and pushed their power out toward a wall adorned with trophies and books. A few beats passed, but soon the wall glowed white, and the pair walked toward it—then through it. Transported to another place, Traci and her mother joined other members of the coven in a small grove that existed in Northern England. Warded against strangers, this space belonged to the coven and was used for sacred rituals and celebrations.

Her coven was another source of comfort and terror. She loved her sisters. She cherished their connection as witches, as daughters of Hecate, and as protectors of light and mother earth. But as much as they were her people, they were strangers, too. The women were powerful. They were secure with their magic, their knowledge, and their practice. Traci was none of those things—a fraud, a charlatan, a fake dime store magician always chasing the ultimate goal.

Her own wants and needs.

She wanted acknowledgment as an individual. Respect, compassion, and patience as a witch. And the unconditional love of her mother. She needed Kassidy. The love of someone who could have anyone in the world yet chose to be with her. Traci knew these thoughts and feelings weren't healthy. She knew the thoughts, feelings, and subsequent decisions were dangerous. Yet she'd moved forward with her plans, with her actions, toward her inevitable doom.

Seeing the five elders of her coven, along with the healer, Myra, brought a dread to Traci's stomach that she'd not felt in a long time. Even with all the things she'd done, these women, their very presence, took her back to a time when she was a little girl, hoping for great things but somehow in the way of everything.

As they all stood in a circle, Traci kept her head down, avoiding eye contact. Shame filled her. As did anger. At them, for judging her. At herself, for what she'd done. At Hecate, for not being the loving goddess she'd been taught about her whole life. At Kassidy, for making her lash out and send her to the underworld.

"No, that's not right. That wasn't her fault," she said to herself.

Yes. Yes it was little witch. It was all her fault. She should have listened and relished being in your presence for all you've done just to be with her. It. Was. All. Her. Fault.

Traci slowly shook her head, trying to deny the voice inside without the others seeing. She wondered, though, if they could sense what was happening. She wondered what her mother had said to them to get them to come. She wouldn't have had to say much. As coven leader, she could convene for any reason. She was not the type to do such a thing, of course. Traci's mother was fair, just, and full of love and compassion for her sisters.

Too bad she didn't have that same love and compassion for you.

"Shut up," Traci said to herself.

The laughter ringing in her head was terrifying. At times, she wasn't fully certain if it was her, or Hecate. Perhaps that was part of the torture the Titan was inflicting in her efforts to be free.

"Sisters," began Mary Leeds, "thank you for coming. Thank you for showing your devotion to the coven, to me, and to my daughter in this time of need."

Traci's heart began to race. Would they remain so devoted once they'd discovered what she'd done? Would her mother defend her? Or would she simply do whatever was best for the coven?

As she'd always done.

The laughter in her head continued.

"Tonight, I must ask for your help," said Mary. "Tonight, I must ask you to join me in helping my child, my life, my love, in finding peace from what troubles her. Tonight, I ask that you help me in strengthening her, as was done in the old days, so that she may battle the demons within and take her rightful place as the powerful witch that she is."

Traci felt a rush of electricity through her body at those words. It was as if her mother was proud of her. It was the first time in a long time that she felt true love from her. She stifled tears and a smile, trying hard to remain humble and stoic. Inside, though, butterflies flew, and her heart grew.

"Are you with me?" asked Mary of the elder witches.

There was a low hum among the witches. It lasted for what seemed an eternity. It was then followed by a collective agreement.

"We are with you."

"Thank you, sister," said Mary.

Traci mouthed the words, "thank you" to her sisters, then watched as her mother turned to Myra, the healer, and nodded.

Myra grabbed a chalice from a high-top table made of stone and walked toward Traci. The witches stood in a circle, around the stone altar. Myra stepped forward, stood next to Traci, then turned to her.

"Come with me, sister."

Traci followed Myra to the center, next to the altar. She felt naked. Standing for all to see. It was in this spot that all witches stood when made sisters of the coven. It was a part of their ascension. Traci had never been given that honor. Her ascension was forced, artificial. No one knew that but her mother, and as coven leader, she could not allow Traci access to such a sacred ceremony. As her mother, she could not allow the knowledge of what Traci had done to reach the coven. It would have ended both their associations with the sisterhood. When the sisters asked why Traci had not participated in an Awakening Ceremony, Mary simply told them that her daughter requested a private ceremony. Knowing the challenges Traci had experienced, the reasoning seemed to satisfy their collective curiosities.

"Take this," said Myra, holding out the chalice.

Traci did as she was told, grabbing the porcelain chalice with both hands. It was cream-colored and adorned with images of nature. The chalice was old, centuries old, handed down from healer to healer, and used only for sacred rituals and complex spells involving the whole of the coven.

"Now, drink," said Myra.

A low hum emanated from the sisters in the circle. Traci looked around, apprehensive at first, but hopeful. Hopeful that this would somehow help. Could this be an actual path toward salvation? Could they, collectively, change her fate?

She drank.

The laughter in her head stopped immediately.

"Continue drinking, sister. Finish it," said Myra.

Traci thought she noticed a hitch in Myra's voice. One of, sadness? Doubt? Concern? Traci let it go, chalking it up to concern over her well-being. Myra was a powerful healer, but that did not mean that there was never concern over her practices. Nothing was ever certain, especially with magic.

Traci finished drinking. Whatever it was had a sweetness to it. There was a bit of an aftertaste, but that was not uncommon with certain mixes. She felt a warmth as the liquid slid down her throat. She recognized some of the ingredients by taste. Including . . . lavender.

"Gah!" exclaimed Traci as she grabbed at her stomach and dropped the chalice. The hum from the sisters continued as she dropped to one knee. Seconds later she was on both knees, cradling her stomach and rocking back and forth.

"Mom," she pleaded as the pain persisted.

Curled up in the fetal position, Traci felt her body rise in the air. Looking around, the sisters had changed positions. Her mother remained at the head. The four remaining elders moved to their respective ritualistic positions—points of the pentagram. They used their powers to lift her and place her upon the altar. As she felt the stone against her body, she felt her legs straighten and her arms move to either side, palms down. The sisters were forcing her to remain still.

"Mom," she said again, through tears.

"Our sister, my daughter, my light, my love, is in pain dear sisters. Her pain, though, will reach beyond her and impact this entire world if we do nothing. And so, I ask you all to help me in binding her powers to keep her and the world safe from harm."

"No. No. Noooooo!" screamed Traci, still feeling the pain in her gut from the potion.

They seek to harm you. They seek to take what is yours by birth. Are these really your sisters?

Traci writhed, shaking her head back and forth. The collective power of the elder witches kept her bound to the altar, but the potion given to her was tearing her up from the inside out.

"Join with me, sisters," said Mary.

Again, a low hum reverberated among the sisters. They all raised their arms, and with that, Traci felt her very essence being pulled away from her body. The pain was excruciating. She screamed aloud, she cried, she begged them to stop. But the coven did not. Her sisters did not.

Her mother did not.

They are taking away your power. Taking away who you are!

"Noooooo!"

Unleash me, little witch. I can save you. I can stop them. I can make them pay!

Traci shook her head, in the throes of agony. She felt as if flesh and muscle were being stripped from her body. She was helpless to fight back. Traci knew that she was going to die. Whether she had her powers or not, that was inevitable. But she did not want to die like this. Powerless, with no dignity, with no love or compassion from those who claimed to be her family. As the pain increased, so did her anger. As her anger increased, so did Hecate's influence. Without warning, Traci stopped moving. The hum amongst the sisters slowed as she closed her eyes. And then she whispered the words.

"Save me."

Traci's eyes burst open, shining bright blue. In an explosion of light and electricity a pulse of energy erupted from her body flinging the elders to the ground. Traci felt her body rise in the air, and as it did, her conscious mind sank down.

Hecate was now in control.

◆　　◆　　◆

Hecate floated above the quintet of elder witches, as they struggled to get up following the energy blast. She looked at them, each of them, and felt, on one hand, a sense of pride. In the part of her that was still benevolent goddess to all witches, she felt warmth and kinship. She felt love and compassion and hope for the continuation of her line, of her magic, of her teachings.

But anger overshadowed those feelings.

"You all turned on her. You turned on one of your own. She who would have supported you in anything. She who would have fought for you, with you, against any enemy. She who only ever sought your friendship, your kinship, your acceptance, your love."

Hecate spoke those last two words as she looked directly at Mary. Lowering herself, she stood atop the stone altar and turned her gaze to the stars above. The moon began to peek out from behind a partly cloudy sky, and its hue brought a smile to Hecate's face.

"You turned on her just as they turned on me," said Hecate.

She lowered her head to stare at them all again, and she saw shock and wonder among them all. All but Mary Leeds, the high priestess. As the other four elders looked at one another, she laughed.

"She hasn't told you? She's told none of you?"

"Goddess, forgive me. I only sought to spare them," said Mary.

As whispers of the word goddess scattered about, Hecate turned to Mary, and with an outstretched arm, she made a fist. Mary's scream was satisfying.

"Spare them? You and your daughter have only damned them."

Eyes aglow, Hecate turned her head, looking again at the elder witches who, one by one, fell to their knees clutching their throats. A beat passed before blue fire erupted from their mouths and eyes. Screams of pain filled the small grove.

"I will spare you," said Hecate, turning her attention back to Mary, "only so you can carry the weight of this for the rest of your days."

Hecate released Mary Leeds, who fell to the ground unconscious. The Titan then rose in the air, looking down at what she'd done. Satisfied, she shimmered out of view as the bodies of witches smoldered from the inside out.

CHAPTER THIRTY-SIX

THE DIVA FOLLOWED THE MASSIVE SURGE OF MAGICAL ENERGY AND took form outside the home of Mary Leeds. She didn't much care if anyone saw her. Humans were beneath her, and she had no problem letting them know that. As she stepped closer to the home, the faint smell of burned flesh filled her nostrils. She imagined the carnage inside, and a sinister smile crossed her lips. Feeling there was no need to be polite and knock, the Diva shimmered out of view, reappearing inside the home.

The residence was quaint. Nice enough for the suburbanites to feel comfortable as they lived droll mundane lives. The Diva wondered what the neighbors would think if they knew this home was the meeting place for a coven of witches. The suburbs provided perfect cover for the practice of witchcraft in a world where such things were shunned and, in some areas, still very illegal.

The Diva stopped at the mantel above the faux fireplace and looked at the photos. The Leeds family seemed happy on film. Mother, daughter, and a son. Curiously there was no father pictured. She also noticed that there were no pictures of the son past a certain age. Maybe sixteen, seventeen, certainly no older than eighteen. Her gaze lingered on the photo of Traci. The Diva marveled at the knowledge that such an innocent-looking girl was helping to usher in the apocalypse. She was also going to be responsible for bringing about the destruction of the Death

God, Kassidy Simmons. All because of one little spell so many years ago.

Her smile returned.

She moved farther into the home and followed the tangy smell of death to a door that led to the basement. The scent became increasingly stronger with each step downward. Reaching the bottom, she looked around and saw nothing. There were no bodies, no sign of struggle or fight, yet the smell was unmistakable. Continuing to follow its pull, the Diva found herself standing next to a wall filled with trophies and awards. Apparently, young Traci, and the boy that must have been her brother, were both studious and athletic.

"How cute," she said, rolling her eyes. After several seconds, she heard the faint sound of air but could not find a space in the wall from which it was escaping. Stepping back, the Diva stretched out her arm, and palm up, pushed energy forward against the wall. Her magic filled the room, and the wall lit up in white light.

Moving forward, she stepped through the wall and beyond the threshold, astounded by what she saw. Standing in an open field she looked around, nodding in approval. She looked up and surmised from the position of the stars above, that the space existed in the hills of Northern England.

"These witches are powerful," said the Diva.

The Diva walked across the open field, and followed the burning smell, till she came to the site that was its source. Around a stone altar lay four women. The elders of the group, no doubt. Upon the altar though was a familiar face. The face from the photos in the home. The face of Mary Leeds.

The Diva stepped forward and looked down upon the woman. The Diva was certain the four women on the ground were dead. Their life forces extinguished for all time, but the same could not be said of Mary. The Diva placed her hand on Mary's forehead and spoke the word, "Awaken."

Mary's eyes popped open at once. She stirred slightly but grimaced in pain.

"Easy, old witch," said the Diva.

The Diva saw some sense of awareness in Mary's eyes. In the legends and myths surrounding ancient and elder gods, she was relatively unknown. It pained her. Infuriated her. Even though, at times, it suited her. She'd quietly orchestrated some of the greatest skirmishes and embarrassing episodes for gods and men through the centuries. A larger part of her wanted the world to recognize her power and importance. So, when someone knew who she was, especially a mortal, she felt great pleasure.

"You," said Mary.

Even if she was only known as a former high school guidance counselor.

"Yes. Me. So good to see you again Miss Leeds."

The Diva smiled wide as shock settled on Mary's face.

"Yes. Oh, yes. I've been here for quite a while. Waiting. Watching. Plotting. And people said I had no patience," said the Diva.

"You . . . are . . . responsible for . . . this."

"This? This what? This death? Oh, dear sister, this was not me."

"You . . . unleashed . . . her," said Mary.

"No. No. I think you have me confused with your daughter."

"You . . . tempted her. Didn't . . . you?"

The Diva stared into the eyes of the old witch, satisfied that the pieces were coming together. Her ego was satiated. She had, in fact, put some things in motion decades ago and it brought her joy to finally talk to someone other than Jacen Lucas about it.

"I've put a great many things in motion here, woman. I have waited centuries for what's to come, and I will see it through."

"You . . . will . . . be stopped," said Mary.

"Doubtful," said the Diva.

Staring up into the sky, the Diva saw the moon overhead in its majestic and blood red glory. She laughed. The glee she felt was unparalleled. After all this time, a Reckoning was coming. One that would see the end of the Twelve and reshape the world with her at the head.

"You're going to die, witch. And your soul is going to be trapped inside this soon-to-be cold and rotting corpse. Gone are the heroes who could stop what I've put into motion. I'm so very sorry for you. Sorry that you'll miss this new era of magic and mayhem."

The Diva chuckled at Mary's pained attempts to move, to attack, to will some sort of energy to get her out of where she was. She chuckled, and then became bored. Placing one hand underneath Mary's head and the other over her mouth and nose, the Diva held tight, pressed slightly, and waited until Mary's beating heart stopped.

"Blessed be," said the Diva.

As the Diva walked away, she waved her hand, and just as the other bodies had, Mary Leeds began burning from the inside out.

CENTURIES AGO

"You have the power to end this!" screamed Hecate.

"I have the power to end a great many things. But this . . ."

Hecate watched Zeus turn his back to her and walk away. Each step increased her anger. She pulled at the chains keeping her hands and arms bound above her. Her steps forward hindered by those and the ones around her ankles. The chains of mortals would do little to stop her. Had a mortal been lucky enough to bind her at all, she would have broken free with the slightest gesture. But these? Hephaestus forged these chains. Responsible for the greatest weapons ever created, Hephaestus' genius knew no limits. Hecate knew her shackles were unbreakable. Yet another sign that the Olympians had turned against her. Despite all the help she'd given, they turned on her.

Even *she* had turned against her.

"Persephone," she whispered as her arms went slack and her head fell.

"She can't help you now, either," said a disembodied voice.

Hecate knew that voice. It was deep, yet soft. Most gods, those who did not truly know him, feared him. He was, after all, the one being capable of killing them all. Many questioned why he did not take his place as King of the Gods. Why had he stepped aside for the likes of Cronus, and later, Zeus? His reply was simple and logical. He was the Death God. He was needed at the end of one's journey, not the beginning, or on the actual life path. If he were King, he could not tend to his duties. Duties that made him everything he was and would ever be.

A cloud of dark gray vapor coalesced across from Hecate. She lifted her head and watched Thanatos take form. Tall, regal, and imposing, Thanatos stood before her in dark purple robes, his blue eyes shining bright. He was among the most beautiful of the gods. It was his station and the power that came with it that made others wary. It was his station that brought him here before her.

"No, she can't," said Hecate. "And I don't know that she even would. She's a coward. Just like all of you."

She saw Thanatos flinch at that. She didn't care. She had supported them, then she dared to hold up a mirror to them, showing the hypocrisy that ran unchecked through Olympus. In the end, Hecate was cast aside easily and condemned to death. Had she been a male, had she been Zeus, none of this would be spoken of. But she was neither male nor the King of the Gods, so she was here, awaiting the Death God to carry out her sentence.

"We are older than them, the twelve," said Hecate. "Yet here we are. Their slaves. Lapdogs. Nothing but playthings and servants for them to use and discard as they see fit. I have known you for centuries, Thanatos. You've been friend and brother over that time. How can you—"

"Not with ease," said the Death God. "There is no joy in me to do this."

"Then don't do it."

"I have no choice!" bellowed Thanatos. "I entered a covenant with the Twelve, just as I did with the Titans before them. I have one function. As the keeper of the Scythe of Cronus, I am charged with maintaining the natural order. I wield that power, so they do not become drunk with theirs, as the gods are prone to do."

"And you think that's what I've done?"

"You bewitched that child and—"

"I did no such thing! How dare you! How dare any of you! When the Twelve fought against the Titans I stood with them, knowing that if they lost, my life was forfeit. When Demeter's daughter was taken, it was I who stepped up to help her. None of the others lifted a finger. Not ever her own father. Her *father*! Who was just as complicit in the abduction as the kidnapper himself. Now I ask you, Death God, where is the justice for their transgression? Why am I here and not them?"

"There is no proof that they—"

"There is no proof that I bewitched Persephone!"

"There is her word," said Thanatos.

"Her word. Her *word*? The word of a woman afraid to stand up to Hades and Zeus. The word of a woman who's lived her life through her mother and never dared to venture away from the thoughts that others put in her head... until me. Until I challenged her to think critically, to question, to wonder. I gave her that, and just like the others she's all but spat at me with her lies."

Hecate sat with those words for a moment. She thought of the days and nights she'd spent with Persephone, talking, exploring magic, dreaming of a world that was different. They'd done nothing more than talk of their feelings. They'd spoken of truths in the celestial world that went ignored and wondered together what, if anything, they should do.

Hades overheard them.

Persephone hated her situation. She hated the fact that she was the wife of a man she did not know, let alone love. The only joy she'd found was her time with Hecate. She'd told the goddess of witchcraft as much. And in the end, Persephone let her fear overpower her heart. Hecate felt the weight of that all over again in this moment.

"I am . . . sorry," said Thanatos.

Hecate laughed.

"You doubt me?"

"Just because you're here, now, without the scythe, doesn't mean you're sorry. Tomorrow, you'll return with it, and you'll end my existence, simply because it's your duty. Like her, you ignore loyalty and friendship and replace it with duty."

"I . . . don't know what to say. I'm sorry you see it that way," said Thanatos.

Hecate laughed again. Tears flowed a bit as she did. When she stopped, she stared at her one-time friend. She held his gaze for several beats, speaking without words, allowing her eyes to express her pain, her anger, and her hatred.

"Know this, Death God. I hate you. I hate you as much as I hate the Twelve. For the rest of your days, you will feel the despair I do. You will never know love. If you have children, they will feel the despair that I do now. Love, true lasting love, will remain out of your reach and just out the grasp of all your offspring. This . . . I swear."

Hecate did not expect Thanatos to tremble or make any pleas. She would have hated him more if he had. He simply inclined his head, gave a short nod, then shimmered away. Out of frustration, she pulled at her chains again and again. Not only did her godly strength do nothing, neither did her magic. Hecate, goddess of magic and witchcraft, was powerless.

"You'll need more than empty words to exact that revenge," said another voice.

From around the corner and out of the shadows walked the ancient deity with whom she shared a disdain for the Twelve.

"Where have you been?" asked Hecate.

"Oh, you know me, my dear. Here and there," said the goddess.

"Trying hard to maintain my mantle as the black sheep of the family."

"Ever the Diva," said Hecate.

"Indeed. But that is not important here. What is important, is getting you out of here so you can exact the revenge you spoke of."

"Time has not healed your anger toward Thanatos?"

"Time has not healed my anger toward many. Certainly not Thanatos. Given what the gods have done to you, they all deserve . . . something. Wouldn't you say?"

Hecate simply nodded.

"I thought you'd agree. I'm going to free you tonight. What you do with your freedom is your business, but I ask of you two things."

"Name them," said Hecate.

"One, that you carry out the curse on Thanatos and his children as you promised."

"And two?"

"That when I call upon you for a favor in the future, you acquiesce, no questions asked."

Hecate stared into the eyes of the goddess. She was desperate for freedom. Desperate to exact her revenge. But did she want to be indebted to this goddess? No good could come from that. Could it? This woman was powerful but unpredictable. She knew loyalty to no one save herself.

"These chains are unbreakable. Only Hephaestus himself can free me."

"Oh, I am well aware," said the goddess. "My love. Come here, please."

From around the darkened corner, Hephaestus limped into view. His skin was covered in soot and sweat. He looked every bit the blacksmith that he was. He also looked . . . enchanted. His eyes, while blue, were cloudy.

"What have you done to him?" asked Hecate.

"Oh," began the goddess, "he thinks I'm Aphrodite. And his love for her knows no bounds. He's willing to do anything for her. Even. Free. You."

Hecate's eyes widened. She had not realized that the goddess had the power to enchant another god. But she was among the first created. A primordial deity with the very powers of Chaos coursing through her veins. Realizing that, the shock lessened. Hecate felt the corners of her mouth curl into a smile. She could be free. She could exact her revenge. And perhaps, just perhaps, her new benefactor would delight in assisting her with clearing her name, while dispensing some mayhem along the way.

"I take it from that smile that you agree," said the goddess.

"I most wholeheartedly do," said Hecate.

"My love," said the goddess, gesturing to Hephaestus to remove the shackles.

Hecate felt immense relief as her arms lowered. Once her legs were free, she stepped forward, closed her eyes, held out her arms, and allowed her powers to rush through her body. After a few beats, her metallic blue eyes shown bright, and she smiled wide. Turning toward the Smith God and the goddess, Hecate bowed slightly in gratitude. When the goddess returned the bow, Hecate felt all concerns about their partnership drift away.

"I'm off to raise some hell," said Hecate.

"I'll see you around."

As the goddess and Hephaestus shimmered away, Hecate exited the cave that was her brief prison. She looked out on the night sky and took a deep breath. Allowing her magic to build, she murmured a few words in an ancient tongue and pointed both hands, palms out, at the moon. As the large, bright white orb turned blood red, she laughed.

"Let's begin," she said.

CHAPTER THIRTY-SEVEN

"THAT'S NOT POSSIBLE. THANATOS HAD NO DAUGHTERS," SAID HADES.

"Yeah, well, it's not like I can do a DNA test, right? But I have it on good authority that he had at least one," said Kassidy.

The silence filled the room. Kassidy wasn't sure how to take that, but she also didn't much care. She did find it curious, though, that Hades, Lord of the Underworld and one of the Twelve, was unaware of her existence. And beyond that, unaware of her recent ascension.

"I guess there's no newsletter on Olympus, or wherever you guys hang out," she said.

"You expect me to believe that you are the daughter of Thanatos. That you killed his second, Azra-El. And then ascended," said Hades with calm skepticism.

"I've got a big shiny glowstick to prove it."

Kassidy allowed her power to fill her. She felt the shift in her eye color and heard audible gasps from both Hades and Persephone. The Scythe of Cronus powered up. Red and purple energy crackled from the blade. To add flair to the moment, Kassidy twirled the blade, performing a kata of sorts to display her mastery of a weapon that was unconventional in battle, at best.

"Impressive," said Persephone.

Kassidy felt genuine admiration from the goddess. She also felt a sense of familiarity. Mostly with her story, nothing more.

Like Kassidy's mother, Persephone had been taken against her will and forced into a marriage that she did not desire. Kassidy empathized with her, acknowledged Persephone with a slight nod, then focused her attention on the scythe, held it in front of her, and released it. The blade hovered for a moment, hummed with energy, then, in a flash of electricity and light, vanished.

"What did you do?" asked Hades.

"I put it away. Some place safe. Some place only I can get to."

"Impressive, indeed," said the underworld lord with a look toward his wife.

Kassidy sensed admiration in him as well. But underneath, there was something else. Confusion, and fear. Hades, was afraid. Of her? At this point, Kassidy was not sure, but it was something to monitor.

"If you are the daughter of Thanatos, as you claim," began Hades, "why are you here? What business do you have in my domain?"

"Trust me, I am not here by choice. In fact, I tried to leave, and I was unable. Something here is blocking me."

"There are no wards or spells that block a god from entering or leaving this domain," said Hades.

"Perhaps she's not who she claims after all," said Persephone, with a wry grin.

Kassidy wasn't quite sure how to take her. The admiration was still there, but there was something else within. It was not confusion and fear, like her consort. Persephone was giving off some aspect of hope, of excitement . . . or wonder. Kassidy filed that away also.

"Look," began Kassidy, "I landed here pretty hard, and I've been unable to leave. Believe me or don't. Either way, just help me get out of here. I'll be out of your hair, and we'll all be happy."

"If what you say is true, tell me how you came to be here," said Hades.

Kassidy hesitated. All of this, the world of gods, was still very new to her. As a Reaper, she had been under the guidance of Azra-El. She learned early on that it was actually Thanatos who was regarded as the Death God, but given that he wasn't around, she, like many Reapers, assumed him to be nothing more than a figurehead. A being worshipped by Reapers because of his role in an ancient mythology. To find out the truth was shocking, to say the least.

As were the subsequent truths that followed.

In any event, recent revelations about herself, her lineage, and this world of gods did not make her anxious to join the immortal union and go to godly cookouts and pool parties. If anything, she was even more wary than before her ascension. She placed no trust in the two standing before her. The fact that Hades was harboring some fear of her, of the blade, was of no consequence. She didn't know him, and she didn't know Persephone, and she wanted nothing to do with whatever drama might result in learning more about them. But she needed to get back. And at this point, she had no choice but to trust.

"I was sent here by a witch," said Kassidy.

"A witch?" asked Hades. "But there is no witch powerful enough to best a god."

"Not anymore," said Persephone.

Kassidy saw an uneasy glance directed at Hades from his wife. There was something more to those words. Something important. It was palpable.

"What does that mean?" asked Kassidy.

Now, the hesitation belonged to the lord and lady of the underworld. After a few beats, Persephone spoke.

"What do you know of the goddess, Hecate?"

returned, "Hecate turned against the Twelve, and a trial was held. The sentence passed was death, which, as you know, can only happen one way with a god."

"The Scythe of Cronus," whispered Kassidy.

"With the help of an unknown immortal, Hecate escaped and began to wreak havoc for centuries. Eventually, she was found, and the sentence carried out."

Kassidy stood in stunned silence, uncertain how to feel about the story. From what she'd heard, and those she read in her mother's journal, nothing about her father seemed redeemable. Yet, he'd helped her. Right before her ascension, those few moments when Azra-El had the upper hand, she'd been cast into the Void. It was there that she heard her father's voice. It was *he* who encouraged *her*. He who reminded her of just who she was and what her legacy was. There was love and compassion in what he'd said.

How can this be the same person?

"So, my father, um . . ." Kassidy let the words trail off and collected herself. "So, if she's gone, then she can't be the one doing this. Wait, why would she be the only one capable of doing this to a god?"

"She was the goddess of witchcraft," said Persephone.

"Right. So, what? That makes her extra powerful?" asked Kassidy. But as she pondered the question even more, awareness sparked. "Oh, shit."

"What is it, Death God. Speak," said Hades.

"The person who sent me here is a witch. Only . . ."

"Only what?" asked Persephone.

"Only, she's not been herself lately. It's almost as if something else is guiding her, pushing her, causing her to do things that I know she would not normally do. She just feels different."

"What do you mean?" asked Hades.

"This particular witch, Traci, I can't sense her at times. I can't feel her emotions consistently, and when I do, it's mostly confusion and anxiety. She's lost time, and in those moments it's like she's become someone else."

Kassidy felt a rush of concern from both beings standing before her. It almost sent her to her knees. She grabbed at her stomach and called to some power within to strengthen her resolve.

"Could it be?" asked Persephone, softly.

"Impossible," said Hades.

"You keep using that word," began Kassidy, "and somehow, you're wrong each time. Tell me what you know. Could it be what?"

Once again, the silence was heavy. Kassidy felt something she'd never felt in an immortal, except maybe Octavia, her aunt. She had not expected to sense it from a true god, though. Yet here it was, emanating from a most unexpected source.

Hades felt shame.

Kassidy trained her eyes on him. She stepped forward, and as she did, she allowed her power to fill her.

"Careful, Death God," said Hades. "This is my domain, and there are rules."

The air around them crackled. Electricity filled the air as the Scythe of Cronus reappeared and flew immediately to Kassidy's open hand.

"I don't give a fuck about your rules. The gods have been fucking with people for far too long. If those are the rules, I'll have no part of it. And, quite frankly, I'll happily use this blade to effect change. Now. Tell me. What. You. Know."

The fear and anxiety in Hades had returned. The hope and

admiration in Persephone had intensified. The goddess wanted Kassidy to act. She wanted her to do . . . something . . . anything. This was indeed interesting.

"Before your father took her life, Hecate cast a final spell. More of a vow, actually," said Hades.

"Go on."

"The spell she cast was one that was supposed to keep her spirit intact so that she could one day return in the body of a descendant. She dispersed her power to her living descendants so that it would exist throughout the blood line and be available for her return. She vowed, upon her return, to destroy the Twelve for their treachery."

A descendant?

"But your father said that the scythe would not even allow her spirit to survive," said Persephone. "Yet, if it was a witch who sent you, and you are truly unable to leave this place on your own, the only being with that knowledge and power was Hecate. Not even we are capable of trapping a god in our own domain."

"If she's come back, what happens to the spirit of the person she inhabits?" asked Kassidy.

"If she's somehow returned," began Hades, "there is no way to save the person she inhabits. Hecate will take complete control."

"There has to be a way."

"There is none," said Persephone. "And you'll know her power is full at the blood moon. An unnaturally occurring blood moon. That is the sign of her return. And . . ."

That pause meant nothing good, Kassidy was certain of it.

"And what?"

"And," began Hades, "so long as that blood moon exists, no soul can leave the body it's in."

"Wait . . . what?" asked Kassidy.

"Souls become trapped. They are unable to move on to the Beyond or to the Void," continued Hades.

"What if the body is dead?" asked Kassidy.

"Then the soul remains trapped in a mindless mass of flesh. The soul is conscious, but it does not control the body. It only provides enough spark to allow the body to fulfil its most basic need," said Hades.

"Sustenance," finished Persephone.

"So, what? Like, zombies?" asked Kassidy.

"Vrykolakas, in the old world. But yes. Zombies," said Hades.

"And as the goddess of witchcraft and sorcery, a natural psychopomp and necromancer, Hecate would be able to control them all," said Persephone.

Kassidy thought back to what Traci said at their last fight. She'd said the blood moon was coming, and she would not be stopped. Was that even Traci? Whether it was, or was not, there was no escaping the current reality. A vengeful Titan was returning with the ability to lead an army of the mindless zombies against . . . anything she wanted them to.

"I have to get out of here," Kassidy said.

"There is nothing stopping you," began Hades, "except maybe for Hecate's power."

"Then perhaps I can help," said Persephone. "I was trained by her. I have my own innate power along with the power of the underworld and some skills taught to me by the goddess herself. I can strengthen yours to help you escape this place."

"Why would you help me? It seemed like you were defending her a few moments ago."

Persephone looked from Kassidy to her husband, and back. There was clear tension.

"Hecate's trial was a farce," said Persephone.

"Hold your—"

"NO!" screamed Persephone. "It was a farce, and you know it. You and your brother lied about her, swayed the others, and because of that, she became what she is."

"And what is that?" asked Kassidy.

"Quite possibly the most dangerous being alive," said Persephone. "I don't want her dead. But I know she has to be stopped. Perhaps, Death God, you are the one to do it."

Kassidy nodded.

"I'll need you to focus. Focus your power, the power of the scythe, and try to find the frequency of my magic. Together, it should propel you from here."

"Okay," said Kassidy. "Wait. One more thing. Can I beat her?"

Kassidy watched as Hades and Persephone shared a look, only to return their gaze to her with shared silence. That silence spoke volumes. Volumes and volumes of dread.

Finally, he spoke.

"If the Scythe of Cronus was unable to destroy her before, I don't know what could possibly stop her now," said Hades.

"What about the Twelve? Can they help me? Can you convince them?" asked Kassidy.

"I will certainly report this, and we will no doubt act. I just don't know to what extent they will trust the daughter of the god who, unconsciously or otherwise, failed in his duty," said Hades.

In anger, Kassidy gripped the scythe even harder. She looked to Persephone and said, "Please get me the fuck out of here."

Persephone gave a nod and began whispering a spell. As she did, Kassidy lowered her head, concentrated, and called more power this time, drawing on the scythe itself to strengthen her. She searched for the frequency Persephone spoke of and felt a vibration in the air. She followed it. Soon, her entire body was aglow in blue flame. The ground beneath her shook, and the walls hummed and crumbled in some areas. As both Persephone and Hades took cover, Kassidy screamed.

And then she was gone.

CHAPTER THIRTY-EIGHT

WHEN JESSIE BURRELL WAS ALIVE, SHE'D BEEN IN THE BUSINESS OF helping others. She'd been known for her ability to be empathetic to strangers at a young age and felt the call to be of service to others throughout her teens and into adulthood. When she'd been tapped to become a Reaper, she jumped at the chance. The opportunity to remain of service to others at yet another crucial moment in their existence—the end—was an opportunity she could not pass up. As a human, she'd seen the best and worst of humanity, and she maintained that even at its worst, humanity was still worth fighting for—worth hoping for.

The image before her now was the first time she'd questioned that belief.

"My god," she'd whispered upon her arrival. Internally she repeated those words. It wasn't until she felt a tear travel down her cheek that she recognized the need to do something. Only, she didn't know what that was. Before her, around a stone altar, lay five women, burned, seemingly from the inside out. Their eyes were missing, nothing but smoldering embers now. Their mouths were open, perhaps from shock, likely from the screams of pain, yet within each mouth, more smoldering embers. Each of them lay on the ground, fully clothed, surrounded by scorched outlines of their bodies.

Jessie had never seen anything like this. She'd only been a Reaper a short time, brought to Azra-El by a Wraith who'd found her dead after she'd shielded an elderly man from harm during a botched store robbery. In a short time she'd escorted hundreds of souls to the Beyond or the Void. Some causes of death had been natural, others not so much. But this? This was something else entirely.

And there was a strange energy in the air.

She'd met Azra-El only one time. He'd given off an energy that was similar, but nowhere near as strong as what she was feeling now. It was his energy magnified one hundred-fold. She didn't know what it was. She'd asked other Reapers who'd admitted to feeling it, too, but none had an explanation. They simply assumed that it was the power of the Primus. But he was dead now. So, who then was responsible for this?

Stretching out with her power, Jessie sent a telepathic message to Cyrus, one of the oldest Reapers. For centuries he'd been charged with guarding the Gladius de Bellum, also known as the Glade, the weapon of the War God, Ares. Recent events made that task unnecessary, and since then, he'd been tasked with serving as guide and mentor to Reapers. Some say he even served as guide and mentor to the Death God herself.

Gossip did not seem to stop in any phase of existence.

Cyrus arrived almost immediately after Jessie made contact. His shock was visible. Subtle, but visible. The fact that someone as old as him could be shaken made Jessie feel a little better.

But not much.

"There are no souls here," said Cyrus.

"No," said Jessie.

"Did you help them already?"

"There were none when I arrived."

"Then how were you called?" asked Cyrus.

"I honestly have no idea. I just felt the pull of power to this location. When I arrived, this is what I found."

"Curious," said Cyrus as he walked the area and checked each body.

Reapers are called to souls at or near death. Most often it's the Reaper that's closest who feels the pull. When they arrive, they meet the soul as it's leaving the body, or they wait a short time until the soul is ready. That connection is made in the Nexus, and it's from there that the Reaper escorts the soul to the Beyond, or the Void. The fact that there were no souls here was disturbing and unnatural.

"What does it mean when we have bodies and no souls?" asked Jessie.

"Nothing good, that I can assure you," said Cyrus.

"What do we do?"

"We—"

Cyrus had abruptly stopped speaking. He was kneeling near a body that seemed to be at the head of the altar. Something about the woman seemed to catch him off guard. Jessie wasn't certain what it was, but his reaction was concerning.

"What is it?" she asked.

"Do you feel that?"

"The energy, right? Yes. It's heavy. It was like the energy of the Primus, but so much more powerful and—"

"Concentrated," finished Cyrus, looking up at Jessie.

She nodded in agreement.

"This is not good."

"You know what it is?"

This time Cyrus nodded. Jessie watched as he slowly stood and closed his eyes. She felt a tingle of energy escaping him. It was nothing more than Reaper magic, but there was an added intensity to it. She wasn't certain what he was doing, but seconds later she felt the hair on the back of her neck stand up. Before she knew it, there was a short flash of light, and then *she* was there.

Jessie had heard stories of the new Death God, but she never imagined she'd see her in person. Her dark hair and metallic blue eyes commanded respect.

"Kassidy, thank you for coming," said Cyrus.

He called her by her name?

"Of course, Cyrus. And . . . I'm sorry for not coming when you requested me before. Things have been rather bat-shit crazy, for lack of a better term. You'll never believe where I just left. There's trouble, and I'm likely going to need your help. We'll get to that later, though. What's happened here?"

She sounded so, ordinary. Jessie wasn't sure what she expected, but it wasn't that. Jessie was so caught up, she hadn't heard Cyrus calling her name. It was at that moment that she realized she'd been staring at Kassidy Simmons since her arrival.

"Jessie!" yelled Cyrus.

"Huh? Um . . . sorry," she said, averting her gaze. "Um . . . what was the question?"

"Tell Kassidy what you found when you arrived."

"Oh . . . right. So, pretty much what you see here. I felt this pull, kind of like what you feel when a soul is ready to move on. It was, I don't know, intermittent, I guess."

"Like static?" asked Kassidy.

"Yeah. Um . . . yes," corrected Jessie, trying not to sound too casual. It garnered a grin from Kassidy.

"Are you okay?" asked Kassidy.

"Yeah. Um, sorry. Yes. Yes, I'm good. It's just . . ."

"Just what?" asked Kassidy.

"I guess I just never expected to meet you. And I didn't expect you to be so—"

"Normal?" finished Kassidy.

Jessie nodded, embarrassed.

"First time meeting a god?" asked Kassidy with a slight grin.

Jessie nodded again, confused at the question.

"It's all good," said Kassidy, still chuckling. "Despite the fact that I'm the Death God, from what I've learned about the others, recently in fact, I'm probably the one you really want to hang out with."

It was the wink after that statement that mostly caught Jessie off guard. The other shock was the fact that there were, in fact, other gods. What kind of world had she gotten herself into?

"So, the pull was intermittent like static, it called you here, and you found this?" asked Kassidy.

Jessie nodded.

"Didn't get a sense that anyone else was here or had recently left?" asked Kassidy, kneeling to inspect the body nearest her.

"I think there was someone else here. Besides these five, there's physical evidence of a sixth person that stood in that spot," said Jessie, pointing to a spot across from the altar. "That person was outside the ring of five and I feel pretty confident they escaped. Or at least, escaped this fate. These poor women were basically cooked from the inside out. Once I got over the shock and surprise of that, I started to feel that residual energy. Like the Primus had."

Jessie felt an unmistakable shift in the Death God at the mention of the Primus. She'd heard the stories, and they'd been repeated so often, with so few changes in the details, that she had no reason to suspect they weren't true. Kassidy Simmons, former Reaper, had dispatched Azra-El. Strangely, there were no parts of Jessie that felt that she should be loyal to Azra-El, so the circumstances leading up to and surrounding his demise were of no consequence. It was just all so weird.

"My apologies," began Jessie, "I didn't mean to—"

"You haven't done anything wrong," said Kassidy. "It's perfectly okay to bring up his name. He was a duplicitous, dark-hearted, piece of shit. But I'm not out to banish people who mention his name nor am I out to erase his name from history. It's all good."

And it was. Jessie felt that as plain as she'd felt the energy in the air.

"If I may?" asked Jessie. "The energy I felt when he was around, the energy that I felt here, I . . . um . . ."

"Feel it in me?" finished Kassidy.

Jessie nodded.

"What you're feeling," began Kassidy, "is god power. You felt it in Azra-El because a large portion of his power came from the god that made him. All Reapers have it, just not in the concentration that he did and certainly nowhere near the concentration that I do. I was a Reaper once, like you. What he didn't know when he made me, though, was that the blood of a god runs through my veins. That's why I was so much stronger than most Reapers. It's also why I was eventually able to dispatch him and his Wraiths. So, what you're feeling here, in this place, means that a god was here. A *god* is responsible for killing these women."

"Perhaps the sixth person that was standing outside the circle?" asked Jessie.

"Gods don't stand outside of circles. They like to be seen. Present company excluded. Whoever that sixth person was, they either managed to get away or they were taken. Let's hope it's the former, not the latter."

"Kassidy," said Cyrus, gesturing for her come to him. "There's a very large concentration in this body."

Jessie moved toward the body, reaching it before Kassidy.

Like the others, it was still smoldering from the inside.

"Oh my god!" exclaimed Kassidy.

"What is it?" asked Cyrus.

Jessie watched Kassidy fall to her knees. Once again, the ultimate power in the Reaper world seemed all too human. Jessie was no empath, but she was quite observant. She'd studied people her entire life, and what she saw here was shock, sadness, and recognition.

Kassidy knew this woman.

"This woman . . . is Mary Leeds," said Kassidy. "She's a witch."

"You knew her?" asked Cyrus.

"She's my girlfriend's mother."

Jessie's heart sank, yet in the back of her mind, she dared to wonder what the Death God would do to whoever was responsible for this. She stopped wondering when she saw Kassidy eyes shift to metallic blue. They grew brighter.

And brighter.

And brighter.

And then, an odd thing happened. Kassidy tilted her head, as if listening for something, or someone. Jessie looked around to see if anyone was approaching, but there was no one. Turning her attention back to the Death God, Jessie felt her pulse quicken at the sight of Kassidy's eyes growing wide with concern.

"Keiron!" screamed Kassidy.

And then she was gone.

Jessie looked to Cyrus for answers, but her mentor simply lowered his head.

"What do we do?" she asked.

"Prepare," said Cyrus.

"For what?"

"I wish I knew."

CHAPTER THIRTY-NINE

KEIRON WAS SOMEWHERE AROUND TEN YEARS OLD WHEN HE discovered he was a son of Cronus. Up to that point he assumed that his athletic prowess, fast healing, and heightened senses were the result of his mother's lineage. It was said that his mother was Philyra, daughter of Oceanus, a Titan. He'd never met her though. He was given the name Chiron at birth, and in the myths and legends of ancient Greece, the people believed he was a centaur—the half horse-half human offspring of a tryst between Cronus, leader of the Titans and Philyra. Those same myths say that Cronus' true wife, Rhea, caught Cronus and Philyra in the act, and the Titan lord transformed into a stallion and galloped away. The Ancient Greeks believed that the transformation resulted in Chiron's half equine appearance, an appearance that so disgusted his mother that she abandoned him.

The truth was much more tragic, and all too human.

Philyra, madly in love with Cronus, expected more from their affair. She expected to be taken as his bride. She thought their son would bring him around to her way of thinking, but it did not. Humiliated and ashamed, she abandoned her son because the very sight of him stirred up feelings of anger.

Keiron was instead raised by a kind man. A man who taught him the art of healing—medicines and herbs. A man who taught him how to be a warrior and a hunter, but also taught him how to love and appreciate music, poetry, and the arts. It was because of that man that Keiron was widely regarded as wise yet fierce. It was that man, that god, Apollo, who made Keiron the man he would become. Keiron was fierce indeed, and very loyal. He was also one who felt deeply. And as he entered the home of Octavia Lord, his friend for centuries, he felt the loss of her in each step he took.

Octavia's home was modest, but it was a true reflection of her. She was a warrior, trained by Keiron, and she was also a student of life, of people, of the arts—an attempt to atone for her own sins and the death and chaos she'd caused from jealousy. She was his oldest friend and confidante. Together they'd worked to ensure Kassidy's safety as a child and watched over her as she grew. The decision to watch over her instead of raising her, or at least telling her of her heritage, may not have been the best, but it seemed right at the time.

And now Octavia was gone.

And he was in her home, packing her things, as the prospect of death and destruction loomed.

"Need a hand?" said a voice from behind.

Keiron turned quickly, hands moved to the small of his back where he kept two onyx daggers, deadly to humans and some immortals, like him.

"Sorry, I didn't mean to startle you."

"Traci? What are you doing here?"

"Yeah, um, I kinda followed you here."

A sense of unease settled in the pit of Keiron's stomach. Part of being the skilled warrior that he was meant that he also had heightened awareness to go along with his senses and athletic ability. The fact that a human, witch or not, could follow him undetected gave him pause. His grief was affecting him. And with so much uncertainty about what was to come, his clouded thinking could mean his very life.

"Is something wrong? Is Kassidy okay?" asked Keiron, trying desperately to regroup and hide his concerns.

"Oh, um . . . she's fine," said Traci.

Keiron noticed a quick shift in her demeanor. Immediately he realized that perhaps that wasn't the question to ask. He'd only known Traci a short time, and in that time only really knew what Kassidy had shared with him. Perhaps she was seeking his help for more than Kassidy. Perhaps she was seeking his help to better understand the chaos that surrounded them all.

"I'm sorry," he said. "I should have been more sensitive. How are *you*, Traci?"

As she stepped farther into Octavia's home, something deeply rooted in Keiron's gut suggested he be on guard. Traci was a witch, he wasn't sure how powerful. Not even Kassidy knew. But there'd never been any occurrence to suggest that she was less than trustworthy. On the surface, she simply was not a threat.

"You know, that's the million-dollar question, isn't it? How am I? How am I coping with my Death God girlfriend and her band of supernatural friends and enemies? I . . . I just don't know, Keiron."

The closer she got to him, the more his gut told him to be prepared, for anything. But all he saw was a young woman casually dressed—seemingly innocent. Nothing to be worried about.

"Why don't we sit and talk," said Keiron, gesturing to the couch.

"No. No, no, no, no, NO!" she replied in escalating tone.

Keiron felt the twist in his gut. The call to his warrior spirit was sounded.

"Okay. We don't have to sit. Tell me what's on your mind."

As Traci walked toward him, he saw a visible shift in her demeanor. Her gait was slow, and she never lost eye contact with him. She grinned, then bit her bottom lip as they stood face to face. Traci placed both hands on his chest, then slowly moved them up to his neck.

"Traci? What are you doing?"

"Mm. Nothing," she said, pulling him in for a deep kiss.

Keiron's mind swam for the briefest of moments before he attempted to pull away. He found, though, that he couldn't. Using all the strength he had, he could not break her hold or the kiss. After what seemed like an eternity, Traci pulled back slightly, then nuzzled his neck. She licked and kissed, and again her grip was like iron.

"Traci? Please!"

She stopped, but she did not break her grasp of him. Instead . . . she sniffed. Once again, the warrior within screamed for him to act, but instead, he called her name again, continuing to insist she stop.

"Traci," began Keiron, "You have to stop this. Come on. Let's sit and—"

The last word never saw the light of day. Keiron's surprise at her behavior was replaced by the shock of a blade buried in his gut. Eyes wide, he looked down as she broke their embrace and saw that the blade was his. He reached for his second dagger, but it was gone.

In the hands of Traci.

Whose eyes had turned metallic blue.

"You have the blood of the Titans in your veins!"

"Traci?" Keiron whispered as he dropped to one knee.

"Who are you?" she demanded, stepping closer.

Keiron felt the dagger twist in his gut as she turned the

weapon and demanded answers. He screamed. He'd not heard his own scream in centuries. It was so foreign to him, and at the same time, the most frightening sound he'd ever encountered.

Is this the end?

"Who are you, damn you?"

His shock kept him silent. He didn't know what to think. He didn't know how to respond. All Keiron knew in this moment was agonizing pain.

"Very well! Keep your secrets. You will die, just as they all will. You all turned against me. Took everything from me—including my very life. I promised you I'd return. I promised you all I'd return and kill you all. And you, will be the first."

In the back of Keiron's mind, awareness trickled in. The words, the strength, the eyes. It was her. She had returned.

"Y-Y-You . . ."

Keiron felt the harsh embrace of the witch before him, followed by the white-hot sensation of his onyx dagger in his back. The last thing he heard was laughter. The last thing he saw was the body of Traci Leeds, inhabited by another, shimmering out of view. As he lay on the floor, looking around, surrounded by the essence of his oldest friend, he whispered a name with as much strength as he could muster.

"K-K-K-Kassidy . . . help. She's returned."

CENTURIES AGO

Hecate once again found herself chained to a rock face, bound by the manacles forged by Hephaestus. The same manacles that nullified her power.

"You've been on the run for centuries. Wreaking havoc on Earth. You've caused wars and countless deaths, all in your desire for vengeance against the Twelve," said Thanatos.

"Is there a point to this?" asked Hecate.

"Why? Why would you do this? You are powerful, and you are wise. Your experience, the respect you'd earned, all of it could have been used to usher in change. Instead, you gave in to your anger, let it fester, let it grow into this hatred—"

"And now, here we are again," said Hecate. "How did you find me?"

Thanatos remained silent. He was protecting someone. He was protecting *him*.

"The Tracker!" she spat. "Damn him!"

The Tracker was practically a legend among the mortals. No one knew his true identity. They only knew that Zeus used him exclusively for special tasks. Tasks that required discretion, cunning, and instinct to survive. It was rumored that the Tracker was also a son of Cronus, but, as with many rumors among the immortals, it just floated around in the ether with no one able or willing to substantiate it.

"Then he too will die at my hands," said Hecate.

Thanatos paced in front of her.

"You were seen with a book. I assume it was your grimoire?" asked Thanatos.

Hecate answered with silence.

"Where is it?"

"Why? Planning to destroy that along with me?"

"I may have to. I don't know what you've done to it. With you gone, there could be repercussions that we are not aware of."

"Could be, indeed," said Hecate, grinning.

Thanatos extended a hand and squeezed. Hecate felt her insides seize. Her lungs and heart felt compressed. Breathing was strained. She didn't even have enough air to let out a scream. Seconds of torture felt like hours. When he released her, she wanted to collapse to the ground, but the overhead chains held her hands causing her to simply slump forward.

"I'm sorry," said Thanatos. "I don't want to do this. It's not my way."

Hecate knew that to be true. He was still prone to outbursts and intense emotional reactions, but never when carrying out his duty as Death God. He respected the journey of life to death and took great pride in ensuring that even those that went to the Void did so with dignity. No, torture was not his way. Which made this time with him that much more heartbreaking.

And infuriating.

"They are using you!" she screamed with as much breath as she could gather. "You have to stop them. Take control. If you won't, then work with me. Work with—"

"I will never work with *her*!" shouted Thanatos.

Hecate stopped breathing for a moment. Not because of Thanatos, but because of his words. He knew. He knew who she was aligned with.

"Thanatos, please. Hear me out," said Hecate.

"There is nothing you can say that will make me align with you two. I should take your life for simply associating with her.

Do you know what she could do? What she's done?"

"Then why don't you kill her, too?"

Silence filled the space between them. Hecate felt her anger swell. She knew all too well the reason that he would not kill the goddess in question.

"She will be dealt with," began Thanatos, "but we are here about you now. Tell me where the grimoire is. Tell me if you've done anything to it before I fulfill my duty."

Hecate spat at his feet.

"Very well," said Thanatos.

As Thanatos reached over his right shoulder to retrieve the Scythe of Cronus, Hecate began whispering. The manacles she wore nullified the physical manifestation of her powers and prevented her from using spells to free herself, but they could not sever her connection with her grimoire. That book was as much a part of her as lightning to Zeus, or the Scythe of Cronus to Thanatos. Her whispers continued as the scythe came to life with a low hum.

"It brings me no pleasure to do this," said Thanatos.

"And I will feel so much pleasure when I return," said Hecate.

She saw awareness in the eyes of the Death God, just as he prepared to swing his blade. When he stopped, she screamed.

"Do it! Do it, damn you!" she bellowed.

Instead, Thanatos held the blade out, and seconds later, a rift formed. Within that rift, Hecate saw a fate worse than death. She saw a world from which she might not return.

"No! No! Not there! Kill me! Kill me as your masters ordered!"

With a sweep of his hand, Thanatos cast Hecate into the rift, then sealed it with the scythe. Even closed, Hecate's screams echoed.

CHAPTER FORTY

"OH NO! NO, NO, NO, NO, NO, NO!"

Kassidy raced to Keiron's side. She did not dare pull the daggers out. She knew the effects of the onyx blade on immortals like him. Before her ascension, she fought Wraiths alongside him and Octavia, and while the odds were an even three on three, the battle took a toll. Two of the three wraiths were dispatched, but both Keiron and Octavia had taken some heavy damage from onyx blades. Octavia's were heavy, but she eventually healed. Keiron's were minor, and he healed faster. That was when she learned that they were both immortal, when she learned Keiron was a son of Cronus.

She hoped that fact would help him now.

"Keiron! Keiron, can you hear me?" she asked, silently pleading with him to wake up.

Had he been mortal, pulling out those daggers would be certain death. He'd bleed out, and she'd be escorting his soul in mere minutes. There was blood, he was covered in it, but in checking his life aura, she saw the golden light intact. It was dim, but present. That was a good sign.

"K-Kass?" he whispered.

"Keiron? Hey, I'm here. I'm here, old man," she said.

"Re-re-respect . . . your . . . elders," said Keiron.

Kassidy laughed through the tears that began to fall. "Just shut it, book man," she said, calling upon a name she'd not used with him in years.

"Kass . . . you need . . . to know . . . what . . . happened . . . here."

Seeing him this weak was hard. So hard that she hadn't even thought to ask who did it. She was so focused on him, his pain, and making him well, that she'd forgotten that this was an attack.

"Let's worry about getting you cared for first. Then we can go after the son of bitch who did this," said Kassidy.

"No . . . Kass . . ."

Kassidy didn't hear him. She reached out with her powers and called the Scythe of Cronus to her. There was a loud pop as electricity and light filled the air. But nothing came.

"Fuck! Not this shit again!"

Kassidy tried again and again. The light show was there, but the blade would not break through. As frustration settled in, she channeled every bit of the strength she had within. In moments, the scythe, her weapon, her tool, was in her hand.

But it was taxing.

"Kass . . ." whispered Keiron, his words going unheard again.

"Alright, all you need to do is concentrate and we'll get you—"

"No!" yelled Keiron as he grabbed Kassidy's arm.

It startled her. His sudden strength, his forceful grab. She didn't think he had enough strength and energy for either. The fact that he'd done so . . . it meant something. Kassidy had known him long enough to know when she needed to shut up and listen. She didn't always do it, but she was getting better.

"I'm listening," she said.

"Traci is . . . in trouble."

Kassidy's heart sank at those words.

"Did she . . . do this . . . ?"

His slow nod of acknowledgment made her stomach tighten. She gripped the scythe harder, both out of anger, and also fear.

What had she done? What was she becoming? *Who*, was she becoming?

"You must . . . understand," began Keiron, "it's not . . . it's not . . ."

"Keiron! Keiron! Stay with me! Let me use the scythe to heal you. I can do this."

"No! You mustn't. The . . . repercussions."

That damned word. What good was being a Death God, with the power to heal and resurrect, if you weren't supposed to use it? Why give them that ability? Kassidy's anger mounted. She didn't want a drink though. She wanted to destroy something. She wanted to fight. She wished there were still Wraiths around. She wished she could get her hands on the big bad causing the current problems. Because it wasn't Traci. It couldn't be.

"Tell me what she said when she did this," said Kassidy.

"It's . . . not . . . her," began Keiron, "it's—"

"Hecate."

Keiron's slow nod provided confirmation. A part of Kassidy felt relief. Relief that her girlfriend had not, in fact, turned evil. That relief was fleeting, though, because instead of simply dealing with a witch, Kassidy would now have to do battle with a god—again. This battle would not likely go the way her fight went with Jaxon. Jaxon was one of the Twelve. Their power was great, individually, but it did not compare to the might of a Death God. Hecate though, was a Titan. And not just any Titan. If not for the combined might of the Twelve, and Thanatos, Hecate would never have been caught, tried, and subsequently killed.

"I don't know what to do," said Kassidy. "I'm not strong enough to battle a Titan. And . . . I can't kill Traci."

"She's . . . already . . . de—"

"No!" Kassidy screamed. "No! I don't accept that! I can heal you now. I can fix her. I can do all that. I just have to find a way to pull Hecate out. Once she's out, we can fight her together. We'll get Jaxon. We can all do it if we work together. Just like the Twelve did before."

"Kassidy," said Keiron.

He got her whole name out this time. When Keiron did that, it was the equivalent of her father, Dan, or her mother, Marlene, calling her by her full name. Keiron was strong. He was fierce. He suffered no beast or monster. And he did not bullshit Kassidy. Ever.

And so, she cried.

The weight of her power was one thing, and she was learning to bear it. She was learning to wield it properly and purposefully. The greater weight, though, was the limitations of her powers. Not so much the things she couldn't do, but the things she *shouldn't* do. Bringing back Anna DeBartolo was one of those things. But she owed a debt. At least, Death owed a debt. And as she was currently assuming that role, she paid it. Healing Keiron with the scythe might be one of those things she shouldn't do as well. She wasn't sure. She had no idea what his fate was, and for the first time she wondered if that was something she should know. Wasn't the death date something a Death God should know? Keiron was immortal. The son of a Titan. He had the ability to heal, but his wounds were grave. With the scythe, she could slow down time, give him time to heal on his own. Would that be manipulation, too?

Then, it hit her.

"Keiron, I need you. I can't lose you. I'm not ready to do this shit without you. I'm going to find a way to get you healed."

"Kassidy . . . no," said Keiron as her eyes shown blue.

A beat passed, and then Kassidy and Keiron both found themselves in the Nexus.

"Wh-wh-what is this?"

"This is my home," said Kassidy. "I may not be allowed to change things out there, in the real world. But this place? This place belongs to me. And I'll be damned if anyone is going to tell me what I can and cannot do in my house."

The daggers remained in Keiron, but there was no more bleeding. At least, not at the rate there was in the real world. Time in the Nexus worked differently. Slowly.

"Stay here. I'll have a Reaper watch over you. When I return for you, I'll have solutions. You're not going anywhere, old man. I won't allow it."

Kassidy watched Keiron's eyes close, and then saw his smile. After contacting a Reaper to watch over him, she called to Cyrus. Moments later, he appeared before her. When he saw Keiron's body, his look darkened.

"Oh, no," he said. "What's happened? What can I do?"

"There's a battle coming, Cyrus. A battle that I have to fight. One that I cannot win by myself."

"I'm here for you, Kassidy. Again, what can I do?"

Kassidy took a moment, quickly running through the thoughts in her mind, weighing all the consequences of her decisions, her actions, reactions, and inactions. She needed to end this. She needed to end it now.

"You were closest to the Glade. It's connected to the War God. I need you to find him."

"As you wish," said Cyrus, before transitioning back to the real world.

As he dematerialized into vapor and left, Kassidy took one last look at Keiron. "I'll fix this," she said.

Then she left the Nexus, mentally preparing for the fight of her life.

CHAPTER FORTY-ONE

KASSIDY MATERIALIZED IN JACOBS GROVE, A LOCAL PARK IN ST. JOHN, New York. The park was nothing spectacular. It was, in fact, not much more than an open field surrounded by a small but lush forest on the eastern and southern ends, a playground on the northern end, and a parking lot to the west. It was not unlike many of the Forest Preserves Kassidy had frequented in the suburbs of Chicago. Jacobs Grove was multifunctional. Everything from soccer to field hockey to football was played there. Summer fairs were common, though they typically consisted of a few food vendors, an occasional beer tent, and rotating local bands. Kassidy had attended a few in her time in the town. They weren't altogether unpleasant. Compared to the fests of Chicago, though, everything seemed to pale in comparison.

Kassidy looked up at the moon, now completely red. News reports went on and on about the unprecedented five-day full moon. Conspiracy theorists went on and on about the progression of the reddening of the majestic heavenly body. They guffawed at the religious community's warning of the end of days, choosing instead to believe a great battle was underway over control of the celestial orb. The battle was, of course, taking place in the underground bunkers built by human-alien hybrids. If not for the truth, and the severity of it, Kassidy would have found it all amusing. Unfortunately, she did not have that luxury. She was on the hunt. She had a Titan to battle.

She had a girlfriend to dispatch.

The thought of it pained her with each step. With what she'd learned from Keiron, from Traci, and later from Hades and Persephone, Kassidy was resigned to the fact that Traci was no longer in control of her body and powers, at least not completely. Now, the most powerful witch in history was taking the reins, determined to exact revenge on those who'd wronged her. Revenge on the Twelve and on Death. And since Kassidy was the current title bearer, she would have to do what her father clearly failed to do.

"Damn you, Thanatos," she said to herself.

In the distance, she saw a lone figure walking toward her. She recognized the form. She even recognized the walk. Did that mean Traci was in control? Was it possible there'd still be time to try and save her?

The hope was there, buried deep under the surface, but Kassidy wasn't sure if it would be enough. As they stood a mere six feet apart, Kassidy felt a loss and sadness she'd not experienced in her lifetime. It was massive. It was oppressive. And it was shared.

Traci was in there.

CHAPTER FORTY-TWO

"HOW DID YOU FIND ME?" ASKED TRACI.

"You know my favorite spot in Chicago, and I know yours in St. John. Plus, I'm a pretty good investigator," said Kassidy.

Kassidy was hesitant. Understandable, given what happened when they last saw each other. If the power of Hecate was enough for Traci to send her to the Underworld, there was no telling what else she may be capable of. As a Titan alone she was formidable, but her power extended even from there. Hecate was the progenitor of generations of mortal magic wielders. Every practitioner from Circe to Merlin was able to manipulate magical energy because they had at least some of her blood in their veins.

But Traci was a direct descendant, and that made her a natural vessel for Hecate's spirit to return. A natural vessel to channel the god power that remained long after her apparent death.

A death at the hands of Thanatos.

What had he done wrong?

This entire situation was, in many ways, similar to her experience with Azra-El. When they fought over twenty years ago, she thought she'd ended him once and for all. Unlike her father, though, she didn't know enough to realize that she'd only severely wounded him. The wounds took decades to heal, and even then required souls to be fed directly to him to accelerate his regeneration. But she'd only been eighteen years old. She didn't know better. Thanatos had been born from Night, literally. He existed long before the Twelve and the Titans. He was Death. There should not have been a mistake. And yet, there clearly was one.

Or was there?

These thoughts passed through her mind as she looked into the eyes of her lover. She looked weathered, but somehow resigned. Kassidy wasn't sure how to take that.

"Wow! Look at you," began Traci, "is this, like, your work outfit? It's kinda bad ass."

Kassidy looked down absently at her clothes. She'd almost forgotten she was wearing her gear.

"Yeah, I guess it's what all the Death Gods are wearing these days."

Kassidy heard a light but anxious laugh from Traci. She didn't need to be an empath to know that there was sadness and regret within. Traci practically wore it on her sleeve.

"Kass. I—"

"I know," began Kassidy, holding a hand up, "it's not you. It's not your fault. I know it's Hecate."

"Yeah, it's her, but it's also me. I'm responsible for this. I made all this happen. I'm so sorry I tried to blame you for everything. I thought if I said that, I'd drive you away. I didn't mean to put you through all this. Everything I've done has been just so selfish. So ignorant. So wrong."

"You're in control now. So, let's work on fixing it," said Kassidy.

There was a long pause. Traci put her head in her hands, then threw her head back, running her fingers through her hair. Kassidy had seen that before, but something about it now seemed . . .

frightening. There was an intensity in it that seemed almost, violent.

Or like it was an act to stifle violence.

"What I told you before was true. About using forbidden magic to accelerate my powers. But I didn't stop when my mother told me too. I found that mentor, and she helped me continue. She helped me grow. And then . . ."

Several beats passed.

"And then what, Trace?"

"And then I found the spell," said Traci, making eye contact with Kassidy for the first time.

Kassidy was again taken aback, but she tried hard not to show her concern. How could she not, though. The beautiful woman she'd met a few months ago in Tully's bar with the chestnut eyes . . . now had eyes of blue. Bright. Metallic. Blue.

"What was the spell for?" asked Kassidy, trying to remain calm.

"It was going to help me find you. I just needed to find you. To thank you. To know you."

"I know, babe. You told me this. You told me the spell didn't work, though. You couldn't find me."

In the moment, Kassidy wasn't sure she was talking to Traci anymore. If she was, she didn't know how much longer she would be.

"No. No, I couldn't. Something was blocking the magic," said Traci.

"I wore something that blocked magic, kept me hidden. I was in trouble and wanted to stay away."

"I didn't realize that. At that age, the thought that you'd want to stay hidden never even occurred to me. Plus, I wasn't that strong anyway. So, selfishly, I went deeper into the forbidden magic."

Kassidy's stomach sank and her knees went slack. She felt her heart speed up as thoughts filled her mind, anticipating the words coming next.

"I found this very ancient spell. It was not only going to strengthen my power, but it had the ability to make me the strongest witch in my line since—"

"Hecate," finished Kassidy.

Traci simply nodded, still maintaining eye contact.

Kassidy did not avert her gaze. A part of her wanted to run. If Traci unleashed like she did before, she knew she'd have to respond, and that response, between resurrected Titan and newly appointed Death God, might not go her way. There was also the potential for collateral damage if the battle extended beyond the park, and harm to the natural order if Kassidy did not come out on top. There was no telling what would happen to the balance between life and death without a Death God in place.

"The spell came with a warning, which I of course ignored. But it only said the power of Hecate would return. It said nothing of Hecate herself. I thought I would essentially be channeling the power of the goddess. It also said that after the conjurer found her heart's desire, the power would return and consume the conjurer by the light of the next full moon. I thought I would just die. Simply wither away. And I was okay with that if it meant I'd have time with you," said Traci.

"So, you performed the spell?"

"I needed to thank you," said Traci.

"But it didn't work?"

"I needed to know you," said Traci, woefully, dropping to her knees.

"It didn't work until the wards on my medallion began to degrade," said Kassidy.

"I needed . . . to love you," said Traci.

"Oh, Trace," said Kassidy, feeling a lump in her throat. Her heart skipped a beat, she clenched and unclenched her fists. She wanted out of this entire situation. But that wasn't possible. In her short time as Death God, Kassidy had learned a great deal about herself and her place in the world. Had she not tracked that Wraith, had she not fought him in that basement, none of this would be happening. If she had not, though, there was no telling what would have become of those girls, those young witches, trapped in his cage.

"All this time, I never had power of my own. Not any *real* power. My abilities were incremental. Since reading from Hecate's grimoire, I've essentially been channeling her power. Making it easier, year after year, for her to return. And now . . . here we are."

"That's what you were keeping from me?" asked Kassidy. "Traci, none of this is your fault. I was manipulated and thrust into an impossible position. What led me to you was the result of decisions made thousands of years ago. So, it's not your fault. It's not mine. We're simply pawns. And in this game, we struggle. In this game, we lose. We lose people, and sometimes, we lose ourselves."

"You sound like my mother," said Traci.

"I'm sure she was a wise woman in her time."

As soon as the words escaped her lips, Kassidy saw an immediate switch in Traci. Traci rose from her knees. Something clicked, and while Kassidy couldn't clearly sense the emotion, she could sense the potential for danger.

"*Was*? What do you mean, *was*?" asked Traci.

Oh fuck. She doesn't know.

"What does that mean, Kass?"

As Traci took steps forward, Kassidy stood vigilant, grounding herself, as she tried to mentally prepare for what could come next. She didn't want to, but she knew she'd have little choice.

"Traci," began Kassidy, "I'm so sorry, but you mom is . . . is gone. She died, love."

Kassidy felt a buildup of energy. So far, it wasn't directed at her, but the powder keg inside Traci was expanding.

"No," said Traci, shaking her head. "No, no, no. That's not possible. I just . . . I just saw . . ."

As the words trailed off, Kassidy prayed that Cyrus was having luck locating Jaxon Burke. If she had any hope of beating Hecate, she would need the help of another god.

"I'm sorry, Traci. It's true."

"Oh, god. What did I do?"

Traci repeated the words and began pacing, short frantic steps. Kassidy was not sure what to do, but she feared this unraveling would signal the last time she'd actually speak to, or hear from, the woman she'd known as Traci Leeds.

"It wasn't you," said Kassidy. "It was Hecate. She's inside you, and she's trying to come out. You have to help me stop her. Please, babe. I need you to help me."

Traci's scream caused Kassidy to cover her ears. It was primal. It was dark. It was otherworldly. The glow of the moonlight seemed to intensify. A red tint now covered the partially snow-covered field. Looking up, she saw the moon was unchanged. The few clouds in the sky absorbed the color. Returning her gaze to Traci, who'd stopped pacing, Kassidy realized that her fear had come true.

It was not Traci.

Not any longer.

The magical energy between them shifted. As Traci brought her head back to face her, there was a shift in her look. It was sinister. There was a smirk. A look of satisfaction. A look of hunger. Hunger for destruction.

"Daughter of Thanatos," said Hecate. "It's good to see you again."

Kassidy looked down and saw Traci's hands aglow. Her body, now controlled by Hecate, was building power. Kassidy's heart raced, but she knew there was no turning back. She would have to fight a Titan *and* lose her love. Reaching out with her own power, she called to the Scythe of Cronus. This time, there was no hesitation. It appeared in an instant. If not for the urgency of her present situation, Kassidy would have thought that curious.

"Perfect," said Hecate.

She would have thought that response was equally curious.

Her sinister laugh made the hair on Kassidy's arms rise. As the laughter continued, she watched as a ball of solid energy was launched at her from the hand of her lover.

CHAPTER FORTY-THREE

KASSIDY STEPPED UP, TOOK A DEFENSIVE POSTURE, AND SPUN THE scythe to deflect the energy blast coming toward her. In all her fights, even the most recent with Ares, she'd never had to face a magic wielder like this. All psychopomps possessed some level of magic. All of it was rooted in the mission of ushering souls to the afterlife or traveling from this plane of existence to the Nexus, or the underworld. Their magic was not used or directed in the manner of witchcraft. It was not used and directed in the form of fire, energy, or psychokinesis. If it was, it was likely that a Reaper could best a witch.

But this was no ordinary witch.

She held sway over the heavens, the earth, the sea, and the underworld. Kassidy was ill prepared to deal with someone with this level of power.

Especially when that person wore the face of someone she loved.

"We don't have to do this," said Kassidy, holding her scythe to the side in a display of friendship. "I know what they did to you, the Twelve. I know they betrayed you. I spoke with Hades and Persephone."

An immediate jolt stabbed Kassidy in the heart. It wasn't a weapon though. It was an emotion. An emotion coming from Hecate. It was the same thing she'd felt when Persephone spoke about the goddess. There was an affection between the two. A love. Not romantic, but something. Persephone projected that love with guilt. Hecate projected it with anger.

"Don't you dare speak her name!" screamed Hecate, as she rose into the air and launched a barrage of fireballs at Kassidy.

Kassidy moved swiftly. Side-stepping one blast, ducking under another, then swatting two down with her scythe. The last, she batted back at Hecate. The Titan simply absorbed it back into her body.

"They took everything from me! She allowed it! And you, daughter of Thanatos? You will pay for what your father did."

Kassidy braced herself as Hecate flew down like a bullet toward her. She threw her scythe down, preparing to catch the goddess and send her flying, but instead, the Titan simply phased through Kassidy's body. Once solidified behind the Death God, Hecate reached back and grabbed Kassidy by the hair, throwing her over her shoulder and into the rock face. Kassidy moaned when she hit it. The move surprised her, the pain angered her, and her eyes went blue. Kassidy transitioned into mist and flew directly at Hecate, engulfing her.

"You have no idea what you're doing, child," said the Titan. "You have this power and no clue how to use it."

Hecate called upon her power and filled the area around her with electricity. As the vapor lit up, Kassidy's scream filled the air. Re-formed, she lay on the ground, curled around herself, steam rising from her clothes. She felt her body rise in the air, and she was once again hurled into the rock face.

Around her, she heard the winds increase. Leaves and debris swirled. She closed her eyes to protect them but felt small pellets of dirt hit her in the face repeatedly. Droplets of water fell from the sky. Daring to look up, she saw the clouds turn dark gray. Lightning flashed. With a great struggle, Kassidy stood and stared at the woman who was once Traci. She looked calm, serene, eyes closed, arms to the side, palms out. The elements did not bother her. She was in full control. Kassidy hoped that somewhere inside Traci still existed.

Reaching out with her empathic power, she tried to connect to the young witch, but she was met with emptiness. There was a void within Hecate where Traci's essence once existed. It was as if it had been carved out and discarded. Sadness welled within her. Then guilt. Followed by anger.

"Looking for your girlfriend? I'm afraid she's long gone. A bargain is a bargain, and she made the ultimate bargain for a chance to meet you."

Hecate's words stung, even more so than the harsh rain attacking her face.

"You . . . you don't have to do this," said Kassidy, again. "The Twelve, they're . . . assholes . . . I get it. But you don't need to destroy the world, to wipe out humanity, over your hatred of them."

Kassidy's words were met with laughter.

"You don't get it, my dear. This isn't about destroying the world. This is about destroying them. Once they're gone this world will be remade, and I will be at the forefront."

"Even you can't stop the Four!" screamed Kassidy.

"Stop them? *Stop* them? Oh, my dear, I mean to control them. The Four are nothing without a fifth to control them. That's my role. *I* am the fifth horseman!"

Her voice echoed as she spoke. Kassidy heard the words as much in her head as with her ears. She was frozen. Wind and rain whipped past, continuing to assault her face. She saw glee in Hecate's face. In Traci's face.

"Traci, I love you," whispered Kassidy.

Kassidy charged Hecate, all the while building up as much power as she could. Tackling the ancient goddess to the ground, Kassidy struck her in the face. Again. And again. And again. The blitz was not just about keeping the witch down; it was also about Kassidy's fury over losing Traci.

And the fury of what she had to do.

As Hecate lay on the ground, moving slowly, Kassidy phased her hand into the witch's body. She searched hard for the soul of the goddess, frantic to make the connection so she could rip it from Traci's body. She knew it would mean the end of Traci's existence. There was no hope of saving her. But she could not let Hecate remain.

"What . . . what are you doing?" screamed Hecate.

"Exactly what I need to," said Kassidy.

Hecate struggled against the Death God. Kassidy felt the resistance, and it was getting stronger by the second. She didn't have much time. She needed more power.

I can't do this! Dammit, I'm not strong enough!

Just then, a bright light appeared next to her. As it dissipated, a lone figure stood. The surge of energy in the air was powerful and familiar. Kassidy felt a tingle of fear inside. But it wasn't coming from Hecate or the new player in this battle. It was coming from herself. She didn't know whether a friend or foe stood before them.

"You!" spat Hecate.

The look on Persephone's face was one of pain. Kassidy felt the weight of it. It was intermixed with love, guilt, and an almost overwhelming sadness. Who was she there to help? That was the question lingering in the back of Kassidy's mind.

"Betrayer!" screamed Hecate.

"I'm sorry," said Persephone.

Then the Underworld Queen locked eyes with Kassidy.

"I will bolster your power with my own," began Persephone, "just as we did before."

Kassidy's eyes widened.

In her mind, she said thank you. In her heart, she whispered a final "I love you" to Traci, as she prepared to rip the vagrant soul of Hecate from her body. With Persephone's power augmenting her own, along with the power of the scythe, Hecate would soon be gone, and the threat of the Four would end. Calling upon all her power, Kassidy called to the Scythe of Cronus. It rose, shakily, and moved toward her hand.

Only to be stopped in midair.

"What the . . ."

Laughter escaped from Hecate again. "Oh, no. We're not doing this," said Hecate.

Hecate pushed her hands up and sent Kassidy flying backward with a psychokinetic thrust. She rose, steepled her fingers, and began to whisper. Kassidy, regaining her composure, again called for the scythe. It would not budge. She attempted to move toward it but was met by an invisible barrier. Above the scythe, the air crackled. Purple lightning came to life and surrounded the ancient weapon.

With a free hand, Hecate pulled Persephone toward the blade of the scythe with great force.

"This is for your betrayal," sneered Hecate.

Persephone was pulled directly into blade, her head severed from her body. The Underworld queen's head and body landed on the ground in an unceremonious thud before bursting into purple flame.

"Noooo!" screamed Kassidy.

"I told you, I will not be stopped. And you! You will suffer the same fate I did," said Hecate.

As she threw her hand outward, Kassidy flew back toward the rock face, only this time, through the power of the ancient weapon, still floating in midair, a dark portal opened. Kassidy felt her body flying toward it. She tried to shimmer away, but found she was unable. She tried to dematerialize into mist, the way all Reapers do. But the power was no longer there.

"Don't do this! Please!" she pleaded.

But her cries were only met with a sinister smile and a final thrust from the ancient goddess' hands.

The last thing Kassidy saw was the Scythe of Cronus flying into the hand of Hecate. With one hand outstretched, Hecate made a fist, and the portal closed.

Kassidy Simmons, Death God, was swallowed by darkness.

EPILOGUE

⊙NE

There was trouble in the world, and Ares, the War God, now known as Jaxon Burke, felt every bit of it. Beaten, broken, and punished by Thanatos, he had been thrust into a future with no memory of who he was. He'd spent the last eight hundred years wandering the earth as a soldier, fighter, and assassin, satisfying a bloodlust of unknown origin.

Unknown until recently.

Thanks to Kassidy Simmons, his memories were restored, and with them, the knowledge of his ancestry, and his celestial station. As the War God, he craved conflict and violence. He was by far the most skilled warrior of Olympus, with the possible exception of his sister, Athena. Where she fought with cunning and precision, he fought with rage and ferocity, almost a feral instinct. In the last century or two, he sought balance. He sought control over his natural instinct to fight and destroy his enemies. It was difficult, though, given mankind's propensity for war as a solution to disputes.

These days it was almost tearing him apart.

He sat cross-legged, eyes closed, hands clasped in his lap, attempting to meditate and control the growing rage inside. Ever since Jacen Lucas orchestrated his abduction outside Anna's home, and told him about some of the dangers coming, Jaxon worked hard to find the necessary balance to be ready to help. If what the Advocate said was true, Kassidy could not afford to fight alongside an unstable War God. But with the unrest in the middle east and the rage sparked in the United States over virtually everything, his ability to control the primal warrior within was stretched. He desperately needed purpose. A mission. A goal. Something, anything, to occupy his mind and soul while at the same time allowing him to satisfy his desire for battle.

He heard the sounds of birds and the sway of the trees in the breeze. He heard the plane overhead, and in the distance a babbling brook. The sounds of nature calmed most people. For Jaxon Burke, it was a slight distraction at best.

Then he felt a shift in the air.

Someone had just arrived.

Out of nowhere.

"Trying to be quiet again?" he asked.

"Trying to be respectful," said Jacen.

A beat passed.

"Is it time?" asked Jaxon.

"It is."

"What do we need to do?"

"We need to find and protect a member of the Four," said Jacen.

"Which one?"

"Famine."

Jaxon levitated, uncrossed his legs, then lowered himself. He slowly opened his eyes and stretched out his hand. Ripples of energy surged, and crackles of red electricity leapt from and surrounded his palm. In seconds, the Gladius de Bellum, also known as the Glade, his weapon, a sword that had seen countless battles and taken thousands of lives, appeared in his hand. He looked from the blade to Jacen, then smiled.

"I'm ready."

TWO

Shay Walker sat at the desk in her home office, sipped her coffee, and stared outside. In the background the news reports were frantic with features about the unprecedented full blood moon that seemed to be unending. Experts in astronomy, religion, history, geology, and even astrology were being interviewed by virtually every news outlet around the world. The second biggest story was the continued unrest in the country of Ki'lal. Assassinations and kidnappings were on the rise in the region. War was imminent, and there seemed to be no hope for compromise.

Despite the unrest in the world, Shay was focused on one thing, and one thing only. Her recent run-in with a vagrant soul attempting to possess her, and her subsequent rescue by a Death God. She had no idea that something like that even existed. Though, perhaps she should have. Growing up she was constantly told how special she was, and how she was destined for great things. In her mind, it was what all parents told their children. It was their way of building confidence and self-esteem. She was also told why she was special, though. Unfortunately, those explanations made absolutely no sense.

Until now.

When Shay woke up the other morning following the incident with the Death God, she found a Reaper in her home. At least, that's what she referred to herself as. Like any good cop, Shay asked more questions.

"So, you kill people and send their souls to heaven or hell?" she'd asked.

"No. We don't kill. We arrive shortly after a body has expired and we then escort the soul of that individual to the afterlife. What you call heaven is the Beyond."

"And the other place? Hell?"

"Hell, as you know it, is actually the Underworld. We don't mess with that place. There is a place though where we usher souls that did not lead the best life. We call that the Void."

"So, the thing that was in me? The thing the lady pulled out of me. That thing went to . . . ?"

"Most likely to the Void," said the Reaper.

Shay recalled the astonishment she'd felt at all that had been shared with her, which of course led to the appropriate follow-up question.

"Should you be telling me this? I mean, should humans know about this? Do humans know about this?" she'd asked.

"Some do. As to why *you*? Kassidy believes there is something special about you. She wasn't sure what it was, but while she was working to extricate the vagrant soul from your body, she felt something."

"Felt what?"

"I don't have an answer to that. But whatever it is, it captured the attention of the Death God, so it must be big," said the Reaper.

The Death God had used the word special, just like her mother and grandmother. She'd grown tired of that word throughout her life, but now it took on an entirely different meaning. First, because she'd caught the attention of a god, and second, because of what had happened with that body at the crime scene. She'd felt something. She didn't know what, but she was certain that woman was dead and only came back to life after she'd made physical contact with the body.

Special.

Special.

Special.

The word repeated itself in her mind as she put down her coffee and grabbed a small potted plant from the office window. It was near death from much neglect, the result of hours and hours on the streets trying to solve a mysterious string of deaths. Shay stared at it while forcing her mind to clear. One by one, she allowed memories to trickle into her head. Memories of times when things inexplicably died in her care, only to strangely return to life. Other memories surfaced of things coming to life in her care that had been seemingly left for dead. Shay reached out and touched the plant. She closed her eyes and concentrated on it, remembering when it was alive and thriving. She felt a tingle when she made contact with it, and when she opened her eyes . . .

. . . nothing happened.

The plant was unchanged.

Shay shook her head and laughed. Partly because she was embarrassed, even though no one else was around her. And partly because the notion of her bringing something back to life was absolutely ridiculous and she couldn't believe she'd entertained the thought.

Buzzzzz! Buzzzzz!

Shay left the office to answer her door. She was greeted by a delivery driver with a package, which she happily signed for. She'd been expecting her order from Kismet Coffee for a few days, and with everything happening the way it was now, she needed the joy the precious brew would bring to her mind, body, and soul.

Shay dropped the box off in the kitchen and returned to her office to finish the cup she'd already begun drinking. After sitting and reaching for the cup, she froze midway. Her plant was alive. It was full of vigor, color, and the sweetest of fragrances. As she stared at it, that damned word popped back in her head and repeated, again . . . and again . . . and again.

Special.
Special.
Special.

THREE

"What have you done?" asked the Diva, angrily.

"I exacted the same punishment on her that was given to me," said Hecate.

Hecate stared at herself in the mirror hanging on the wall of the Diva's temporary home in Athens, Greece. The face staring back at her wasn't hers. The hair, the eyes, the smile, were those of a stranger, but at least it was attractive. It was a face that she could wear comfortably. She could always cast a spell to change her appearance, but she felt she could work on that later. After the gods were dead and the world was in her grasp.

"Why would you do that?" asked the Diva.

Hecate ignored the question and walked to the window of the hotel suite. The night was young, but the full blood moon brought a late-night wildness to the city. She was beyond pleased. After being away so long, it felt good to be back in the place she had long considered home.

"It's good to be back in the city, isn't it?" asked Hecate, rhetorically.

From behind, she sensed the Diva channeling her power. There was a vibration in the air between them and flare up of energy.

"Sister, please," began Hecate as she turned to face the Diva, "there's no need for all that."

"Then answer me, damn you! You know we need the Death God. The Four is not complete without her."

"The Four is not complete as it is. You've lost the War God, and you have no idea where Famine is yet. So, my action against Kassidy Simmons is irrelevant."

"Irrelevant? Irrelevant?! Without the Death God, the Four are nothing!" screamed the Diva.

"And what is it that makes a Death God, sister? Hmm?"

There was silence between them. Hecate felt the anger coming from the Diva, and it only invigorated her. The Lost One, now the Diva, was always petulant when she didn't get her way. She was a cunning strategist, especially when it came to formulating plans for mischief and mayhem. But when things did not progress according to her plan, she reverted to nothing more than a godling. It was both sad and amusing. Hecate was having so much fun simply being alive that she relished the amusing aspects of this exchange.

"Let me answer that for you," said Hecate. "A Death God is first and foremost a psychopomp. Without the ability to engage souls and enter the realms of the Nexus and the Underworld, they are nothing. Now, aside from Thanatos, who do you know with the ability to travel to both of those realms?"

A moment passed before realization seemed to wash over the Diva's face. With that realization came a smirk.

"And then of course, there's the ability to wield this."

Hecate waved her hand and the Scythe of Cronus appeared. She looked at the Diva, whose face shifted to astonishment. She took great pleasure in that. Hecate was not seeking to antagonize or start a conflict with the Diva. But she wanted to make it clear that she was not going to be used, either. She was an equal partner in their shared plan. Though, with the scythe in her grasp, that equality did shift slightly in her favor.

"I can't believe it," said the Diva.

"Everything will work out," began Hecate, "just have faith."

"And Simmons? We truly don't need her? She won't be a problem?"

"Not only will she not be a problem, but we'll also never have to worry about Kassidy Simmons again."

Both women smiled.

"Now ... let's take your little potion from your scientist friend and go resurrect Pestilence. There's work to be done."

FOUR

Kassidy shifted from side to side and felt the intrusive sting of something sharp against her back. There was a softness beneath her head, and a cool compress on her eyes. She reached up to remove it and slowly opened her eyes.

She no longer saw darkness.

Instead, she saw a fiery red-orange sky with dark gray-black clouds. Purple lightning flashed, but it was not accompanied by thunder. Instead, a low, consistent hum traveled on the warm breeze. She sat up with great hesitation and some occasional pain. Confusion put those sensations on back burner. To her right, there was a mountain range in the distance. Ahead, there was nothing. Just wasteland. To her left was a body of water, black as coal, with angry, crashing waves that made no sound. The ground upon which she was lying was solid rock. Jagged in some places, but it was all she could see in every direction. She suspected the mountain range in the distance was just an extension of the rough surface.

She attempted to stand. Pressing her hand down to the surface, she felt nothing but pain followed by intense fatigue. Her head spun. As the dizziness took hold, she resumed her horizontal position and returned the compress to her eyes. Her thoughts swirled. Anger and sadness filled her. She tried to push it all back long enough to give herself time to recover and figure out her next move.

It took some time for the dizziness to subside. When it did, she removed her compress and simply sat upright. In the distance, she saw a figure moving toward her. As it neared, she saw that it was a man. Adrenalin shot through her. If he was a threat, she wasn't sure she could defend herself. She called upon her power to will her hand into a scythe to offer some semblance of protection.

Nothing happened.

She attempted again and again, becoming more desperate with each step the stranger took, but nothing happened. With more concentration she attempted to shimmer from her current position to another location, preferably standing, ready to defend herself.

Again, nothing.

She was powerless, and she had little strength to stand, let alone defend herself.

The man was only a few feet away now. He stopped and assessed her. He was tall and strong. Not just fit, but strong. Chiseled. Almost as if he were made of the same material as the ground upon which she sat. His skin was dark, his facial hair light and somehow well-manicured. The hair did not hide the scars. There was one on his right cheek and a jagged scar across his left eye.

He moved closer, and with each step his smile seemed to widen.

Kassidy felt a pounding in her skull, as if someone were trying to crack it open. She grabbed at her head with both hands and cried out. No sound escaped yet she felt the vibration in her throat. The throbbing continued when she felt hands upon hers. They were surprisingly soft, gentle, in both feel and intention. Kassidy dared to open her eyes and saw the stranger now, directly in front of her, offering comfort. She was still fearful. She had no power, no voice, and no one to come to her aid.

Yet she allowed this stranger to take her hands away to replace them with his own. He massaged her temples then put his head against hers. Suddenly, the throbbing stopped. There was static, as if a signal was trying to break through. The stranger gestured to her to breathe, to relax.

She did.

The static stopped.

A voice spoke in her mind.

"Can you hear me, Kassidy?"

She looked around for a source of the echoed voice, but only saw the stranger before her. His mouth had not moved. She heard the words again.

"Can you hear me, Kassidy?"

Confusion enveloped her. The stranger looked at her, tapped his temple, and smiled.

"Is that you?" she asked in her mind.

The stranger nodded.

"How? How is that possible? And how do you know me? Who are you?"

The stranger took Kassidy's hand and placed it against his chest, directly over his heart. She felt no heartbeat, but there was something about his touch that was familiar. He took a deep breath, and the next words she heard shook Kassidy to her core.

"My name," he began, "is Thanatos."

The shock of those words sent Kassidy on a tour of her entire life. Everything, good and bad, flashed before her, until finally, she was brought back to the moment at hand. Several beats passed before she finally spoke.

"Holy sh—"

ACKNOWLEDGMENTS

I've mentioned before that while writing is a solitary endeavor, everything that goes into the final product is not. It truly takes a village. This novel, *Death's Despair*, was particularly challenging as I dealt with many issues outside of my writing world. Issues that, for a time, took me to a place in which the craft I enjoyed so much became a chore, instead of a joy. It's in those moments that I was able to fully lean into support from my "village". Family, friends, readers, fellow writers, publishers, and podcasters, I thank you. Without your encouragement, this book would not exist. Without bearing witness to the joy in your individual successes, I would not have felt inspired. Without your support of me, and love for Kassidy, you would likely not be reading this page.

I have had the honor of creating, and being embraced by, a community. A community of writers, readers, and interviewers, both digitally and in print. I have to thank Ona Russell for inviting me to be a part of the inaugural season of her interview series, *Authors in the Tent*. Thank you to S. Faxon, for inviting me to be a guest on your podcast, *Cheers, Dears!* Joseph Kerney of *Fiction Ink Flow*, I thoroughly enjoyed our conversation. I hope to join you again. Michelle, the Coffee Fitness Unicorn, I can't thank you enough for having me on your podcast. That was crazy fun! And to your other half, Brandi, I am so grateful for the digital art and graphics you created to promote Kassidy Simmons and her adventures. To fellow author Khalid Uddin, thank you for having me as a guest on, *Mr. Write Now*. J. Dianne Dotson, friend and fellow author, our conversation on your interview series *Fantasy Author Chat*, was a blast. And lastly, thank you to the *Semi Sages of the Pages*. Our conversation on mystery novels got the wheels turning.

To the folks that helped make this book possible, my deepest gratitude. My publishers Holly Kammier and Jessica Therrien continue to be the best partners an author can have. My editor, Molly Lewis, sticks with me on this crazy urban fantasy journey. Thank you for helping steer this ship and making sure that I stay true to Kassidy and her story. To all the Acorn Publishing staff that have touched some portion of this novel and those before it, you have my heartfelt gratitude. And lastly, if you love the covers as much as I do, please join me in thanking the great Damonza Book Cover Design Team.

And to my readers, you all are amazing! You've read, you've laughed, you've cried, and you've probably screamed at me at times. I heard you as I sipped bourbon. You also shared your love of this world with others, and I cannot put into words what that's meant to me. Kassidy and I appreciate you all! Stay tuned! There's more to come!

Cheers y'all!

ABOUT THE AUTHOR

Dennis K. Crosby is the award-winning author of the Amazon bestselling urban fantasy novel, *Death's Legacy*, and its follow up, *Death's Debt*. With a degree in Criminal Justice, he spent six years working as a Private Investigator. His love of learning about, and better understanding people, led him to pursue a master's degree in Forensic Psychology. During his studies, Dennis transitioned to social service, and since 2008, he has worked primarily with men and women experiencing challenges with mental health, addiction, and housing insecurity. He continues to be a staunch advocate of mental health reform, social justice, and efforts to combat homelessness.

Dennis earned his MFA from National University in 2018, and since the launch of his novels Dennis has served as guest speaker and panelist at various events. He's been a guest on several podcasts and has seven published short stories in various anthologies. *Death's Despair* is book three in his Kassidy Simmons series.

Dennis grew up in Oak Park, IL, but the self-proclaimed geek currently lives and writes in San Diego, CA.